RADICAL ACCEPTANCE

Radical Acceptance

A novel
by

BONNIE E. CARLSON

Adelaide Books
New York / Lisbon
2019

RADICAL ACCEPTANCE
A novel
By Bonnie E. Carlson

Published by Adelaide Books, New York / Lisbon
adelaidebooks.org
Editor-in-Chief
Stevan V. Nikolic

For any information, please address Adelaide Books
at info@adelaidebooks.org
or write to:
Adelaide Books
244 Fifth Ave. Suite D27
New York, NY, 10001

ISBN-10: 1-951214-40-4
ISBN-13: 978-1-951214-40-1

Printed in the United States of America

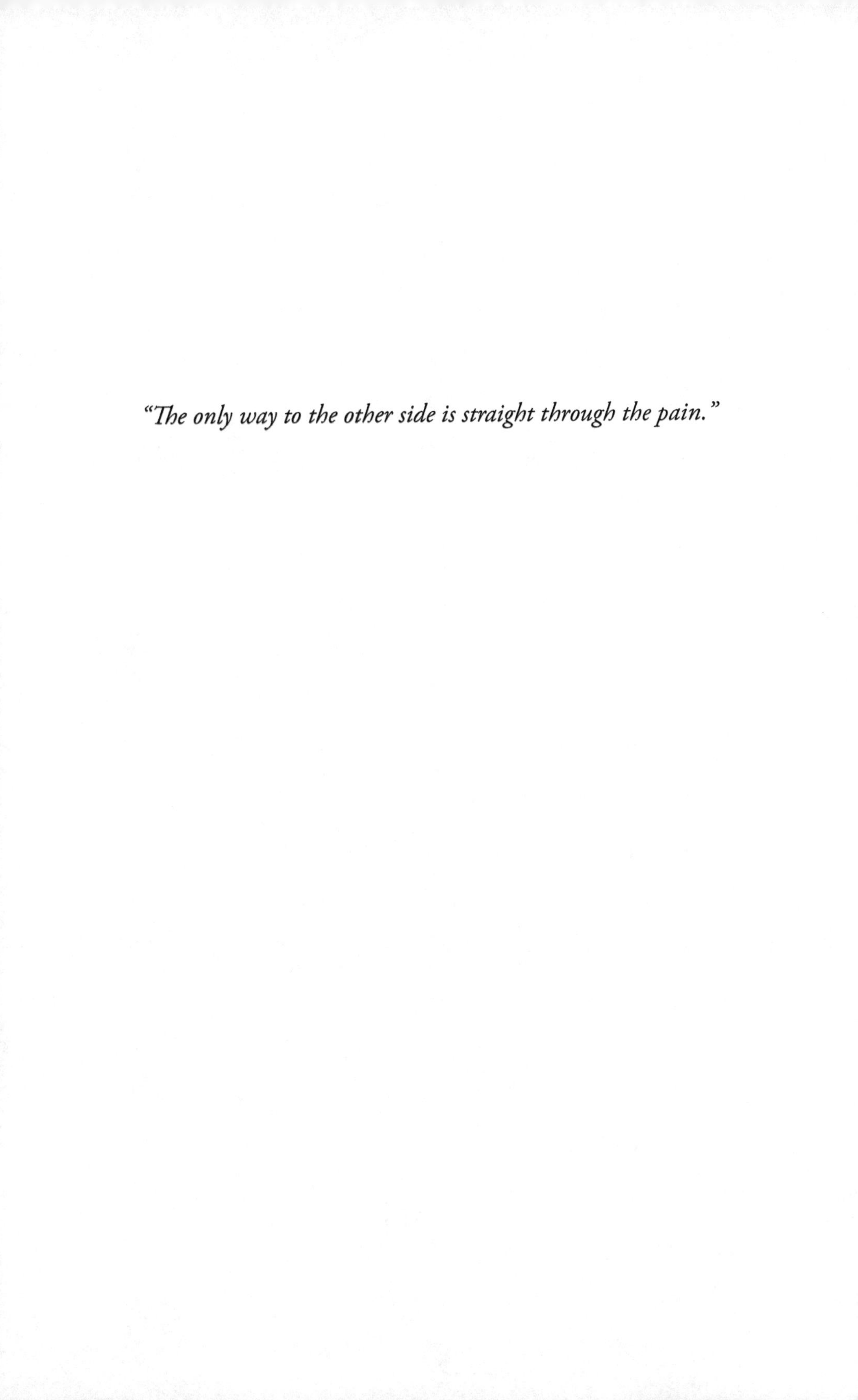
"The only way to the other side is straight through the pain."

*"Humans are notoriously bad at resisting temptation,
especially . . . if we're busy, tired, or stressed."*

— David Desteno

Buckeye, Arizona

October 2016

"Peterson, you've got mail."

"Fat chance. I've had zero mail in the month I've been here. Hardly anybody even knows I'm in here."

Laurel sprawled on her rack in Sunstate Women's Correctional Facility. She leaned back against the thin pillow, her outstretched legs covered against the Arizona winter with a threadbare gray blanket.

"Hurry up," her bunkie, Guzman, said. "You'd better get over there quick or the window will close."

Curiosity piqued, Laurel leapt up, shoved her feet into the clunky vinyl boots that made her feet sweat, even in the Arizona winter. She zipped up her gray hoodie and rushed out to the mail window. Shivering against the chilly wind sweeping across the barren, dusty yard, she arrived out of breath just as the corrugated metal window rumbled shut. Dammit.

"Wait!" *They saw me coming. Would it have killed them to wait ten more seconds to give me that letter? These guards just got off on being mean. Oh well, guess I can wait another day to find out who it's from.*

The next morning, she woke at five-thirty and followed her usual routine: a walk over to breakfast followed by a full day working at the print shop, and teaching GED classes after work. This time, though, she raced over in time to pick up her mail. A line had already formed. She waited ten minutes for her turn, tapping her foot nonstop. Prison was all about waiting.

"Laurel Peterson," she announced to the correctional officer behind the window. He handed her a white, legal-sized envelope, already sliced opened. "Wait, how come somebody opened it?"

"Inmate, is this your first piece of mail?" The officer shook his head in disgust. "Every piece of mail is opened first to make sure there's no contraband in there, remember?"

Seething, Laurel grabbed it and stomped away. She noticed right away the return address did not include a name. It came from Cal Tech in Pasadena. *Hmm, strange*, she thought. She'd already decided she'd wait to return to her cube before she read it. Privacy was worth the five-minute walk.

Good, Guzman wasn't there. She plopped down and pulled out the single page. She started trembling as she read its three typed sentences. The letter dropped to the floor as she lurched across the five feet to the lidless toilet, fell to her knees, and puked up the remnants of her lunch.

PART I: TEMPTATION

Getting sober is hard; staying sober is harder.

Chapter 1

February 2016

Boy, she could sure use a drink. Yeah, right. That'd be pretty idiotic, especially here at work. How exactly would that help anything? She'd still have that ridiculous new deadline from her boss. And, she'd still miss that hike she desperately craved, simply to find out what her mother needed. What a crappy day.

It didn't start out so bad, although she arrived late to work, again, after another miserable night's sleep. She was already sweaty. Menopause sucked. Laurel sprinted through the door at the graphic design agency where she worked, heart racing. She tossed her purse and briefcase on her desk, grabbed some coffee, and headed for the conference room.

She looked pretty good today, if she did think so herself. Skinny black jeans that accentuated her height and lanky frame, and the coral cashmere sweater complemented her auburn hair. The designer silk scarf added flair. If she could just stop sweating, her makeup might even look good for more than half an hour.

Breathe, she urged herself silently, *you've got this!*

She strode into the conference room where her team waited. "Morning guys. Sorry I'm late. Accident on the 51."

She'd moved to back to Scottsdale from Miami just four months ago. Another new beginning. It was a chance to start over in the place she grew up. She'd get it right this time.

"Okay, so let's begin." Laurel lightly clapped her hands together once. "As you know, the client has us on a tight deadline—"

Shit, she forgot the stuff. "Hold on a sec. Be right back."

She rushed back to her desk and rifled through her briefcase, eventually finding the notes she'd worked on at home over the weekend. She raced back to the conference room. Four sets of eyes looked up expectantly.

"Let's start by reviewing the plans so far. Luke, you start."

All eyes turned to Luke, the handsome thirty-something, newest member of the team. "As you all know, we decided—actually Laurel came up with the idea—that we'd design the Desert Arroyo Industries magazine using a new approach. We've discussed layout and text but haven't tackled the graphics yet."

"Great summary, Luke. She looked around the table. Next steps?"

Thea, the in-house Photoshop expert, leaned forward. "We'd brainstormed some layout ideas, but I don't think we made any final decisions."

"I agree. We had a bunch of good ideas, but we didn't settle on anything." Spiky-haired Ross always had to put his two cents in.

Laurel studied what she'd worked on over the weekend. "So, let's start with those ideas and finalize what we're going to do."

Fiery discussion ensued, debating the pros and cons of possible designs. They eliminated two fairly quickly.

Laurel observed the team and assessed their progress. Part of her role involved getting the team to work together more effectively. She'd put a stop to the guys running roughshod over the women like they used to.

The discussion turned heated at one point, with Ross, Julia, and Nikki favoring one option, and Luke and Thea the other. When the momentum stalled, Laurel interrupted.

"Enough! Let's compromise by retaining the best features of both designs?"

Ross objected. "I don't see how that's gonna work."

Nikki twirled a lock of her long, wavy red hair around her index finger. "Sure, it could, we could use—"

Laurel waded in. "Come on, guys. I want you all, as a team, to *make* it work. Figure out the best features of each layout and incorporate them into the final design. We need to move on to the content, the text, and we haven't even started to discuss social media applications. Work it out, okay?"

Ross glanced around the table. "Give us a couple of hours."

Laurel stood. "Okay then, let's reconvene after lunch with a decision and some ideas about the content."

As the team returned to their common space, Laurel overheard Nikki say, "You know guys, she can be a pain sometimes—like, I hate how often she's late—but when push comes to shove she's got terrific ideas. I never would've thought of combining aspects of the two ideas."

Ross stood at the head of the line, holding the door for the rest of the crew. "It hasn't worked yet."

When Laurel returned to her desk she found an email from her boss, the owner of this small Phoenix agency. He needed to see her today. She bit her lip. Crap, what was this about? Instantly she felt herself starting to tear up. God, menopause was a bitch.

She retrieved a phone message from her mother next.

"How come I never hear from you? There's some stuff I need to discuss. Call me."

Not so much as a, "How are you doing?" Well, she couldn't call her back now. She walked down the hall to Logan's office and asked his assistant if he was in. She waved Laurel into his office. Logan had his back to the door, typing fast at his standing desk.

"Knock, knock. You wanted to see me?"

"G'morning, Laurel." He spoke over his shoulder, still typing on his laptop. "Yeah, have a seat."

Laurel flopped down in an uncomfortable molded plastic chair.

"How are things going with the team?"

"I've got them all working effectively together."

Logan still pounded away on his keyboard.

So rude not to look at her. "Ross and Luke don't seem quite as competitive with each other and aren't so busy trying to dominate the women. They're doing okay."

What was this meeting really about?

He finally slammed his laptop shut and faced her. "So, I just got a call from the client on your Desert Arroyo Industries project, and they're really eager to move things along—"

"Logan, we're on track—"

"Hold on. Let me finish." Both palms faced her, in a stop gesture. He pulled up a chair so close to her she could smell his pricey cologne. "Things have changed at their end. They need the completed magazine in a week or two."

Wow, she hadn't seen that coming. "Geez, I don't know, Logan . . . a week? Out of the question. Two, maybe . . . I'll have to see what the team thinks. They're finalizing the layout now, and we're going to meet this afternoon. I'll do my best."

Logan Bishop was a dynamo, ten years her junior. He'd spun off his agency from a much larger one where he had been one of the execs.

"Laurel, it's important. As you know, Desert Arroyo is potentially a big client with a lot more work coming down the pike if we make 'em happy on this one. I don't have to tell you how competitive it is out there. Get back to me after you meet with the team. Let me know the plan."

"Will do."

Shit, could the team pull this off?

At lunchtime, she ate a salad at her desk and called her mom back. Her mother Joanne refused to explain what she wanted. "Not when you're at the office. Just come by tonight."

Crap. So much for hiking after work. She had to let off steam somehow, after getting slammed with a new deadline. She rubbed at the tightness in the muscles at the back of her neck.

She left work at five-thirty and headed north on the 51, watching at the pink and gray sunset. The desert was such a welcome change after muggy Miami. As she continued into posh Carefree, she chuckled about the goofy names of its winding roads. Languid Lane, ha!

What was so urgent with her mother? The nearby mountains were thick with towering saguaros and prickly cholla cactus. A resentment brewed in her gut at having to sacrifice that hike to find out what her mother wanted.

She pulled into the long, curving driveway, the Cheetos-colored flowers of acacia trees floating to the ground, their sweet fragrance wafting in the breeze. Why hadn't she visited more often since she'd moved to Scottsdale?

She rang the bell next to the carved mesquite wooden door. She tapped her foot on the flagstone, wondering about the command performance, her stomach growling. Would her mom feed her dinner? As she started to knock, Joanne opened the door.

She still couldn't get over how attractive her mother was, even in her mid-seventies. Her gray hair was short and stylish. And she was thin—too thin?—somehow managing to still look good, even in jeans and a sweatshirt.

"Hey, Mom, how's it going?"

"Shitty, if you want to know the truth."

Okay, here we go.

"What's wrong?"

Why was she always so prickly? It would have been nice if she'd even gone through the motions of asking about how she was doing. Mom was lucky to live in such an elegant home at this stage of her life. Original artwork, beautiful Oriental rugs on dark hardwood floors.

Joanne walked slowly, hunched over, like it hurt to walk. "Let's go in the kitchen and sit down."

"Okay. Is Bill around?"

Probably. She could hear the TV blaring in the background and wondered if her mother's husband had a hearing problem.

"Dozing. That's what I wanted to talk to you about."

Laurel sat across from her mother at the kitchen table. Her mother's hands shook as she lifted a glass of water to her lips. Tremors? She hoped she hadn't started drinking again. She waited for her mother to continue, fingering the fuzzy leaves of an African violet plant on the table.

"We just got back from the doctor. Bill has mid- to late-stage Alzheimer's disease."

Crap. Mom finally manages to find a decent guy, and he turns out to have dementia. Laurel chose her words carefully.

"Mom, that's awful. I'm so sorry. Had you suspected it?"

"Yep, totally forgetful all the time. Mind like a sieve." Her mother's hand still trembled, despite trying to hide it in the sleeve of her sweatshirt.

How in the world had her mother managed to land a guy like Bill rich enough to own this gorgeous house in Carefree? If she'd spent more time here she might know. "So, Mom, how did you meet Bill anyway?"

"Remember when I was a receptionist at the Four Seasons spa? Bill used to come in for massages. Eventually we got friendly—he was pretty lonely—and he asked me out. After about a year of dating he asked me to marry him. Great guy, probably better than I deserve."

Isn't that the truth? Laurel stared into Joanne's eyes. Her chocolate brown eyes looked so inviting. But she always had an agenda.

"Of course, I said yes. Had no idea he was losing his mind. I just thought his forgetfulness was old age—he's seventy-eight. His loser kids want nothing to do with him. The cynical part of me thinks he wanted a caretaker. The other part of me says he's a nice guy, didn't know, and just my bad luck. Doesn't matter. It is what it is."

"I'm really sorry, Mom. Is there something I can do?"

"You bet there is. I'm gonna need a lot of help with this. I know you just moved here a few months ago but, so far, you've been no help at all."

Well, shit, she'd never asked for any help. Her speech sounded different, softer. Laurel had to strain to hear what she said, so different from the screaming she remembered from childhood. Joanne had never been easy to get along with, but she acted more irritable than usual.

"Okay, Mom, sorry I haven't been more helpful. What would you like me to do?"

"For starters, you can come over next Saturday morning. I have some stuff I need your help with."

Joanne got up gingerly, went to the refrigerator and poured herself some iced tea. Laurel's stomach growled loudly.

"Mom, can I have a glass, too?" Obviously she wouldn't get fed here, since Joanne wouldn't even bother to pour her a lousy glass of tea.

Joanne sat back down and waved toward the refrigerator. "Help yourself."

Laurel got up, grabbed a glass from the cabinet, and poured some tea. "I can come this weekend, but Saturday won't work. I chair an AA meeting on Saturday mornings." *Damn, she's going to take up half my weekend.* "And, I volunteer at the animal shelter on Saturday afternoon." But, this was her mother, and this is what daughters were supposed to do. "I guess I can come on Sunday morning."

How was she going to finish all that work she'd brought home?

"Sunday morning would be fine. Earlier would be better."

"Okay, I'll shoot for nine."

By the time Laurel arrived home after she stopped to grab dinner, it was already eight-thirty. Exhausted, she dragged herself up the stairs to her apartment, the nicest she'd ever lived in. It felt so good to be home, to relax. First thing, she lit a eucalyptus candle.

She walked into the den and plopped down on her white linen sofa in front of the TV. Nestling into the couch, she surrounded herself with brightly colored pillows and started in on her salad. She needed to relax after the visit with Mom.

When she realized another day had passed without exercising, she let out a big sigh. Then, another hot flash. Instant sweat. Would these never stop? At least she wasn't in front of the team. She hated feeling on the verge of tears when somebody even looked at her funny.

She took a quick trip into the kitchen for a towel to wipe off the sweat and turned on the overhead fan. She sat down again to eat and her cat jumped into her lap.

"Oh, Winston, you must be starved. Let me get you some dinner."

She filled his bowl with dry food and poured him fresh water. Her lease didn't allow pets, but she already had Winston when she moved from Miami and wasn't about to give him up. He didn't go outside, and she'd just have to chance the rental company finding out.

She listened to Winston crunch his food and returned to finish her salad and watch TV. Unable to stop obsessing about her mother, she grabbed her laptop. Mom was sure in a bad way. She logged onto the Mayo Clinic website and searched on her mother's symptoms. After a few minutes, she slammed her laptop shut.

"Crap, I can't believe it."

First Bill with Alzheimer's, and now this. She groaned. It looks like they were all in for a rough ride.

Chapter 2

Laurel would have traded her last Gucci handbag to have someone else to take over this Alcoholics Anonymous meeting. Eight-fifteen on Saturday morning? What was she thinking when she agreed to chair? *Man, I sure could have used another couple of hours of shuteye.* After her tough week at work, though, and then her mother's bombshell about old Bill losing his marbles, she really needed a meeting. She parked her old black BMW and punched in the code to unlock the door at the North Scottsdale Presbyterian Church. She found the big tub of materials and set up the gray metal folding chairs.

So, here she was, ready or not. God grant me the serenity not to lose my shit.

Twenty women showed up, ranging in age from their early twenties to sixties. Some dressed quite casually; others were dressed to the hilt on a Saturday morning —typical North Scottsdale—full makeup, artfully applied, with designer clothing and handbags. She scoffed and felt out of place, dressed in the Gap jeans she had thrown on after yet another lousy night's sleep, along with a wrinkled denim work shirt and sneakers. Once again, her laundry had piled up. Her straight auburn hair, clean but with gray roots showing, needed a good cut. She wished she'd left time for makeup to disguise the dark circles under her eyes.

Laurel called the meeting to order and read the "Preamble" and "How it Works." She asked if there were any newcomers present, any visitors, or anyone coming back. One woman raised her hand.

"My name is Bailey, alcoholic and addict. Coming back."

Code for "I've had a relapse."

Then a woman named Louise told her story, detailing when she started drinking, how she drank, and her last DUI and divorce. Louise chose gratitude as the topic for discussion. Laurel mentally rolled her eyes. Each woman shared around the circle for a couple minutes on gratitude.

Bailey's turn came next. Bleached, almost-white hair with four inches of dark roots showing, red-rimmed eyes visible despite heavy black liner and mascara, she exhaled a cigarette breath and said in a broken voice, "Bailey. Alcoholic. This is day five."

She received a burst of clapping and "we're glad you're here's" and "keep coming back's." The young woman clearly struggled not to dissolve into tears.

"I feel like absolute crap. Been in and out of treatment, and in and out of AA. Not feeling a whole lotta gratitude right now."

Dead silence.

"But, I guess I'd have to say I'm grateful to be alive. And… that's about it. Oh, and I need a new sponsor."

Laurel considered passing, like Bailey, not feeling all that grateful. It wouldn't look good for the chair to pass, so she quickly came up with a perfunctory share.

"Laurel, alcoholic. Bailey, welcome back. You're in a safe place. I'm grateful for the life I get to have if I don't drink."

The sharing ended with the Serenity Prayer. Laurel asked for help with the chairs. When she left a few women still remained, talking, so she asked them to turn the lights and lock up.

Laurel walked out into the bright February sunshine, relieved that commitment was over with, so she could sleep in on future Saturdays. Although she'd attended this meeting for weeks, she'd never connected with anybody. She hadn't made a single friend since moving to Scottsdale. Maybe that was starting to get old. Maybe being so disconnected from people wasn't working anymore. Was she starting to get lonely?

Then she noticed Bailey smoking a cigarette around the corner of the building. Much younger than Laurel, her puffy face betrayed a scowl.

Laurel walked over. "Hey, Bailey. How's it going?"

"Shitty. I have a ton of medical problems. Forced to move in with my sister. I'm just waiting for her to show up and give me a ride home."

"At least you *have* a sister who's willing to let you live with her."

That conjured up memories of the time she had no choice but to move in with her own sister, a real low point in her life. Remembering those dark days made her shudder. Oh God, what if she had to move in with her mother? What a nightmare that'd be.

"I suppose it can always be worse that it is."

She could hear the voice of her former sponsor as they walked toward the parking lot. *Reach out, Laurel.* "Want to get coffee sometime?"

"Not sure if I can. I can't drive, so my sister's carting me around to meetings and doctor's appointments. Can't ask her to drive me someplace to get coffee, too."

"What if I pick you for a meeting Monday or Tuesday? We can go to the meeting and hit Starbucks afterwards. I'll drive you home after that."

"Seriously?" She dropped her cig and crushed it into the asphalt.

"Pick you up at five on Monday?" That meant leaving work a bit early. She'd have to sneak out without her boss noticing, already having second thoughts about her offer to have coffee.

Bailey gave Laurel her contact info and walked over to the Infinity SUV pulling into the parking lot.

Laurel glanced around. The temperature was warming up. Big puffy white clouds scudded across the cerulean sky, casting interesting shadows on the mountains. She needed to get outdoors and hike off all the worry and stress of work and her mom.

Greeted by the cacophony of dozens of barking dogs and meowing cats, Laurel entered the Man's Best Friends no-kill animal shelter where she started volunteering a couple months ago. Laurel adored dogs, but had never owned one since most of the apartments she lived in wouldn't allow them. So, she settled for Winston, her cat. Spending a chunk of each Saturday at the shelter was the next best thing. She could finally come there without tears filling her eyes when she saw all these rescued pets.

She reported to Sydney, with her Goth eye makeup and piercings. "Hi, Syd, what do you have for me today"?

"Got a pack of dogs that need walking. A few people are scheduled to come by for meet-and-greets." She pointed to the back. "You can walk those two in that last cage. If you want to help talk up the dogs to potential adopters, that'd be great. We've got a full house, so we need adoptions."

Laurel walked to the back and saw two mongrels, one medium-sized and one small. The larger one, *"Buddy,"* according to the sign, had a sleek, brown coat and pointed ears. He wagged his skinny pointed tail like crazy. As soon as she approached, the little white fluffy puffball started to bark and jump up and down.

"Hi there," she said, looking over at the other sign. *"Cloud?"* People were weird.

As she attached their leashes she recognized a black woman a few cages away, who was also prepping a couple of dogs ready to walk. By the time Laurel had leashed her two squirming pups, the woman walked over.

"Want to walk together? I'm Caroline Spenser."

"Howdy. I'm Laurel. Okay. I think I've seen you before. How long've you been volunteering?"

"A few months. Just moved to Scottsdale from LA less than a year ago. Thought it might be a good way to meet people who love animals the way I do."

Caroline looked to be in her forties, short, but very powerfully built.

"Have you got a dog?"

"Nah. I'd love to, but my schedule just wouldn't work with an animal that needs a lot of attention."

On the street, Laurel walked two abreast with Caroline, the dogs leading the way. The McDowell Mountains loomed up on their left.

Laurel admired the way Caroline carried herself. She seemed very self-assured. Why couldn't she be like that? "What do you do for work?"

"I'm a nurse practitioner. Moved here to help set up an orthopedic practice. Sometimes I have to work long hours. Leaving a dog at home alone just wouldn't be fair to the dog. How about you?"

"Graphic artist. Wish I could have a dog, but my apartment is no pets. I had to sneak in my cat. I honestly cannot fathom how people can abuse or abandon their pets. They should be shot. Winston is my family. No way I could deliberately hurt him or give him up."

"I hear you, girl. Makes me so mad the crap people do to their animals. Hey, be careful!"

Laurel had somehow let her dogs get tangled up with Caroline's two. She didn't have to raise her voice like that. "Sorry."

Laurel headed back up the hill toward the shelter, keeping a safe distance from Caroline. They dropped off the dogs and Sydney gave each of them a dog to talk up for the meet-and-greets.

After her shift ended, Laurel walked back to her car, and turned when she heard her name called out.

"Hey, Laurel! Wait up."

Caroline jogged over. "Any interest in getting some lunch?"

Did she want to do this? "Uh, sure, I guess I've got time for that. I'm gonna hike this afternoon, but I've got time for lunch before that. Where to?"

"There's a little coffee shop just down the road called Jolta Java. Been there?"

"No, but I'll follow you."

Caroline had the neatest hair, dark brown, very short and very curly. Her skin was the color of mocha, highlighting her almost-black eyes, sparkling through round, black-rimmed glasses. Something elfin about her appealed to Laurel.

She arrived at the packed Jolta Java Café where Caroline had already scored a table. It held a different kind of vibe than Starbucks, funkier. On the deep eggplant-colored walls, oil paintings hung—not very good ones. The other customers didn't look like typical North Scottsdale. Instead, they were young, LGBT, hip, kind of edgy. Looked like Sydney's kind of place. The heady smell of coffee permeated the air.

Laurel scanned the menu posted on the wall. "Need some carbs before I hike. Thinking about an everything bagel. And, a latte. How about you?"

"Coffee. If I'm gonna eat, it's gotta be a salad. I'd give anything to be as thin as you are. Do you exercise a lot?"

Laurel scoffed. "Hah! Barely. I hike as often as I can, or at least walk. Been threatening to join a gym, but still haven't done it. Always letting work get in the way. How about you? You look really toned. Bet you work out."

"I do, constantly fighting the battle of the bulge. Where do you usually hike?"

"Mostly I take one of the trailheads in the McDowell Sonoran Preserve, right nearby." She pointed out the window toward the mountains.

When the barista called their numbers, they picked up their coffee and food.

After they sat, Caroline raised the volume of her voice to speak over the background noise. "How crowded is it?"

Laurel took another mouthful of bagel and chewed it thoughtfully. "This time of year, it gets busy."

"Maybe I could join you sometime. I much prefer doing cardio outside. I've been using a bike in my apartment, or the treadmill, but hiking sounds more fun."

"I love it. My favorite part of living in the desert. You free this afternoon?"

"That won't work. I'm Skyping with my son, who's still in LA with my ex."

After exchanging small talk and finishing their meals, Caroline stood up to leave. "Thanks for joining me. I really meant what I said about hiking. Here's my number. Text me."

Boy, she was kind of pushy.

"Okay," Laurel said, pulling out her phone and entering Caroline's number. "Maybe after work sometime."

She waved goodbye, regretting that she'd mentioned hiking. Caroline seemed nice, but she preferred the solitude of hiking alone, being able to decompress after work.

Just after nine on Sunday morning, after Joanne didn't answer the door, Laurel used her key to get in. As soon as she walked in she heard a moaning sound. She rushed into the kitchen and found her mother lying on the floor.

"Mom, my God, what happened?"

"I fell during the night and couldn't get up. I've been yelling for Bill, but he hasn't heard me. Come on, help me up!"

Biting her tongue, Laurel bent down, gently grabbed her mother's arms, and helped her to her feet. Her mother's light weight surprised her.

"Are you okay? How long have you been here?" What was that smell? Had her mother peed herself?

"I guess I'm okay. I hurt everywhere, though. Came in to get a glass of water and slipped. Then I just couldn't get up."

Laurel surveyed her mother. "Mom, I think we should get you to urgent care, have a doctor look at you. Look at this bruise on your arm."

"No way!" her mother insisted, hunched over, hair sticking out every which way. "Nothing's broken. It'll just be a waste of time and another friggin' medical bill."

"Are you sure? It would be safer to have you checked out." Laurel wished for the hundredth time that her mother wasn't so difficult.

Joanne stumbled out of the room. "I need to change."

"Do you need help, Mom?"

"No, but you could get started on the cleaning and laundry."

"Just tell me what to do."

Under her mother's direction, Laurel threw in a load of laundry and completed the dusting. She started in on the vacuuming. The vacuum cleaner was on its last legs, hardly picking anything up. Mom really needed a new one, but she wasn't about to suggest it. After she threw the wet laundry into the dryer, she heard the front door open.

Laurel walked into the foyer. "Bill, where have you been? Are you okay?"

"I'm okay. Just decided to take a walk. I must have gotten lost."

Maybe that explained why he didn't hear Mom. How long had he been gone?

She found Joanne sitting in the kitchen.

"Want something to eat?"

"That'd be nice."

Laurel opened the fridge and started rooting around. Slim pickings. No lunchmeat. A small hunk of cheddar cheese. What had these two been eating? "Mom, there's not all that much in here that we can eat. When was the last time you went grocery shopping?"

Joanne sat hunched over at the table. "Can't remember."

"All I can find in here is cheese. Are there crackers? Or, what about some soup?"

"Not sure. Check up in that cabinet." She pointed in the direction of the likely location.

Laurel found Ritz crackers and poured two cans of tomato soup into a saucepan.

"Is Bill going to join us?"

"Probably. Go ask him." She obviously didn't want to get up.

Her tremors hadn't gone away. Plus, Laurel still had trouble understanding her speech.

Laurel went to find Bill. She came back into the kitchen. "Says he's not hungry. I'm worried, because he said he was out walking while you were lying on the kitchen floor."

"So that's what happened to him."

Laurel had a bad feeling about the two of them living there by themselves. She poured the warmed-up soup into two bowls and got out the cheese and crackers. As they started to eat, she thought about her search of the Mayo Clinic website. She needed to raise the possibility of her mother having Parkinson's disease, but was unsure where to start. She worried Joanne would get angry at her if she was right about the diagnosis, even though it wasn't Laurel's fault. If Joanne did have Parkinson's, though, the sooner she started on some medication, the better off she'd be.

"Mom, there's something I'd like to talk to you about." She paused while mustering the courage to begin, noticing how stale the crackers were. "It looks like your hands shake quite a—"

"That's just getting old."

"Please let me finish, Mom." She fought to keep the annoyance out of her voice. "It's not just getting old. Plus, I'm concerned about how you fell this morning and couldn't get up. That's dangerous. It must have been scary lying there on the floor and not being able to do anything."

Laurel finished a piece of moldy-tasting cheese. "I've been searching the Internet and doing some reading, and I think there's a chance you might have Parkinson's disease—"

"Nonsense! What makes you think that?"

Joanne had barely touched her lunch.

Laurel took a deep breath. "I've noticed that besides the tremor in your hands, you've also become kind of bent over when you walk. And, you look kind of stiff—rigidity is a symptom."

She paused, waiting to see how her mother would react. Joanne listened, looking like she might interrupt and get defensive, but she let her daughter continue.

Laurel took a couple of spoonsful of soup. "I also read that another symptom of Parkinson's is depression. You seem kind of depr—"

"Of course, I'm depressed!" Joanne's faced reddened. "Who wouldn't be under the circumstances? I just found out Bill has Alzheimer's!"

"Okay, okay, I'm not arguing your life is a bed of roses. All I'm trying to say is you seem to show some symptoms of Parkinson's disease and you should go to your doctor to get evaluated. Maybe there are medications that would help. I think we should get you checked out."

Why am I even trying to help her if she's going to fight me? I'm never going get her approval, no matter what I do.

She decided not to mention that another later symptom of the disease is dementia. If Joanne did have Parkinson's, she'd find out soon enough.

"Will you at least agree to let me make an appointment with your doctor?"

Joanne sighed. "I don't need to make a doctor's appointment."

Laurel could hear the resignation in her voice.

"I saw my primary care doctor last month. You're right. He thinks I have Parkinson's."

Dang, then why was she arguing? "Mom, that's really terrible." What else could she say? "Somehow, we're going to get through this together."

Did she believe that?

Laurel talked herself into hugging her mother goodbye, despite knowing that Joanne avoided physical affection. Driving home, she obsessed. Could this be the chance to finally work out her relationship with her mother? To put the past behind them and try to have a "normal" relationship?

In the meantime, how would she marshal the energy to help her mother every week, while dealing with the new deadline at work, and doing what she needed to do to stay sober?

Chapter 3

Laurel and her team worked twelve-hour days, rushing to meet Desert Arroyo Industries' new deadline. Everyone got along, pitched in, did their part. Laurel felt proud of the team, and her boss Logan congratulated them on meeting the earlier deadline.

"Hey, Laurel!" Luke leaned against her office door frame on Friday afternoon. "Put down that pen and come out to celebrate with us. We did it!"

His goofy smile made it dangerously tempting, but she couldn't. "Yes! We got it done, Luke! Amazing teamwork. But my cat will starve without me. You guys go on and have fun." *Better get my butt to an AA meeting tonight.* She found one at eight o'clock and, after dinner, drove to the Lutheran Church on Frank Lloyd Wright Boulevard.

By the time the meeting ended, her previous desire for a drink had evaporated. Now all she craved was twelve hours of sleep. Tomorrow was the dreaded drive to Carefree and helping her mother.

At her mother's, Joanne mentioned the usual housework she needed help with, but also asked her to go to CVS to pick up some prescriptions for herself and Bill. After dusting and vac-uuming, Laurel drove the short distance to the pharmacy. One of the prescriptions wasn't ready, so she browsed a while and sat down to wait, watching people come and go. While she played on her phone, a man arrived to drop off some prescriptions and wait for them. He looked about her age and could have been attractive, but looked raggedy: hair disheveled, two-day's growth of beard, eyes sunken and bloodshot, messy clothes that looked like they'd stayed in the dryer for days.

He sat down next to her in the only available chair. In two minutes, he was snoring like a buzz saw. Soon she heard the pharmacy tech call out "Scott Harris," but nobody answered. After they called the name a second time, she jiggled the man with her elbow. He woke with a start.

"Are you Scott Harris?"

He rubbed his eyes. "Yeah, why?"

"They just called your name. I think your prescriptions are ready."

They called Joanne's name and Laurel stood up to get the medications. Scott walked to the counter with her.

"Man, I must've been out cold. I wasn't snoring was I?"

Laurel laughed. "Yeah, you were. I think people in the front of the store could hear you."

Was she flirting with this scruffy-looking guy?

He groaned. "Oh, no. How embarrassing."

"Just kidding. You *were* snoring, but I doubt people up front could hear you."

They left the store together. As they parted to go to their sep-arate cars, Scott playfully winked at her. "Don't tell anyone, okay?"

She unlocked her car she looked back over her shoulder at him. "Our little secret."

You bet she was flirting.

Laurel spent the rest of the day doing chores at her apartment and running errands. Weekend chores made her itch to hit a trail. She needed to move, but the day was already gone. Saturday night, she watched a movie on demand, grateful to have Winston purring in her lap.

She was googling trail maps when Caroline texted. "Hike tomorrow?"

Good timing.

On Sunday, Laurel pulled into a parking spot at a strip mall. Caroline was already waiting.

Laurel gestured for Caroline to ride with her. "Happy Sunday. Hop in, I'll drive."

Caroline climbed in. "What a gorgeous day. I had no plans for the day, so I'm thrilled you were available. Perfect day for a hike. Look at that blue sky."

"I know, right? This is why we moved to Arizona."

Laurel drove a short distance on Via Linda, turning left onto 128th Street across from Mountainside Middle School. The street dead-ended at a short trail that connected to the Sunrise Trail, one of Laurel's favorites. On one side, high-end homes lined the road, with open desert on the other. They got out and started hiking up the trail.

Caroline stumbled, almost falling. "Wow, this trail is really rocky."

"Major downside of this set of trails. But, wait till we get onto the Sunrise Trail and go up the ridge. The views are stunning." Even the brown band of pollution couldn't overcome the brilliance of the endless sky.

They connected with the Sunrise Trail and took the right fork, toward the ridge. The trail got steeper.

Caroline stopped and looked around. "I can't believe how gorgeous it is here." Teddy bear and buckhorn chollas, and saguaros surrounded them. "It's a lot greener that I expected."

"Because of all the rain this winter."

Caroline leaned over, pointing a finger toward a teddy bear, a.k.a. "jumping" cholla.

Laurel seized her arm "Stop! Don't touch it!"

"Jeez, I wasn't gonna. What would happen if I did?"

"The spines look pointed on the ends, but they're actually barbed. If you touch them they hook into your skin. Hard to get out and hurt like a son of a bitch."

"Good thing you grabbed my arm. I had no clue. Thanks."

They hiked in silence for a while, and Laurel felt the tight muscles in her shoulders and back relax with the exertion. Twenty minutes later she looked back at Caroline.

"How're you doing?"

"Love it here, other than the rocky trail. Great choice. Where'd you move from?"

"Miami, four months ago. Before that, New York, and Boston. How long had you lived in LA before you moved here?"

"Since college."

They rested for a second and drank their water. A gentle breeze had kicked up.

"Where'd you grow up?" asked Laurel.

"New York City. My parents immigrated from Jamaica. They were smothering . . . helicopter parents before there was a name for it. So, when it was time to go to college, I wanted to move as far away as possible. Ended up at UCLA. I majored in health sciences, which qualified me to do nothing." Caroline put the cap back on her water bottle. "So, I completed EMT training after college, where I met my husband. Ex-husband. After we did the EMT thing for a while, we both decided to go back to school. I ended up in a program for nurse practitioners. Kind of ironic, 'cause my mother's a nurse, and I wanted to be nothing like her. How about you?"

"I had a crappy childhood."

"What do you mean?"

"Well, for starters, I have two brothers and one sister, and between the four of us there are three different fathers. Not one of them stuck around." She didn't want to get into her dysfunctional childhood. Why had she opened that door?

"Wow, that's tough. What are they up to now?"

Laurel resumed the lead after their rest. "Funny you should ask. One brother's dead, killed in a drug deal gone bad, and the other brother's in prison." Time to change the subject. "Look at all the buzzards. Must be something dead over there."

"What about your sister?"

"From what my mom says, I guess she's a prostitute. I haven't seen her in about twenty years." *Gotta shut this down.*

"So how did you get to be so successful—you're a graphic artist, right?"

Shit, she'd opened a hornet's nest.

They rounded a bend and she glanced up the mountain-side completely blanketed in Mexican gold poppies. Purple lupines and several other purple and blue flowers added more color. Laurel grabbed Caroline's arm.

"Look! I've been waiting the entire four months I've lived here to see these wildflowers."

Despite the ever-steepening incline of the trail, Laurel kept up a quick pace. Both women started to sweat. Laurel pulled out a bandanna and wiped her brow.

Caroline sucked in deep breaths, her chest heaving. "Wish I'd thought to bring one of those. Can we rest a sec'?" They stopped for another break, sipping more water. When she had caught her breath, Carolyn said, "So, before we stopped, I was asking you how you ended up doing so well."

Darn, she wasn't going to give up, was she? Finally, Laurel said, a little too sharply, "It's a long story for another day."

"Sorry," Caroline said. "Didn't mean to be intrusive."

Laurel didn't respond and started walking again, relieved that the steepness of the trail made it difficult to talk.

After a series of steep switchbacks, the ridge came into view. Guilt niggled at her about the way she'd cut off the conversation. Finally, she said, "Caroline, I'm sorry I snapped at you back there. It's just that . . . it wasn't just my childhood that was bad . . . my adult life—"

"You know what? You don't owe me any explanations."

I know I don't, so how come I feel like I do?

"Really," Caroline continued. "Sometimes I can be too pushy, and I guess this is one of those—"

"Let's just leave it at this for today. From the outside my life might look okay—good job, nice apartment, nice clothes, yada yada—but the reality is I'm about two steps away from being a train wreck. I just feel like I'm not able to talk about it right now—"

"Oh look. I think we're at the top!"

Thank God Caroline changed the subject. Laurel looked ahead, to the other side of the ridge. She stared down into a large, deep canyon, with a narrow trail snaking down, and a view all the way to Fountain Hills. Looking in the direction from which they'd just hiked, the cities of Scottsdale and Phoenix stretched out in the distance, the eye-popping view she'd told Caroline about.

Neither said anything more about Laurel's childhood. On the way back down the trail, the conversation returned to the animal shelter and other innocuous topics.

This is why I don't make friends. They want to know too much. I just don't want to go there.

The following Saturday Laurel trekked up to her mom's again. A new routine began: do the housework and laundry, run errands. She did the grocery shopping and stopped at CVS. She couldn't believe it when she saw the same guy there, in the chair again, waiting. He sat reading a mystery.

She walked to the counter and said her mother's name. After she paid, she walked over to the guy. "Look who's here."

He looked up. "Oh, wow. Hi. Remind me of your name again?"

"Laurel Peterson."

"That's right. I'm Scott Harris. Hey, at least this time I wasn't snoring."

She laughed and sat down. He looked better today. His graying sandy hair was combed, although it needed cutting, and he wore ironed khakis and a crisp white polo shirt.

"Seriously though, I've been taking care of my dad, who's, uh… been real sick, and I hadn't been sleeping—"

"No need to apologize. I've been helping out a sick mom, so I get it."

They sat looking at each other. She liked his soft gray eyes. Then, both started to talk at the same time. They laughed.

"You go first," she said.

"Maybe you'd like to get coffee sometime. I can't get away for long, and I need to plan, but it would be great to talk to somebody who understands this stuff."

Should she say yes? She could sure use a sympathetic ear. Maybe he could give her some tips on caring for sick parents.

"I'd like that."

They exchanged numbers and Scott said he'd contact her soon.

A few days later, Scott texted her about having coffee. They made arrangements to meet at a Starbucks at five-thirty in the evening. She arrived first and found a quiet table in the back. The aroma of coffee greeted her as soon as she walked in. It was quiet, dark, and almost empty. She watched Scott hurry in. He looked like he might have been physically fit at some point, but now had a paunch.

"Hi, have you ordered yet?"

"No, I was waiting for you. Let's do it."

They walked to the counter. Laurel ordered a decaf mocha, Scott a black coffee. They made small talk over the noise of the coffee grinders while they waited.

When the drinks arrived, Laurel gestured to his cup. "Wow, I'm impressed you can drink caffeinated coffee this late. I'm afraid my caffeine-drinking days are numbered, certainly at this hour."

"I can drink caffeinated coffee twenty-four/seven. It's the only way to deal with taking care of Dad. He's up at all hours needing my help. I tend to grab a couple hours of sleep here and there when I can. Even with all the caffeine, I don't have any problem sleeping, 'cause I'm bone tired all the time."

They walked back to their table.

Laurel blew on her mocha to cool it. "What's wrong with your dad?"

"Diagnosed with stage three prostate/colon cancer three months ago. Spent three weeks in the hospital, then two weeks in a nursing home before being discharged. When I lost my job six months ago, I moved in with him to help him out. It's so humiliating to be fifty-five years old and living back home with a parent, even if I am caring for him."

"Boy, that sounds tough."

"How about you? You mentioned you were taking care of your mother."

"Not exactly taking care of her. More like helping her out. Right after she learned her husband had Alzheimer's, she found out she has Parkinson's. Just diagnosed actually. So, I'm going to Carefree every weekend to give them a hand."

Sure hope I don't end up in his shoes. Scott looked despondent, so Laurel decided to change the subject. "So, you've lived in Arizona for six months?"

"A little longer. Moved here from Massachusetts when I got laid off. I was having a hard time making ends meet on unemployment. Dad encouraged me to move here, saying the economy had recovered and there were jobs. I've been applying for jobs like crazy, but nothing's come through. I wasn't intending to live with him, but when he got sick, that's how it turned out." He stopped to sip his coffee. "At first, I thought he might get better, but it doesn't look that way."

Laurel mulled that over. His circumstances sounded way worse than hers. Seemed like a nice guy though.

Scott finished his coffee. He sighed and sat back in his chair, looking less harried despite the caffeine. "What's your job like?"

She spoke briefly about work—the big project, the deadline, her high-pressure boss—not wanting to get into it too much, since Scott seemed upset about not working.

Abruptly, Scott looked at his watch. "Sorry, but I've got to leave already. I've got someone staying with Dad who could only come for a short time. Maybe next time, with a little planning, I'll have more time."

Is this guy worth pursuing? Friend, maybe?

A week later, Scott texted again, inviting her for coffee later in the evening. What a relief he wasn't inviting her out for a drink. They returned to the same Starbucks.

Again, she arrived first and found a table, the place was virtually empty. As soon as he walked in, she could tell something was wrong. His hair was mussed, face pale, and huge bags under his eyes.

As soon as he sat down, she asked, "How are you?"

"Been better. Pretty exhausted. Dad was hospitalized again with another crisis." He shared details of what had happened, his voice cracking and tears glistening in his eyes. He shook his head slightly as if to clear it. "How are things at your end?"

"About the same. Nothing like what you've been going through. It sounds totally stressful. Honestly, I don't know how you're handling it. Don't think I could."

She thought about her project and pressure at work, which drove her nuts. Should she talk to him about it? With a terminally ill father, he didn't need to hear that right then.

"You'd be surprised what you can handle if you have to," he said.

They bought their coffees and sat at the table farthest from the door.

He stared down at his black caffeinated coffee. "Aside from Dad, what I'm most worried about is that I might start drinking again."

She let the out-of-the-blue comment sit there, unsure how to respond. That explained why he hadn't asked her out for a drink. She toyed with mentioning her own drinking problem.

Laurel played with her napkin. "Have you ever gone to AA?"

He took a big swig of coffee. "Once."

Now she felt like she had to mention her own drinking, but the words stuck in her throat. An uncomfortable silence settled in. She took a big breath and said, "I'm a recovering alcoholic myself. Been sober almost two years." This time. "I go to AA meetings myself."

"Well, I'm not sure I'm an alcoholic. Plus, going to meetings right now would be next to impossible, and I don't think that meeting helped."

After another silence, she asked, "What made you think you needed to stop?"

Why couldn't she keep her mouth shut?

"'Cause I was drinking every day. I got worried something might happen to Dad and I'd be too wasted to help him."

He couldn't make eye contact, and gazed over at the counter where someone ordered.

She swallowed hard. "Yep, that would be bad. Were there times in the past where you drank too much?"

Now she was really pushing her luck.

"Of course. I had two marriages blow up in my face, because of my drinking and drugging, I made some bad decisions about relationships. My second marriage lasted awhile, and we had a child, a girl I never even see." He looked off into the distance. "She's in her twenties now . . ."

That tugged Laurel back into unwelcome memories of her own past. When she tuned back in to the conversation, she heard, "… that second marriage was bad. We did some really hurtful things to each other. Looking back on it, I see she was pretty nutso. I was probably abusive to her. Especially after I'd been drinking. Not really physical abuse, but plenty of emotional. She kept up her part of the bargain, too."

Probably abusive? Uh oh, red flag. "Meaning what?"

"We egged each other on. And, kept coming back for more, long after we should have split."

Been there, done that.

"She always said she stayed for our daughter. But, looking back on it, I can see Jennifer did not benefit one iota from our staying together for so long. By the time I got outta there, Jennifer was thirteen and wanted nothing to do with me. So, I split, looking to get as far away as possible."

By then, the sounds of a vacuum cleaner signaled that Starbucks was closing. The noise made it impossible to talk, so they got up to leave, and walked to the parking lot.

She pulled out her car keys. "So, how did you stop drinking without treatment or AA? I've had trouble pulling it off even with *both* treatment *and* meetings."

"Long story. I gotta get back. I enjoyed talking though."

"Would you be interested in taking a hike sometime?"

"Sure, I'd like that. If I can find someone to stay with Dad. Lemme give you a call in a few days when I have a better sense of what's going on."

Laurel got into her car. Where was this headed? Then she heard the voice of a former sponsor warning about starting relationships early in sobriety.

Chapter 4

The last conversation with Scott got Laurel thinking about her tenuous connection to AA. After dragging her feet for four months, she reluctantly decided she should finally get an AA sponsor in Scottsdale. She forced herself to return to the Saturday morning meeting she'd chaired a month ago. A woman named Starr celebrated twenty-three years sober, so Laurel asked her to be her sponsor after the meeting. Starr agreed, her earnest hazel eyes crinkling when she smiled, and they made an arrangement to get together the next day.

Laurel showed up on Sunday at three o'clock at a tea shop chosen by Starr, relieved that the place was almost empty. Starr, with her wavy, shoulder-length grayish-blonde hair, had already arrived and nursed some green tea. They got right down to work.

"I think we should get to know each other a bit first," Starr said. "Why don't you start by telling me about yourself."

Laurel explained her recent move back to the valley from Miami and her job as a graphic designer.

"And, you've been sober how long?"

"Almost two years. This time."

"So, you've tried to get sober before?"

Laurel glanced around the room to make sure no one could hear their conversation. "Many times. I've been trying to get sober since my mid-thirties. Been in and out of several rehabs, and in and out of AA."

"Sounds like you've worked pretty hard at it." Starr sipped her tea and leaned back in her chair. "Maybe we should start at the beginning, so I can understand how you've gotten to this point. What was your childhood like?"

Crap, first Caroline, and now Starr. She really didn't want to get into this. "How is that relevant to making amends, which is what I wanted help with?"

"Before you can get to that point, you need to have completed the other steps."

"I already did some with a previous sponsor." She squirmed in her seat, not in the mood to go back over all that stuff.

"Maybe so, but for me to be able help you, I need to understand where you're coming from. I need to understand more about you than what you just told me. Why are you so reluctant to talk about your childhood?"

Laurel inhaled the mint aroma from her tea and massaged her temples. "Let's just say I'd prefer not to get into it unless I have to."

"The more reluctant you are to talk about it, the more you probably need to."

How would she know?

"Was there alcoholism or drug abuse in your family?"

Man, this lady was not going to quit. "Both. My mother drank heavily—probably alcoholically—when I was growing up. And, all of my siblings are heavy drinkers and probably use drugs, too."

"You don't sound sure."

"I'm sure about one brother who dealt drugs and is dead because of a drug deal gone bad. The other one is in prison for who knows what. I lost track of him ages ago." She stopped and gazed off into the distance. "My sister, I'm not sure. Haven't seen her in probably twenty years." She stopped again, and Starr gave her some time to continue. "I guess you could say that, given my upbringing, I was pretty much destined to become an alcoholic."

Starr leaned forward and stared at her. When Laurel didn't continue she asked, "So, what was it about that childhood that produced all these substance abusers?"

"You're not going to give up, are you?"

Starr shook her head. "Nope."

Heaving a big sigh, Laurel began. "I grew up in South Phoenix. The four of us had three different fathers. My older brothers saw their dad occasionally when they were little, but that's it. My younger sister and I never saw our fathers. I wouldn't know my so-called father if I bumped into him on the street."

She paused, remembering the crummy apartments they lived in, the three schools she had attended by sixth grade.

"We moved around a lot. I'm not going to go into all the details, but I'll tell you the story of how we all ended up in foster care. That should give you a pretty good idea of what it was like."

Smoke billowed out of the kitchen. My older brothers Paul and Lucas started yelling, and soon we heard sirens. Running down the stairs to the parking lot, we collided with the firefighters dragging up hoses and axes. They sprayed the kitchen, where flames licked at the doorway, threatening to engulf the living room.

When the fire was out, we went back inside. In the smoky living room, a burly firefighter wearing heavy, black gear and huge boots rushed over to Paul.

"Where's your mother?" he asked gruffly.

Paul shook so badly he could barely talk. "Um, we... don't know."

"You don't know where your mother is?" Before Paul could answer, the firefighter asked, more gently, "Who's in charge?"

Ten-year-old Lucas pointed to Paul.

The firefighter pressed his lips together and turned back to Paul. "How old are you?"

"Twelve."

"When did she leave?"

Lucas, the big mouth, answered. "A couple hours ago?"

"And, you have no idea where she is?" he asked, his eyes widening.

I had just turned eight and, trying to be helpful, piped up, "She usually goes to the Towne Bar."

The firefighter glared at us. Were we in trouble? The boys sure were. Mom told them not to cook. They were so stupid. Why did they have to make grilled cheese? It stunk in here.

"Has she ever done that before?" All three of us older kids nodded yes. "And, you have no way to reach her?" I shook my head no.

Betsy, only five, started to whimper. "Laurel, where's Mommy?"

The concerned firefighter shook his head and gestured to his co-worker to come over. "Joe, better call Child Protective Services."

The firefighters until a man and a woman arrived from CPS. It was almost eleven at night, and Mom still wasn't home.

The kitchen was smoky, stinky, and soaking wet. Poor Betsy's favorite teddy bear lay on the floor, a filthy, sodden mess. Mom was going to be really mad.

Mr. Williams and Mrs. Bartollini sat us down in the living room and asked us the same questions the firefighters had asked, plus a lot more, and we gave them the same answers. We didn't know enough to lie, not yet.

Just then, Mom sailed in, reeking of booze.

We stayed with neighbors that night, but the fire triggered a full-scale child protective investigation. Mom knew she was in deep shit and decided to take matters into her own hands. The next day she had all four of us kids pack plastic bags with a change of clothes and our pajamas. She gave each of us a sandwich and a candy bar, and Paul a twenty-dollar bill. Then she drove us to the Greyhound station and put us on a bus to Nebraska to stay with Aunt Alice and Uncle Joe, whom we'd never met. Mom wrote a phone number on a piece of paper, kissed us goodbye, and told Paul to call the number when we got to Lincoln. Her parting words were "For God's sake, don't lose that phone number!"

Forty hours later we finally arrived, hungry and exhausted. Poor Betsy was a mess. Paul called Aunt Alice and explained, as best he could, why we were there. I could hear Uncle Joe in the background saying, "They came by themselves?" We waited more than an hour for Aunt Alice and Uncle Joe to come get us in their rundown, rusted, red pickup truck. They piled us into the back and drove another hour to Denton, a little farm town outside of Lincoln. We barely got settled in and met our three cousins, when we heard loud arguing as Alice and Joe fought over the nerve of Alice's sister, Joanne, to send her four kids to stay with them without even so much as a phone call. Now, Mom was in trouble.

Aunt Alice loaded us on the bus back to Phoenix the very next day. That's how Paul, Lucas, Betsy, and I ended up in foster care.

Starr raised her eyebrows and shook her head. "Holy cow. Okay, I can understand why you were reluctant to get into that. And, you're right, I think that gives me a flavor for what it must have been like. But, here's what I've been wondering. How did you end up as a graphic artist, coming from that background?"

"Even though we moved a lot, I loved school and always did well. Teachers always liked me. I discovered my artistic ability in junior high and some teachers took an interest in me. Even though I got kind of wild by the time I was in high school, I had good enough grades to get into Arizona State and earn a scholarship. That was my ticket out. I probably could have gone away, but I decided to stay in Phoenix because I worried about my younger sister. So, I got jobs that paid my living expenses and made it through ASU."

"Wow, good for you. That's impressive." Starr beamed at her.

"I'm not saying I didn't party—everyone did—but I had to keep up my grades to keep that scholarship." She stopped and stared down at her lap, fiddling with a spoon. "And I tried to keep an eye on Betsy. The boys were long gone, but by the time she was sixteen she had dropped out of high school . . ." Her voice faded away as she thought about her poor little sister. She shook her head. "She was already on her way to being lost by then."

Laurel looked at her watch. Two hours had passed.

Starr carried her cup to the counter and sat back down. "By the way, I'm thinking it might be a good idea for you to find a therapist. Sounds like you've got some issues."

On the basis of this single conversation, she thinks I have issues? Laurel's cheeks flamed with indignation.

"No way! I saw plenty of counselors in those rehabs I was in. Mostly men. Bunch of jerks. Not a single one ever helped me with anything. Absolutely not happening."

She bullies me into talking about my shitty childhood and then tells me I have issues? Laurel stood and shoved back her chair.

"It's nothing to be defensive about," Starr said. "Everyone can benefit from professional help."

Chapter 5

Laurel bumped into Starr at a meeting the following week, ambivalent about whether she wanted her to be her sponsor after that first meeting. She seemed too intrusive.

Starr asked her right away when she wanted to meet again. They agreed to meet one evening after dinner at the same tea shop.

Once settled at a table in the corner, Starr leaned slightly in. "I think we should start at the beginning and go through all the steps together."

Laurel groaned. "Really, I did them with a previous sponsor."

After going back and forth, they agreed on a compromise. They would start working on steps six and seven, which had to do with character defects.

Starr got right down to business. "So, what do you see as your character defects?"

"First of all, I hate that term 'character defects.' It sounds so fixed, so permanent."

"But, the program is all about changing them, so AA doesn't see them as permanent at all. But, we have to identify what they are if we're going to change them."

Laurel still resisted getting into this. She needed help on making amends to her mother, that's it. And, now she felt pressured into looking at herself.

When she didn't respond right away, Starr had go another go at it. "By the way, if it helps, you can look at them as flaws or weaknesses. Plus, I always insist that my sponsees identify strengths. If you'd rather start with that, we can, but we're going to get to those flaws sooner or later. You have to if you want to stay sober."

Discomfort settled into her belly. Could she trust Starr? She stared into her tea. "Well, for starters, I have a real problem trusting people."

"Okay, I get that, given your history. What else?"

"I tend to isolate. I've always been a loner. But, I realized a couple weeks ago that I'm lonely, so maybe that's not working anymore."

"Hmm, doesn't trust and isolates. Do you think they might be related?"

Laurel started laughing.

Starr added honey to her green tea. "What?"

"The way you asked it made it seem so obvious, yet I've never put it together before. Because, duh, another one of my character defects, I guess, is lack of self-awareness."

"I'd agree with that, which is why, last week, I suggested you might think about therapy . . ."

"And, I got all huffy and defensive about it."

"Yep. All annoyed and offended."

Laurel thought about that. "I can get like that, especially when I hear things about myself I don't want to acknowledge."

"Well, maybe it's time you opened up to suggestions and recognized you might need professional help. Doesn't mean you're weak, you know, it means you're human."

Maybe Starr was right. "Okay, I'll think about it. I've told you I have demons, and there's even more I haven't mentioned."

"Okay. Any other thoughts?"

Laurel finished her tea. "The other thing I've been really bad about is lying."

"What's that all about?"

"Well, it goes way back. Started when I was a kid. My brothers and I, we all lied, all the time. Mom lied, too. I thought it was normal."

"Hmm."

"Once my drinking got to be an issue, I just continued lying . . . as natural as breathing. Seemed like I was always trying to get out of something, to cover my tracks. Lying at school, at work, or to my boyfriends. Like, no, I haven't been drinking, or I only had two. It became completely habitual."

Starr stared intently at Laurel. "You know you've got to stop that if you're ever going to quit drinking once and for all, right?"

"Yeah, I do . . ." Laurel grabbed her purse. "One last thing. I don't deal well with stress. I get overwhelmed really easily and keep it all inside. I drink instead of telling someone or trying to cope in a healthy way. If I'm honest, I have to admit that drinking's been pretty much my only coping strategy."

"Wow! Big realization. I'm proud of you, Laurel. Now we're getting somewhere."

Laurel and Scott had been texting or talking every couple of days. He'd started to grow on her. Laurel decided it was time for a real date. So, she invited Scott to dinner at her apartment. He had to make arrangements to get away for a whole evening, but finally the night arrived. Laurel's stomach did flip-flops as she tried to remember her last date.

When he arrived at six-thirty, he leaned over and softly kissed her cheek as he handed her a bottle of sparkling cranapple juice and a bunch of colorful flowers. Laurel appreciated the haircut, and that he'd dressed up in a blue linen shirt and pressed khakis. He complimented her on her dress. Laurel hardly ever wore dresses, but this was a real date, right?

Laurel took the juice and flowers. "Thanks for these. Come on in. Have a seat." Laurel pointed to her sofa.

"Smells good in here. What're you cooking?"

She put the flowers in a vase. "I probably should have asked you if you liked fish, 'cause I've made salmon with pesto sauce, rice, and salad."

Scott grinned. "Sounds yummy. I'll eat basically anything someone other than me prepares."

She poured the sparkling juice into wineglasses and handed one to him. "Unless you'd like Pellegrino?"

"No, this is great. Nice apartment. You have a flair for decorating."

Scott helped himself to crackers and two kinds of cheese on the coffee table. "It's so nice to get away for an evening and relax. Thanks for inviting me."

Laurel sat down next to Scott on the sofa. "How're things with your dad?"

"He's back from the hospital, but it doesn't look good."

"I'm so sorry." She wanted to reach over and take his hand, but hesitated.

"How's your mom doing?"

"You know, about the same. She's pretty miserable right now between her own symptoms and Bill's dementia." She wondered how his not drinking was going but, for once, managed to keep her mouth shut. He'd brought a nonalcoholic drink, after all.

After a few minutes of small talk, they sat down to dinner.

Scott chowed down on his salmon. "Everything is delicious. You're a great cook, you know that?"

"Not really, but thanks. This was pretty easy. I don't cook very often, living alone. It was a nice change to have someone to cook for."

"Well, you can cook for me anytime."

They finished eating and Laurel carried their dishes into the kitchen. "How about some dessert and coffee? It's got to be decaf though."

Scott laughed. "Fine, if you insist, but you know how I feel about decaf. What's for dessert? Something sinfully rich and bad for you, I hope."

"Brownies—not homemade though—and vanilla ice cream."

"Totally fits the bill. Bring it on."

Laurel rose to prepare the coffee and dessert. "Shall we move back into the living room?"

"Absolutely. Can I help with anything? Dishes? Getting the brownies ready?"

Wow, he offers to help with dishes.

"Nice try," Laurel said, laughing. "You just want a shot at those brownies. You're going to have to wait a few minutes, while I make the coffee."

She puttered in the kitchen and brought the coffee and brownies into the living room. She sat down next to him, close enough that their knees touched. A shiver of electricity coursed up her thigh. When she picked up her coffee she noticed her palms sweating. It surprised her how much she liked this guy.

After they finished their coffee and dessert, she carried the dishes into the kitchen and returned to sit next to him. This time she snuggled closer. He put his arm around her.

Scott said, "This has been such a nice evening—"

"Oh no, you're not leaving, are you? It's not even nine o'clock."

"No, I'm not leaving yet," he said, looking intently into her eyes. "But, I wanted you to know how much I was enjoying myself."

She felt hot, her heart thumping in her chest. "Me too, I'm so glad you came."

He leaned over and kissed her, taking her face gently into both hands. She kissed him back. They made out for a while—he was a great kisser—and Laurel found herself very aroused. He put his hand under her shirt to fondle her breasts.

Okay, time to improve the venue.

She took his hand and pulled him up from the sofa, coaxing him toward the bedroom. "Can you stay for a while longer?"

"I thought you'd never ask."

"Oh, you rascal, you. Someone might get the impression you'd planned this out ahead of time.

"Who, *moi?*"

So, they moved into Laurel's bedroom. Her breath quickened. She couldn't remember the last time she'd made love sober. Booze sure made this a lot easier.

They sat down on the bed. He held her and kissed her, long, slow and passionate. She started to get all tingly inside, having forgotten how good sex felt.

"And, look what I remembered to bring."

He took a condom out of his pocket.

Afterwards, they lay on Laurel's bed until it was time for Scott to go. He apologized for having to leave, saying he'd left his niece in charge of looking after his father and he had to be home by eleven.

"Thank you," Laurel said. "It was so-o-o-o nice."

He kissed her goodbye at the front door and promised to call or text when he had a moment. "I feel bad about leaving you with the dishes."

"No worries. Not much cleanup."

He's so considerate. Maybe this one's a keeper.

Chapter 6

Laurel and Starr met a third time. Laurel finally felt ready to work on the eighth and ninth steps: making a list of people her drinking had harmed, then actually making amends to them.

"What made you decide you needed to finally start making amends?" Starr asked.

Laurel sipped her mint tea, and vaguely registered the murmur of employees talking in the background. "Living here in Scottsdale near my mother in Carefree, after living on the other side of the country for a long time . . . I, uh, probably owe her amends."

"Okay, but let's start at the beginning and figure out who's on the list."

They spent an hour coming up with a list of people she had harmed as a result of her long drinking career. It made sense to start with her mother since the others, like her sister, lived elsewhere.

"Okay, I'll get started on it."

Laurel got together for coffee a second time with Caroline after Scott came over. They sat at the same café after volunteering at the shelter again. Thank goodness Caroline had not suggested getting together for a drink after work or anything like that, because she had no intention of sharing her drinking history or status as an alcoholic. Yet, she enjoyed Caroline and appreciated that she apparently got the message that Laurel wasn't ready to go into detail about her past.

Go slow, she warned herself.

It was one thing to talk to Starr about that stuff, but another . . .

On the other hand, Laurel had talked about her mom's Parkinson's and how difficult Joanne could be. She needed to talk to someone about how conflicted she always felt about it. She constantly feared it would overwhelm her—physically, in terms of the time involved, but also emotionally. Her resentment toward her mother kept cropping up, the anger still consuming her when she thought about the lousy childhood she endured, especially foster care and what happened to her there.

No way Laurel would get into that with Caroline. Instead, she focused on the symptoms of the Parkinson's itself, and Bill's Alzheimer's, and all she did on weekends to help her mother.

In the meantime, she worked on the amends she'd promised to start. She chafed at having to do it. Her mother had certainly done more to hurt Laurel growing up than Laurel had harmed her mother as an adult. Feeling stuck, she called Starr to ask whether she really had to do this.

"Did you harm your mother as a result of your drinking?"

"Yeah, we already talked about that. But, she was a shitty mother. She completely fucked up my childhood! She's probably the biggest reason I became an alcoholic. Hell, she should be making amends to me!"

"You're really gonna play the blame game? Maybe you're not ready for this."

"Why?" Laurel pretty much knew the answer.

"Why? Because this about taking responsibility for what *you* did, regardless of what the *other person* might have done to you. It's not about who was worse."

"Oka-a-a-y. I'll give it another try." God, she dreaded it.

"Remember that the word 'amend' actually means change, rather than apologize. Apologies are fine, but most people we've harmed while drinking really just want to see we've changed. So, fess up to the things you did that hurt your mother, and say you're sorry. But, show her how you have cha—"

"I *have* changed!" Laurel insisted. She paced around her apartment, agitated. Winston raced to avoid getting stepped on.

"Can your mother see those changes?"

Laurel raised her voice with annoyance. "How do I know? She *should* be able to! I mean, I've been helping her and Bill every weekend since she asked. Driving them to doctor's appointments and running errands for them, cleaning… stuff like that."

"Good. Last thing I want to mention before you set out to do this," Starr said, "Most people find it really tough to make amends to someone who has also hurt us, like your mother."

Laurel listened intently.

"She might not be all that receptive. She might not forgive you or be gracious in any way. Remember, you're not trying to work out all the problems between you and your mom. The whole point of this is to take responsibility, so *you'll* feel better. And, to find out if there are things you need to do. Are you ready for that?"

Laurel slaved over the amends all week, listing all the bad things she had done to her mother over the years, like having a previous sponsor call Joanne to come pick up Laurel from the Emergency Room after a bad relapse. She dreaded sitting down with her mom, wary about how she would react. But, she wanted to get it over with on the weekend while she helped with chores and errands. Hopefully, Starr was right and she'd feel better afterward.

When she arrived on Saturday morning Laurel stood in the spacious foyer. "Mom, have you got a few minutes? There're some things I'd like to talk to you about."

They walked into the kitchen. Joanne sat at the table. "What's on your mind? If you're going to ask for money, forget it, I don't have any to lend."

After past relapses, when she'd lost jobs, Laurel had sometimes hit her mom up for loans.

"No, nothing like that. Why don't we sit down and have a cup of tea?"

Laurel busied herself filling the kettle and finding mugs and teabags and honey, buying time. She rehearsed, in her head, her amends.

"I know I did some things to you when I was drinking…"

Joanne tsked. "Laurel, I am really not up for this." She still seemed very wobbly, and irritable, as usual.

Standing at the counter, all of her muscles tensed, Laurel took a breath, turned to her mother, and tried again. "Mom, will you please listen for a minute?" *Stop being impatient. Take your time, and stop whining.* "As part of my . . . recovery, I'm supposed to make amends to people I harmed with my, uh, drinking."

Joanne's eyes narrowed. "Well, you sure hurt me enough over the years. Do you have any idea what a pain in the ass it was having to rescue you so many times?" She slammed her fist on the table.

Laurel jumped.

Joanne pursed her lips. "I expected that kind of shit out of the rest of them, but not out of you. Do you have any idea what that was like?"

Both Paul, her surviving older brother, and her younger sister Betsy were a total mess. Always had been. Joanne got no help whatsoever out of them.

Laurel closed her eyes and took another deep breath. Her stomach twisted in knots. This was going to be even harder than she thought.

"Mom, I'm deeply sorry for that. You're absolutely right, I have no idea how hard that was. I have no excuses. I put you in difficult situations over the years—"

Joanne pounded her fist on the table again. "Damn right you did! I can't even count the number of times you pulled that kind of bullshit. Laurel, when are you going to get your act together once and for all? I *need* you now."

Struggling not to raise her voice, despite Joanne's shouting, Laurel said, "I *know* you need me, and I *am* getting my act together. I haven't had a drink in almost two years. I've been going to as many meetings as I can. And, I've tried to be as helpful as I can with you and Bill."

Joanne stood up. "You need to know that there's *nothing* you can do to make up for all the crap you've pulled over the years. I don't care how many doctor's appointments you drive us to!"

"You know, Mom, you weren't exactly in the running for the mother of the year award yourself. Sending us to Aunt Alice after the fire…"

Shit, I just did exactly what Starr warned me against.

"We're done! Get out of my house!" Joanne hobbled out of the kitchen.

Laurel took a sip of tea and tears ran down her cheeks. Though pissed at her mother for being so unforgiving, she also was angry at herself for doing what Starr had cautioned her not to do. Her attempt at amends had gone about as badly as it could. Her mother would never forgive her, and she handled her end of it poorly. Maybe Starr was right, she wasn't ready.

She went to work and attended an AA meeting once a week through the end of April.

Scott had contacted her two or three times a week. Then, a week after their dinner at her apartment, nothing. She called and texted him repeatedly, but he never responded.

"Scott, why aren't you taking my calls, I'm worried about you. Are you okay? Is your dad okay?" she texted.

He didn't respond. How hard could it be to answer her texts, to tell her something had happened and he didn't have time to talk? She couldn't believe he'd ghosted her, that he'd just break up with her—after the relationship they'd developed, after they'd slept together—without even telling her why.

When she wasn't working, she moped around the house and tried to play with Winston. Even hiking didn't interest her. She obsessed about Scott at work. Why wasn't he calling back? What was going on? Couldn't he see how upset she was, how hurt? It drove her crazy.

She texted, *"Please tell me what's going on. Don't I deserve that at least?"*

As one week became two, her initial worry morphed into annoyance.

"Why are you being such an asshole? If I did something wrong, can't you at least tell me?"

Eventually, he texted back, *"Leave me alone. Please back off!"*

To which she responded, *"Fuck you!"*

By then her anger consumed her. It was all she could think about. She had actually started to trust this guy.

"Winston, why did I let myself get sucked in by this guy? He seemed so nice. Then he just drops off the face of the Earth? What a jerk! Why do men have to be such assholes? No more relationships, Winston. You hear that? No more guys, just you."

Chapter 7

Despite it being May already, Laurel came down with a bad cold. When her throat started to feel scratchy while getting ready for bed, she knew she was in trouble. The minute she woke up, the sneezing started. She went to work anyhow—too much had to get done. By the time she dragged herself home at eight, her throat screamed fire and she could barely swallow. The coughing began after dinner and she hacked all night, hardly sleeping.

When she dragged herself out of bed the next day, it felt like she'd been hit by a truck. Her head throbbed and she ached all over. The flu, maybe? She couldn't tell, but it didn't matter. She was really sick and didn't have the luxury of staying home. Instead she worked hard not to spread her germs around, feeling like total crap. Her mood sucked. Grouchy and irritable to her team. They happily stayed away.

The world looked black. She despised colds.

And yet, after weeks of hard work, the firm had landed a big, lucrative contract for all the graphics needs of Desert Arroyo Industries. Laurel's boss couldn't have been happier with her and her team.

More projects landed on her desk and work pressures mounted. She and her crew worked insane hours. Most nights she either stayed until eight o'clock, or took work home with her, slaving away until she couldn't keep her eyes open. Waking up every night with menopausal night sweats drained her, not to mention the coughing and being unable to breathe. When Friday night rolled around she hauled herself home and crashed, too exhausted to find an AA meeting. Saturday mornings she slept in, meeting be damned.

To celebrate landing the big Desert Arroyo contract, Logan announced a blowout party at his house for a Saturday night in mid-May, inviting the agency staff as well as a ton of people from Desert Arroyo. A fancy party was the last thing Laurel needed, but Logan expected it from his team leader.

She spent most of the day Saturday at her mother's, despite still feeling shitty, helping her clean, picking up prescriptions, shopping.

"Make sure you don't leave any of your cold germs and snotty tissues around," Joanne warned.

Neither said anything about the argument they'd had two weeks earlier when Laurel tried to make amends. They waded through tension as thick as mud. Joanne's Parkinson's had advanced—she had trouble walking now—but Laurel could barely dredge up sympathy, resenting being there in light of her mother's lack of gratitude and refusal to accept her amends. So, she did the minimum required and kept her mouth shut.

I can't believe she expects this kind of help from me, considering her lousy parenting. If you could even call it that. And, not a single thank you for all my help.

No matter how hard she tried, Laurel could not stop obsessing about Scott. She berated herself because she'd let him into her life. She'd actually started trusting that jerk! Then, he dumped her without explanation. How did she manage to find so many fucked-up guys?

She couldn't get work out of her head, either. She knew obsessing about all this stuff didn't do her any good, but she couldn't stop. And, now she had to go to this stupid party.

Driving back from her mother's, the thought of a drink flitted across her mind. Just one, to take the edge off. To get rid of these body aches, the sore throat. No, she wasn't going to sink to that. Maybe she should find a meeting. Forget it, she didn't have time, needed to get ready for the party. She longed for the predictable relief and relaxation a drink would provide, the taste of the vodka, icy cold, with a twist of lemon. She didn't want to get wasted, just to get lost in that delicious, floaty feeling after a couple drinks.

No way, don't even go there. What good is that going to do? Just go to this party, get it over with, and move on. With each liquor store she passed, the craving got stronger. Then, without giving it another thought, she pulled into a strip mall and bought a pint of vodka. Not a fifth, just a pint. *I'm only going to have one, later, while I'm getting dressed.*

She needed just a little something to take the edge off and get through this party, to stop obsessing about Scott. To stop thinking about her stupid mother. To pull the plug on those thoughts. How else was she supposed to make small talk with all those Desert Arroyo executives?

As soon as she walked in the door at four o'clock she got a lemon out of the fridge, plopped ice in a glass, and poured herself a tall one, putting the rest of the Stoli into the freezer. At five, with the Stoli all nice and frosty, she made a second. And, at seven, while getting dressed, a third.

She drove to the party, savoring that sense of ease and comfort, of relief. No pain. She could do this now.

Logan sure knew how to throw an extravagant party. He lived in a gorgeous ten-thousand-square-foot mansion in Silverleaf, built into the side of the McDowell Mountains, with neighboring billionaires and professional athletes. From that elevation, after dark, guests could view a million gems of sparkling colored lights in the valley below. Sliding glass doors covered the entire back of the house, opening onto a yard that dazzled—an enormous negative edge pool with a waterfall, palm trees, and full outdoor kitchen. The agency must be doing really well for him to be able to live like this.

Waiters in tuxes served fancy hors d'oeuvres—caviar and sushi—from silver trays. An open bar beckoned. Tasteful jazz played in the background. About twenty-five people, her staff, as well as other people from work and Desert Arroyo execs, dressed in designer clothes and partied away. She felt comfortable in the form-fitting black cocktail dress showcasing her trim figure, with her chestnut hair shiny, her makeup perfect. Usually she hated these kinds of affairs, but tonight she felt relaxed, almost enjoying herself. She had another vodka with a twist when she arrived, and later the champagne flowed freely.

By ten-thirty, she had put in her required appearance and said her goodbyes.

As she waited for the valet to bring her car around, she noticed she had more than a little buzz going. *Better open all my windows to drive down the winding roads through Silverleaf, so the cool night air will sober me up.*

But she had trouble controlling the car. *You need to drive super carefully*, she warned herself. But, no matter how hard she tried, she had trouble keeping the car on the road, weaving left then right.

She heard the sirens before she noticed the blue and red lights flashing behind her.

Shit, they were pulling over! She moved over to the side of the road and stopped, her heart drumming in her chest.

Instantly, a Scottsdale police officer stood beside the car. Her hands shook so badly she had trouble turning off the ignition.

"Ma'am, I need to see your license, registration, and proof of insurance."

A polite, handsome young officer shone a big flashlight around inside the car.

Damn, I hope I have them. As if that was the worst of her problems. Laurel got her license out of her purse and fumbled through the crap in her glove box, finally finding her registration and insurance card. She handed them all over. Her hands still shook, and sweat poured down her face and from her armpits. The other cop walked around the car. So far, she hadn't uttered a word. Time had stopped dead in its tracks.

"Where've you been tonight, Ms. Peterson?"

"To a party at my boss's house in Silverleaf." Could he smell the booze?

"And, where are you going?"

"Home, to my apartment, on Bell Road." *Don't say anything more than you have to*, she warned herself.

"Do you know why we stopped you?"

She shook her head no.

"Because you were driving fifteen miles per hour and your car was swerving all over the road. How much have you had to drink?"

"Two drinks." *Oh God, I am so screwed!*

"Ma'am, I can smell alcohol on your breath and your speech is slurred. I need to ask you to get out of the car."

Try to act normal. Getting out of the car, she had trouble keeping her balance.

He held a rectangular black plastic thing up to her face with a clear tube sticking out of the top.

Oh no, a breathalyzer!

"Ma'am, take a deep breath and breathe into this tube."

She was so freaked out, she had trouble breathing at all, much less taking a deep breath. When she blew into the device, nothing registered.

The cop said, "Ma'am, you need to take a deep breath and try again."

She did, but couldn't see the reading.

"Okay, now I'm going to conduct a field sobriety test. First, I'd like you to stand on one leg."

He must be kidding.

No matter how hard she tried, she could barely lift one foot off the ground a few inches without losing her balance. She tried not to shake. Could they see how badly she was sweating?

"Okay, the last thing I'm going to ask you to do is to walk along this painted line here over to my partner."

She tried to follow his instructions, but could barely put one foot in front of the other on that line with nothing to hold onto. *Oh man, I am so drunk.*

He walked back to the police car while his partner stayed with her. Finally, he came back.

"Ma'am, I'm arresting you on suspicion of driving while under the influence, and taking you into custody. You're too intoxicated to drive. We're going to take you downtown for a blood test."

As if on another planet, she listened to him read her Miranda rights. His partner handcuffed her hands behind her back and told her to get into the back seat of their cruiser. She felt dizzy and thought she might vomit. What had she done to herself? As soon as the door closed, she started to cry.

A perfect storm.

Chapter 8

The officers drove Laurel, handcuffed in the back seat of their car, downtown to the Scottsdale Police Station. They arrived after midnight. An officer helped her out of the car, holding her up, because she could barely walk. He led her into a small windowless room where a phlebotomist drew blood while she sat, numb, and tried to stop shaking.

After an eternity, a female cop entered the room and told Laurel they were charging her with extreme DUI due to her high blood alcohol level—0.22, almost three times the legal limit of .08. Furthermore, she said, a computer search revealed she had two previous DUI charges, one in Florida and one in Massachusetts.

"Because this is your third, you will likely face two separate charges. Extreme DUI and aggravated DUI. Arizona's got some of the toughest DUI laws in the country. Ms. Peterson, you are in a lot of trouble"—as if Laurel didn't know—"and I'd suggest you contact an attorney."

Struggling to focus, slurring her words, Laurel mumbled, "Don't have one."

She needed to lie down, to make this all go away. Her head throbbed. Was she going to puke? She hated puking. Scanning the room, she found a small, black plastic waste basket, in case she needed it.

The female cop left and returned with her cell phone, along with typed list of lawyers specializing in DUI.

If only her head would stop spinning.

Laurel studied the list, seeing double. Putting her left hand over one eye, she found a name at random and called the number.

A groggy-sounding man answered. "Mickey Lane."

"Hi, my name is Laurel Peterson." Barely intelligible. "I've just been arrested for DUI in Scottsdale—"

"Can you speak up? I can't understand you."

"I've just been arrested for DUI. I'm at the Scottsdale Police Department right now. I don't know what to do next."

Mickey told her he'd meet with her in court on Monday morning. She wasn't sure what to expect, but it wasn't that.

"You mean I'm stuck here until Monday?" Those party hors d'oeuvres now lurked at the back of her throat.

When she got off the phone, the female cop told her she'd be spending the night in lockup. "Do you need to call anyone?"

Laurel shook her head.

"Come with me."

She followed the officer down a long corridor to a cell in the back of the station, relieved to see it empty. She felt too physically horrible to even consider how much trouble she was in. There'd be plenty of time for that tomorrow . . . and the day after that. Meanwhile, it was a relief to lie down on the cot and just pass out.

After a fitful sleep, disturbed by bizarre dreams, Laurel awoke on Sunday morning. Where the hell was she? It all came crashing down on her.

Oh God, I've fucked up so bad!

As she struggled to remember exactly what happened the day before, an officer arrived with some water, asking if she wanted breakfast. She shook her pounding head no, still too nauseous to eat.

"What happens now?"

"You stay here until court first thing tomorrow morning," answered a new cop, a dark-skinned Latino guy with a beard.

Great, stuck here all day. Shit, she was supposed to be at her mother's today. "Can I have my phone back for a few minutes?"

When he brought her the phone she saw a voicemail from Mom. She called her back to say she wasn't feeling well and, of course, her mother let her know how pissed off she was. Laurel didn't even consider telling her about the relapse and the DUI. She simply apologized and said she'd try to come in the evening during the week to do what she couldn't do on Sunday.

Next, she left a message at her office that she had a family emergency and wouldn't be in on Monday.

She yelled for the officer. "Do you want my phone back?"

"Nah, you can hold onto it. Ready to eat yet?"

"Uh-uh. Any chance I could get a couple of Advils?

"Lemme see what I can find."

She spent the morning ruminating about the mess she was in, finally calling her lawyer again.

"Mickey Lane."

"Hi, this is Laurel Peterson again. I talked to you late last night about my DUI."

He paused a beat. "Oh yeah, right. Where are you?"

"Still in the Scottsdale Police lockup until tomorrow. Could we talk before I meet you in court?"

"Uh, okay, I guess. Shoot."

Laurel asked about how much trouble she was in, explaining to him again what happened and what the charges were, since he didn't have her paperwork yet.

"Assuming you're correct about what the charges are, Ms. Peterson, you're in a shitload of trouble. We'll find out for sure tomorrow morning at your initial appearance. Your first big problem is that your BAC was 0.22, which is considered a 'super extreme' DUI in Arizona. Although that's still considered a misdemeanor—"

Hearing the word misdemeanor, Laurel exhaled a quick—too quick—sigh of relief. She relaxed her shoulders.

"It comes with very hefty fines, up to twenty-five hundred dollars, and a non-negotiable forty-five days in jail."

He paused when he heard Laurel's sharp intake of breath.

"Jail? You've got to be kidding me." She had trouble catching her breath and fought to hold back the tears.

"Do you have any other DUIs?"

"Um, two, both misdemeanors. In other states, though."

"When?"

"Uh, one three years ago and one . . . let's see . . . about six years ago."

"Then that's your biggest problem. If this is your third DUI within eighty-four months—seven years—then that means that this charge gets upgraded, so to speak, to aggravated DUI—"

"Wait, what? Even though first two were misdemeanors and they were in different states?"

"Doesn't matter. We'll see what happens tomorrow, but I'm pretty sure they're going to charge you with aggravated DUI, which is a Class 4 felony."

"Which means what?" Suddenly she remembered the female cop's words from last night: aggravated DUI.

"If you're convicted, which you most certainly will be because of the breathalyzer, assuming the blood test confirms it, your license will be revoked, and you could go to prison for up to two years."

Her whole mind exploded.

"Prison? You can't be serious! Two years? No. That can't be right. How can that be?" Sitting alone, on her cot, in the windowless, dingy lockup, Laurel started trembling and sobbing. "But, can't we fight it? Surely you can do something."

"Laurel—can I call you Laurel?—you need to understand that these are very serious charges and you don't really have a leg to stand on. Fighting it, going to court, would require some kind of defense—which you don't have—and probably ten grand. Even if you had ten grand, there's no point. You won't win, because you don't have a case."

Too stunned to speak, her mind racing like a stallion, Laurel tried to get her head around this thing. Jail? Prison? But, wait, didn't he say "could go," not "will go?" *Oh my God. I can't believe where drinking has finally taken me. This cannot be happening.* She had to find a way to make this disaster go away.

The next morning, a white van transported her to a nearby downtown courtroom to hear the charges. She met Mickey Lane, a hunched over, sad-looking, middle-aged guy, with bags beneath his eyes, bald, with a gray comb-over.

They waited in the back of the courtroom, Laurel still in her party dress, now all wrinkled, with mascara running down her cheeks. Mickey wore a rumpled dark suit. The courtroom looked pretty much like the ones seen during her previous DUIs and what you saw on TV. At the front, a judge perched on an elevated platform. In front of him sat two rectangular wooden tables, one for the defense and one for the prosecution, in her case an assistant district attorney, ADA, from Maricopa County. On the right side, a raised platform featured two rows of seats for the jury, empty this morning. This one looked newer than other courtrooms she'd been in.

The arraignment lasted less than three minutes. The ADA read the charges. Mickey nailed it. There were two separate charges, one for extreme DUI and one for aggravated DUI, both felonies. The judge released her on her own recognizance, so no bail. Upon learning she'd recently moved to Scottsdale, though, he cautioned her not to leave town. Mickey noted she was employed—at least for the time being—and not a flight risk. Then they were done, for now. Still, even though it came off exactly as Mickey had led her to expect, she felt wounded. It confirmed her worst fears: She might be facing jail and even prison.

Afterward, Mickey drove her to his nearby office on a side street in downtown Scottsdale. She followed him into the building, a knot in her chest. They entered a small waiting area with an empty receptionist's desk.

"Have a seat in my office," he said, pointing into a small room. The whole place looked shabby, the beige carpeting dirty and worn, the off-white walls scuffed and in need of a paint job. Obviously, not a high-powered attorney.

She took a seat across from a large desk. Covered in multiple, disorganized piles of papers, almost no surface area visible. It gave her a bad feeling.

Mickey sat down at his desk and cleared away some of the piles.

She pulled herself together enough to speak. "So, what happens next?"

"We negotiate with the DA for a plea agreement. Once we agree, there'll be an arraignment where the plea is entered. Then you'll be sentenced. By pleading guilty right away, they might be open to reduce the penalties somewhat, so you're not facing the absolute worst."

She started to ask about the absolute worst and changed her mind. Too scary. She shook her head to try to clear her mind and looked up.

"So, what is this going to cost me?"

"Assuming we agree that I'm going to represent you, my retainer for DUI cases is four thousand dollars."

She whistled. Four grand! Was he kidding? Already in debt because of things she did before she got sober the last time, where would she get that kind of money?

"I'll take a credit card. I doubt it'll run a whole lot more than that, assuming we proceed as I've suggested with the plea agreement. There's some paperwork I need you to fill out before you leave, a contract and some other things."

Handing him her Visa card, she felt like a zombie. He charged it and handed it back to her. She filled out all the paperwork, totaling up in her mind what this whole shit storm would cost her. She still had no idea she would be charged for the privilege of going to jail and being on probation after prison.

Mickey offered to drive her the short distance to get her car, the nicest thing that had happened to her in the previous forty-eight hours.

She paid one-hundred seventy-five dollars to pick up her car, and sat in the car, sobbing, unable to drive, the implications of the whole disaster soaking into her pores. How the hell would she get out of this one? She couldn't believe she'd finally done something so bad that she might go to jail. She berated herself. *Why didn't you learn from the other DUIs? Man, I could really use a drink. Shit! You idiot, how can you still want to drink?*

Finally, she had the most rational thought she'd had since she drank that first vodka. She needed to get to a meeting. She had to figure out how to stop drinking once and for all.

She got home early Monday afternoon, took a shower and ate something. While driving to her mother's in Carefree, she debated telling her what happened. Right then, Laurel craved only to be numb, totally numb, to make this insanity go away, if only for a few brief moments.

As she approached Bill and Joanne's house with a lump in her throat, she felt the familiar dread overtaking her. Drinking always made her a complete wreck. Once inside, wresting up her courage, Laurel began.

"Mom, I have something I need to tell you. On Saturday, after I left here, I started drinking—"

"Laurel—"

"Please, Mom, let me finish. Sometimes I get so overwhelmed with everything that I just give in to the craving." *Stop whining.*

"You know what, Laurel? I don't want to hear it. I have my own problems. Do you think having Parkinson's is a picnic? Or, how about taking care of a husband who wanders off and gets lost? How much fun do you think that is? You need to man up and just get sober!" she said. "I did it years ago, and there's no reason you can't too. Just stop drinking, once and for all!"

If only she could. At a loss for words, Laurel wondered what should she take on first: why she couldn't stop drinking, or how bad her mother's situation was. She'd been selfishly focused on her own problems, forgetting about others' challenges.

"Mom, I'm sorry. You're right. You do have your own problems, and my problems are largely of my own making. But, I think the way for us to get through this is to help each other."

"You're damn right you're gonna help me."

Laurel dissolved into tears. "Mom, I'm going to have to go to jail. I was arrested the other night for DUI, my third. I might even have to go to prison! I don't know what I'm going to do."

"Laurel, I can't believe what a fuckup you've turned out to be."

As she drove home from her mother's, Laurel started feeling sorry for herself. Mom was right, she was a fuckup. Thinking like that, though, wouldn't get her anywhere.

When she arrived home, she called Starr and asked if they could meet up at the seven-thirty meeting. Starr couldn't make it, but they arranged a phone call at nine o'clock. Laurel hoped she might have a sympathetic word. She needed someone who could help her figure out how she could get through the next terrifying phase of her life.

After the meeting, she called Starr back.

"Laurel, how are you?"

After a long pause, fighting off tears, Laurel told her about the last couple weeks: Scott breaking up with her, having the amends she tried to make to her mother blow up in her face, the crazy hours at work. And finally, she told her about the relapse and getting arrested.

"I'm a total mess!"

"Wow, I had no idea all that stuff was going on. I thought you were doing pretty well. Man, your drinking has really taken you to a whole new bottom, hasn't it?"

"Yes, it has. Oh, Starr, what am I going to do?" Laurel wailed.

She sat on the sofa in her apartment, Winston on her lap. Her carrying on had just scared him half to death.

"Well, first, have you been to a meeting since the incident?"

"Just came back from one, and I know I need to start going every day again. I'm not drinking, and I know I can't drink anymore. It just kicks my ass every time."

"Okay, so you're not drinking, that's good. What happens next in your case?"

"My lawyer said I have no case at all, no defense I mean, with the BAC reading being so high and this being my third DUI—"

"Third?" Starr groaned. "Oh, Laurel . . . "

"I know. I've totally screwed myself."

She started to sob. Finally, she stopped crying enough to explain to Starr everything she knew about what was about to happen—court, jail, prison.

"How come both jail and prison?"

"I guess one of my charges—I'm not even sure which one—carries an automatic jail sentence—but because they're felonies, I'll be going for longer than a year. That means prison, I guess."

Her life was about to change in ways she could never have imagined. Could it get any worse?

Chapter 9

Memorial Day weekend fast approached. Three days off with nothing to do was dangerous. She started planning how to fill that time. Maybe go to the office for part of it, and she certainly had to make a meeting each day . . . but what else could she do? Would Caroline be around?

Wednesday morning, as she walked into the office, Logan's secretary stopped her and said he wanted to see her. Uh oh, what now? She headed over to his office. Talking on the phone, he waved her in. As she waited for him to get off his phone, butterflies fluttered in her stomach.

"Have a seat and close the door."

Shit! This couldn't be good. She sat down, trying to calm her stomach, a knot in her chest. She held her hands together in her lap so Logan couldn't see them shaking.

"It's come to my attention that you had a DUI late Saturday night, I assume on your way home from my party. I'm not completely surprised, because I think it was pretty obvious to lots of people there that you'd had too much to drink—"

"Logan, everyone was—"

"Drinking. Sure, they were, Laurel, it was a party. But, not everyone got drunk and got arrested for DUI on the way home."

Sweat poured off her face. Avoiding eye contact, she saw herself floating on the ceiling, peering down on this scene, like some kind of bad dream she couldn't wake up from. It felt like an out-of-body experience, and kept getting worse.

Laurel's brain raced, trying to figure out how to respond. She couldn't manage to put a sentence together.

Obviously exasperated, Logan said, "You have nothing more to say?"

She shook her head. She just couldn't come up with something that wouldn't make it worse. She wanted to scream, "This is so unfair!"

"Well, I'm sorry, but I feel like I have no choice but to terminate you. I can't risk losing an important new client because of a management-level employee behaving unprofessionally at a work function. Not to mention your arrest appearing in the local paper—"

The newspaper? It hit her like a sucker punch. "Wait, no—" she blurted out.

"I'm sorry, but you'll need to clean out your desk by the end of the day."

The end of the day! That statement shocked Laurel right out of her paralysis. "Logan, wait, please let me say something here."

He nodded for her to go ahead.

"Look, I'll admit, I did have too much to drink, and I was arrested." She considered telling him she was an alcoholic, that she had gone back to AA. In the end, all she said was, "Please, I'm begging you. Just let me work until I start my jail sentence, in a month or so. Or, at least until you can find a replacement."

She couldn't believe she was talking to her boss about a jail sentence. *Please, God, let me wake up from this nightmare.*

Logan shook his head slowly.

"Please, at least think about it. Wouldn't it be better to have me around while you're searching for someone to replace me?" *Lose the whiny tone, Laurel.*

"I've already decided that Ross will replace you."

That little snake!

"Fine, but please consider giving me a month before you fire me. Please, Logan. I've done a good job since I've been here."

She hated begging.

Laurel squirmed in her seat while Logan said nothing. Should she continue to beg—so not her style—or just keep her mouth shut? Maybe she'd already said too much.

He sighed. "Okay, I'll let you know on Tuesday, after the holiday weekend."

Finally, she dredged up the nerve to say, simply, "Thanks for considering my request."

Begging was so humiliating. She walked out of his office, raw, shell-shocked, physically wounded. As she returned to her desk, she passed the room where the team worked, and overheard Nikki.

"Ross, you're such a rat. I can't believe you actually went to Lo—"

So, it was Ross. That slithering bottom feeder! When she got to her desk, she couldn't focus on any of the projects she needed to be working on. She thought about leaving for the day, but it was still early, and it would look bad. No, she had to stay put and at least appear to be working.

Instead of delving into her projects, she decided to take matters into her own hands, to think things through, to plan for what would happen next. Her sublet lease ended at the end of June. Convenient… by then she'd probably be in jail, and maybe on her way to prison. So, she wouldn't need it—and couldn't afford it—since she wouldn't be working. Wait, didn't Bill's house have a casita? Maybe she could stay there for a while if she had to.

What about her car? Bill's house had a three-car garage, so she could probably leave it there. Oh, crap. Her furniture. She didn't want to sell or give all her belongings away. She had accumulated them over many years, some from trips abroad, too nice to give away. At some point, she'd be on her own again, and it would cost a fortune to replace all that. Okay, she had to talk to her mother about that, too. Between the garage and the casita there'd probably be room to store her stuff. But, wait, what about Winston? Mom hated cats, so that wouldn't work. Only two other options: Starr and Caroline.

She thought about calling Caroline, but rejected the idea. Caroline, of course, knew nothing of any of this. Not even about her being in recovery. She didn't feel ready to go there yet. She did call Starr, though, to touch base and tell her the latest bad news: losing her job.

What else could go wrong? She found out soon enough. Starr said she couldn't possibly take Laurel's cat, especially since it was unclear how long Laurel would be gone. She already had a cat, and a dog.

Okay, Laurel, don't get bogged down. Just put one foot in front of the next. At lunchtime, she found a noon AA meeting nearby. She'd be late, but better to catch part of it, given her shitty day.

The meeting cleared her head enough to return to work and actually get something done. She slept well that night for the first time since the relapse. Having a plan made sense. She needed to feel she had some modicum of control to face the dark days ahead. If she didn't drink, maybe, just maybe, she could get through this.

Thursday. She just had to get through today and Friday before the weekend. Laurel called her mother and offered to drive up on the weekend and help her and Bill with whatever they needed. Wait 'til she found out the real reason for the visit.

That afternoon Caroline texted her about a hike on the weekend.

Laurel studied the text, trying to decide whether to feel relieved or worried about it. She did need to talk to Caroline about the possibility of taking Winston—maybe for as long as a couple of years. But, she dreaded having to explain what happened, which meant talking about her past. Every time she started to trust someone, she felt like she got slapped down, most recently by Scott's disappearance.

But right then, she needed a friend, someone she could talk to and hopefully look after Winston for a while. Okay, if she told her tale of woe to Caroline, what's the worst that could happen? She could refuse to take Winston and act like a bitch when she heard Laurel's pathetic story. Since Laurel would be off to jail soon anyhow, no biggie. She'd survived worse.

So, she invited Caroline to dinner at her place, worried that when she spilled her guts, she might be a hot mess. She didn't want to be in a restaurant, for sure, or even at Caroline's apartment.

The relief she felt when the plans with Caroline fell into place surprised her. The next big hurdle: talking to her mother about storing her stuff there and staying in the casita if the worst-case scenario came to pass. Ugh.

Which is better, she wondered, to be optimistic that the worst might not happen, setting yourself up for a big disappointment when it did, or to be more negative about the future by accepting the worst-case scenario right now? Too existential for her to handle at the moment.

Dreading the prospect of seeing her mother and asking for help, Laurel drove to Carefree on Saturday morning. She argued with herself on the way there, trying to convince herself that maybe this time would be different, but she remembered how badly the last two visits had gone.

She completed the usual chores and errands. At one o'clock, leaving the dryer whirring away, she took a break and found a new AA meeting in Carefree. By three o'clock, exhausted, she began to regret having invited Caroline for dinner, because she still faced the hardest part of the visit.

She finally asked her mother to sit down in the kitchen for an iced tea with her. "How've you been feeling, Mom? I mean with the Parkinson's and all."

"Pretty shitty. I don't think the medication is helping, and it's expensive."

The tremors had worsened, and Joanne's speech was even harder to understand. Now her breathing sounded labored.

Laurel ignored all that. "Well, you don't seem to be too much worse. Maybe that's the best you can hope for." Immediately, she regretted saying it, and prepared for her mother to lash out. But Joanne didn't react.

Laurel heard snoring from the other room. "How's Bill doing? Seems like he's barely around when I visit. He's gotten so thin. He's either sleeping or just sitting in front of the TV."

"Yep. That's all he does. I have a hard time getting him to eat anything. He can't get dressed or ready for bed, or do anything without help from me. But, so far, he still knows who I am."

"Have you thought about having someone come in every day, or even every few days, to help with him? Could he afford that?"

"He can afford it. That's not the problem. He doesn't like the idea of strangers in the house or handling him. I don't think anyone my age likes that idea."

"I understand. But Mom, really, I think you're going to have to consider that option. With your own health problems, I'm not sure how much longer you can handle him alone."

"You're right, but he's been so good to me I hate to force him into something he really doesn't want to do." She took a sip of her tea. "How about some of those chocolate chip cookies you bought?"

Laurel got up to get the cookies. It felt good to get up and walk around. She felt antsy at the prospect of changing the subject to her own problems.

She opened the package of Pepperidge Farm cookies, her mom's favorite, and finally marshaled enough courage. "Mom, I need help with a couple of things that won't cost you anything." She stopped to weigh her mother's response.

Joanne's eyes narrowed. "Like what?"

"Well, for one thing, when I go to jail"—avoiding the mention of prison—"I'm gonna need someplace to store my car. Could I park it in your driveway or garage?"

Joanne started in on her third cookie. "I guess that wouldn't be a problem . . ."

"The other issue is my furniture. My lease is up in June, and by then I should be in jail."

"You're gonna give up your apartment?"

Now Laurel started fidgeting and squirming in her seat. She didn't say anything right away, knowing her mother would freak out at the word "prison."

"Aren't you gonna need it after jail?"

"Here's the thing, Mom. Someone at work ratted me out, told the boss I got arrested for DUI, and he fired me."

Joanne's head whipped up. "Oh Jesus!"

"I know. I'm in deep shit. But, it might not have even mattered that much because, after jail, my lawyer said I'm probably going to prison."

"Prison? Are you kidding me? I'm gonna have two no-good kids in prison? What in hell did I do to deserve this?" Joanne's voice became as loud as she could manage. "Dammit Laurel, just when I needed your help!"

"I know, Mom, it really sucks." Laurel held back tears, knowing her mother associated crying with weakness. For the first time, it dawned on her that her screw-up affected someone other than herself. "Hopefully I'll only be in prison for about a year."

She knew this was likely a lowball estimate of her sentence, but she couldn't bear to upset her mother any more than she already had.

"We're gonna get through this, Mom," Laurel said, as much to herself as to her mother. She leaned across the table and grabbed her mother's hand, about as much physical affection as her mother could tolerate. "As soon as I'm out, I promise I'll be as helpful as I possibly can."

Of course, Laurel failed to take into account where she'd likely be living—nowhere near Carefree—or the fact that her driver's license would be suspended or revoked.

Joanne groaned. "So. Your furniture. I'm not sure there's enough space to fit it all. Of course, I've never been invited to your apartment, so I don't know how much you have."

Laurel ignored the dig. "Well, I think between the garage and the extra bedrooms I can probably squeeze it all in. Plus, isn't there a casita? Is that furnished?" Her backdoor way of finding out about the casita's availability.

"Yeah, there's a casita. Haven't really been out there in a while. I think it's furnished, but there's probably some space there, too."

That's all Laurel needed to know about the casita for now: that there was one. She decided to avoid mentioning that she might need to stay there for a short time. Her mother had surprised her. Joanne agreed to let her store her car and possessions there.

Best not to push her luck.

She looked at her watch, hugely relieved. "Already after four. Gotta go. I have a friend coming for dinner. Thanks, Mom. I appreciate you letting me store my car and stuff here. I'll be back next weekend to help. Just keep track of what you need me to do. I know I fucked up on this one, I do, but I'm gonna do better. Promise."

She considered giving her a quick kiss or hug and decided against it.

Chapter 10

Back at the apartment, preparing for Caroline's visit, Laurel asked herself, *When was the last time you had a girlfriend for dinner? Miami, maybe? Shit, when was the last time you even had a friend?*

She cleaned for the second time that Saturday, vacuuming and dusting. Before she showered, she surveyed her beloved apartment. It struck her: I am about to lose it all, this beautiful apartment, the job I really like. She started drifting toward despondency, but stopped herself.

Laurel, knock it off. You fucked up. But feeling sorry for yourself, sitting on the pity pot, is not going to help. Get a grip! You invited Caroline for dinner. You need to find a temporary home for Winston. Get it together to do what you need to do.

She did. By the time Caroline arrived at six-thirty she was set. The apartment was ready, the dinner was ready, and she was ready. When the doorbell rang, she had plucked up her courage to do whatever it took to let her new friend know what happened and how she needed her help.

She had no idea how it would turn out.

"Hi, Laurel. Thanks for inviting me over."

Caroline handed over a plate of crudités, wedges of whole-wheat pita, and hummus, while she held onto the fruit tart for dessert. She looked very summery in a breezy navy tank top and white linen drawstring pants.

Laurel grabbed the appetizers. "Hi there. Thanks for all the goodies. Why don't you have a seat while I get us something cold to drink?" In the awkward moment when guests expected the host to ask, "White or red?" Laurel asked, "Do you like Pellegrino and lime? I also have some pomegranate juice I could add to make a spritzer."

Caroline sat on the white linen sofa. "Pellegrino and lime with a dash of pomegranate would be perfect. Boy, it's already getting pretty hot outside, isn't it?"

Laurel bustled in the kitchen to prepare their drinks, serving them in thick, Mexican, blue-rimmed glasses. She brought over Caroline's plate of veggies and hummus, and put it on the coffee table.

Her friend took her drink. "Ooh, that looks so refreshing, the red against the blue. I'm starved." She helped herself to carrot sticks, red peppers, and hummus, and dove right to the point. "So, you said you needed to talk. What's going on?"

A big gulp of her drink eased the lump in Laurel's throat. "When we were hiking . . . No, let me start again." She couldn't look Caroline in the eye or figure out how to say this succinctly, and still be honest. "I guess I'll just say it straight out. What I haven't told you yet is that I'm an alcoholic." She looked up for Caroline's reaction. "A chronic alcoholic. To make a very long story short, I was almost two years sober when we first met. Then a week ago, at a mandatory party at my boss's house, I got shit-faced drunk and was arrested for DUI on my way home. And, now I'm really down in the weeds."

Once again, she found herself fighting back tears. It seemed like every time she turned around she was crying or trying not to cry. Plus, soaked with sweat. Damned hot flashes.

Neither said anything for a beat. Caroline's eyes looked gentle.

"Laurel. I had no idea." Her voice registered softly in the silence. "I'm so sorry. Do you want to talk about how much trouble? Actually, before you do, let me just say, I'll probably understand a lot better than you might think."

Doubtful. "Okay, I will, but let's cook dinner first and we can talk over dinner. Want to help me grill the chicken on the balcony? It'll be hot out there, though."

"Sure. Let me know how I can help."

Laurel went into the kitchen to retrieve the chicken, marinating in a spicy lemon-olive oil mix. "Would you grab that plate of vegetables on the second shelf?"

They took their drinks out to the small, shady balcony looking out onto treetops. Laurel had placed colorful flowers in Mexican ceramic pots and added a couple of houseplants. Birds warbled in the background.

Carolyn put her legs up on a striped chaise lounge. "It's nice out here. Surprisingly comfortable."

Laurel fired up the Weber and they cooked their dinner, the smell of grilled chicken and rosemary perfuming the air. They made small talk until the food was ready, with Caroline tactfully avoiding any specific questions about Laurel's situation.

They went inside and sat in the dining area. Laurel added a brown and wild rice dish to the grilled meat, and zucchini, eggplant, and peppers. As soon as they each served themselves, Laurel shared the details of the arrest, the discovery of the other two DUIs, and the separate "super extreme" charge. The whole sordid thing, nothing held back. She hoped she wouldn't regret it.

Caroline's first response stunned her. "Oh no, I can't believe you did that."

"Come on, Caroline. Please don't judge me. I fucked up! I know that," Laurel said, her voice rising, her words rushing out so fast Caroline blinked several times. "I take responsibility for that. When I get overwhelmed, I freak out and I drink. That guy Scott I told you about and really liked, he ghosted me—gone, no explanation. I was working, like, seventy hours a week, exhausted, and trying to help my mother who's going downhill. I know it's not an excuse, but it's an explan—"

"Wait! Hold on. I wasn't judging you at all. Or, at least I didn't mean to. Honestly. I get it, I really do." Caroline took a second serving of vegetables. "So, what does all that mean?"

Laurel carried the plates into the kitchen. "I'm like a zombie in a nightmare I can't wake up from. Seems like every time I turn around something new and horrible happens. Want some decaf?"

"That would be great. What do you mean?"

"When I went into work on Tuesday, my boss fired me."

"What? Why?"

"One of the guys who reports to me, who I've always suspected wanted my job, ratted me out. Told the boss I got arrested after his party. They publish DUIs in the local paper, apparently. And, guess who's gonna get my job when I'm gone?"

"That guy. So, how long do you have before you're out?"

"Originally he said immediately—"

"Wait. What? That's so unfair."

"I tried to negotiate for a month, or until I go to jail."

"You're going to jail?"

"Every DUI conviction in this state leads to jail time. Hang on a sec while I grind the coffee beans."

Soon, the smell of fresh ground coffee filled the air.

When the grinding noise stopped Caroline continued. "You're kidding."

"Wish I was. But, it gets worse, way worse."

"Oh, no. I'm afraid to ask."

"I'm most likely going to prison."

When Laurel dropped that bomb, Caroline said nothing. She got up, went into the kitchen and hugged her. "You probably won't believe this, but I can totally relate."

"Let's get our coffee and go into the living room." What did she mean she could totally relate? "Do you want some of the tart now or later?"

Caroline laughed. "When it comes to dessert I'm pretty much always gonna say now. That's why I struggle with my weight."

Laurel sliced two pieces of tart, admiring the dark chocolate drizzle over the brightly colored berries, kiwi fruit, and mandarin oranges. She poured the coffee and carried everything into the living room.

Laurel sipped her coffee. "When you said you could relate, what did you mean?"

"I'm in recovery, too. Five years ago, I developed an Oxy-Contin problem after knee surgery. It was unbelievably easy to get my hands on it, working in an orthopedic practice. At first, I just stole samples. Eventually, I stole pages from the doc's prescription pads and wrote my own scripts. I even used at work. Of course, inevitably, I got caught."

Her story stunned Laurel . . . the last thing she expected. Somehow, as twisted as it seemed, it almost comforted her to hear about someone else who had also screwed up big time.

"Oh, boy. So, what happened?"

"Gigantic shit storm. Stealing drug prescriptions is a felony, so I was arrested. I pled it down to a misdemeanor, but I had to go into a long-term program for nurses with addiction issues. Took a year to complete the program and I have to be supervised for a l-o-o-o-ng time. My new bosses are okay with it. I essentially landed on my feet.

"But…" She stopped for emphasis. "I lost my marriage. Duane just didn't understand addiction. Couldn't get why I just didn't stop once it became a problem. Couldn't accept me as a recovering person. Couldn't forgive me. Eventually, I said enough is enough and walked. By that time, it was mutual."

Laurel stared into Caroline's dark brown eyes for a minute. "Wow, quite a story. Never in a million years did I expect this conversation would lead here. I've been a nervous wreck trying to summon up the courage to tell you about me." Laurel paused, trying to digest all she'd just heard. "Do you still go to meetings?"

"Absolutely. Sometimes I go to NA meetings, and sometimes I go to the Fellowship Club down at Scottsdale Road and Shea. A lot of the people in those AA meetings also have drug problems." Caroline finished off the last of her tart, licking her lips. "That was *delicioso*."

"Do you consider yourself an alcoholic?"

Caroline took a sip of coffee. "Sort of."

Laurel laughed. "Meaning what?"

"Well, booze really wasn't my drug of choice. Opiates were, but I know if I drink there's a chance I'd start to use again, so I can't risk drinking."

"I *hope* I have finally accepted that once and for all. If going to jail and prison doesn't convince me of that, I don't know what will."

Time for the big ask.

"I know I don't know you very well, Caroline, but I have a huge favor to ask. Is there any chance you could take care of my cat Winston while I'm gone? It could be as long as a couple years, I guess. Hopefully not that long, but . . ."

"Geez, I don't know, Laurel." She tugged at her earlobe. "I've never had a cat. Always been more of a dog person. Can I meet him?"

"Sure. He's probably hiding. Since I've always lived alone with him, he's pretty shy. He's kinda old, too. Fifteen. He's healthy, but if you can't do it, I think I'm gonna have to turn him over to the shelter. I would totally hate to be one of those people who does that, but I don't really have any other options. Let me see if I can find him."

Laurel left for a couple minutes, finally dragging poor Winston out from under the bed where he'd been hiding.

"Listen Winston. No squirming or struggling or trying to get away. We gotta make Caroline see what a nice guy you are."

She sat down on the sofa with him in her lap. Quite large, almost eighteen pounds, he looked even larger because he had such long, silky gray fur. She petted his soft white paws and the white spot on his bib. He finally settled down and started purring, which he sometimes did when he was scared, like now.

"He's very affectionate. Come on over and sit next to me."

Caroline came over and Winston let her pet him, continuing to purr. "He's a *big* boy."

"Yeah, he is. But, he's no trouble, really. He's so good. The most loyal male in my whole life. Please just think about it, okay?"

"Okay, I will. I know you're really in a bind. I should probably get going, Laurel. This was a great evening, really, even if you did have such bad news to share. You're gonna get through this, you are. Keep going to meetings. Thanks so much. I'll be in touch. Or call me, anytime, really."

Would she take Winston?

Chapter 11

Laurel returned to work on the first Tuesday in June, refreshed after the holiday weekend, praying Logan would let her keep her job for a month, or until she went to jail. For once, luck was her friend. Against his better judgment, he decided she could work until the end of the month, acknowledging she'd done a good job since she started. She felt ridiculously grateful, almost embarrassing herself, and him, as she thanked him.

June passed in a whirlwind. Laurel still worked seventy hours a week and went to help her mother every weekend. Helping out acted as insurance against Joanne changing her mind about providing needed storage space there, and because Laurel knew she needed one remaining big favor. . . Even though staying in the casita wouldn't be a huge inconvenience, since it was a totally separate space, it was still an imposition. She scavenged boxes and made arrangements to move at the end of the month, busy every second.

She attended an AA meeting almost every day and talked to Starr often. She had to accept, once and for all, her powerlessness over alcohol. Between being arrested and losing her job, she had no doubt about how totally unmanageable her life had become.

Mickey Lane called to say he'd negotiated a plea agreement with the ADA, with a tentative date set for the end of the month at the Superior Court in downtown Phoenix. This assumed she agreed to the plea: forty-five days in Tent City jail, followed by sixteen months at the state women's prison, with credit for time served. So, fourteen-and-a-half months in prison. Also, she'd suffer a suspended driver's license for at least year following prison, plus two years on probation.

It hit her like a tsunami. "Oh, God! Really? That's the best you could do?" She couldn't believe it. She thought she had prepared for this. Her worse fear. Locked up for a year and a half. How would she survive that?

"Laurel, this is a good deal! You could've gotten two years. You've got to be realistic. The jail time, license suspension, and probation are statutory—not negotiable."

Laurel moaned. "Okay, okay. I hear you. You told me this is what I was looking at. I've been trying to prepare myself for it, but it's still a shock to hear you say it. When do you think I'll actually go to jail?"

"Not for a while. There's at least one more court date after the one at the end of the month, for sentencing. I'll try to get on the judge's calendar as quickly as I can, but it'll probably be mid to late July. You'll go to Tent City immediately after that. So, you'll have to be ready."

"All right. Thanks."

She hadn't heard from Caroline since Memorial Day weekend and still didn't have an answer about whether she'd take Winston. She assumed the worst and dreaded having to put him in the shelter, knowing how stressful it would be for him and how unlikely an older cat like him would ever get adopted.

In a text conversation, they agreed to have coffee on Saturday, after volunteering at the shelter. Once they sat down with their coffees at Jolta Java, Laurel asked Caroline if she'd decided about taking Winston.

"I have. I'll take him on a trial basis, with the understanding that if it doesn't work, I'd have your permission to bring him to the shelter." Caroline fiddled with her earring, avoiding looking at Laurel. "I know it's not what you hoped for, but never having had a cat, I feel like I need an escape hatch if it doesn't work out, since you won't be available. And, since it's for such a long time." Finally, she looked up for Laurel's response.

"Thank you. That's a reasonable compromise. I should have a little time—maybe just a couple of days—between jail and prison, and I'll be back in touch then." She couldn't believe herself talking like this, so matter-of-fact, about going to jail and prison. Like she was leaving for vacation or something. "I won't be able to drive, but I'd love to see how he's doing… to visit him before I go prison."

Starr had helped her with the acceptance of all of this.

"Sure, I'll come get you. Do you know yet how long that's gonna be?"

"Pretty much what I expected. With credit for the month and a half in jail, fourteen and a half months in the women's prison."

"Aw, Laurel, I'm so sorry."

"Don't be. It actually could have been worse. My sponsor's been working with me on taking responsibility for my actions. And, a bizarre thing is happening in my head. Now that I've accepted that I'm going away, I just want it to get started."

Laurel told Caroline about her lease ending and moving to her mother's casita.

"Nice of her to let you stay there."

"Haven't asked her yet."

Movers would come at the end of June, giving Laurel a couple of days to clean her apartment and finish up at work. To save money, she packed everything herself. So, she was over-the-top busy with work and getting ready for the move the last week in June. Between that and procrastinating about asking her mother about the casita, Laurel's guts churned. Finally, the weekend before she had to move, she broached the subject while in Carefree helping out.

Joanne wasn't thrilled, as expected, saying Laurel asked too much of her. But, in the end, she agreed, along with a reminder that no one had stayed there in years.

"Probably filthy."

Well, Laurel would just have to deal with it. One more thing for her to-do list. As the last couple weeks got busier and busier, she considered skipping meetings, just to give herself a little more time, but she knew Starr—and Caroline—were holding her feet to the fire. She'd committed to go to at least five a week. She did.

Her day in Superior Court played out as expected. At the end of June, the judge accepted her plea agreement, with her sentencing hearing scheduled for mid-July. She'd report to jail the next day. Surreal.

The move was chaos. Everything got carted over on Sunday. Her apartment had to be super clean, because she needed her two-thousand five-hundred-dollar security deposit back. With no savings, she needed all the cash she could get her hands on, especially her final paycheck, to make it through the next year and half of not working and paying her lawyer. She'd been doing pretty well on reducing her credit card debt until she had to put his retainer on her card.

By the time she finished cleaning her apartment, it was eight o'clock, and she still had to drive to her mother's. She arrived, exhausted, vacuum cleaner in hand, knowing she still faced cleaning the casita. Joanne had it right: barely furnished and filthy.

Nonetheless, she had a free place to stay until she went to jail. Eight hundred feet square, with a double bed, love seat, and one comfortable chair. A tiny bathroom, with a sink, toilet and shower stall. Every surface needed cleaning.

So, at eight-thirty Monday night she got to work. While the bedding washed, she vacuumed, dusted, and cleaned the bathroom. By ten-thirty, when she took her clean sheets and coverlet out of the dryer, the place was finally habitable. After making the bed, she took stock: this would work. Small, but the huge windows made it bright. She'd spruce it up a bit with some of her things, like brightly colored pillows, now stored in the garage, and she'd be good to go for a while. She had her laptop and iPad, books, and privacy. No Internet and no cable, but she'd be okay. Good practice for jail and prison. Or, so she hoped. She collapsed into bed and set her alarm for her last day at work on Tuesday.

Not working was weird, but Laurel settled into a new routine in the casita, helping her mother and Bill. She expected this period before Tent City to be like a mini-vacation. Take a long walk in the morning before it got too hot, catch up on reading. How wrong she was. Taking care of her mother and Bill filled her day. Joanne made it clear that if Laurel lived in the casita, she'd have major responsibilities around the house, and Laurel agreed. She cooked every night, did the shopping and other errands, cleaned, and took Joanne and Bill to various doctor's appointments. What would they do when she left?

Every day, she attended an AA meeting, regularly met with Starr, and got together for coffee or dinner with Caroline. Her friendship with Caroline deepened now that she didn't have to hide a huge part of her life.

A week before her sentencing hearing, Laurel had her final meeting with her attorney. The month had flown by. Mickey informed her she'd be sentenced to Sunstate, which she'd never heard of.

Laurel sat in silence, absorbing the finality of it. Despite her expectations, the confirmation jolted her. She didn't know what to say. "Sunstate?"

"Sunstate Women's Correctional Facility, the women's prison in Buckeye, on the west side of the valley."

"Sounds horrible."

Mickey snapped back with, "Frankly, Laurel, given your previous DUI convictions and your blood alcohol, I think it's an okay deal. Not a sweet one, but it could've been a lot worse. You'll be out in a little over a year with credit for the time you spend in Tent City. You can deal with that. And, with any luck, it'll be minimum security." Again, he said—this time almost apologetically, "It could be a lot worse, Laurel."

She sat with that a while. "And after that?"

"Like I said, two years on probation. Meeting with your probation officer regularly. No drinking, of course. Random drug and alcohol tests. Probably mandatory participation in a substance abuse program. Maybe community service. Any other questions?"

"Is prison going to be worse or better than jail?"

"Interesting question. Depends on what you mean by better or worse. There'll be some programming in prison, 'cause people stay there longer. Food might be a bit better, but don't get your hopes up." He paused for a minute. "Let's see, you'll be with pretty much the same group of people every day, unlike jail where it's constant turnover. Not sure whether that's better or worse. There'll be counselors there, so you'll have someone you can talk to if you need to. And if you're interested in getting sober, I think they have AA meetings."

"*Of course,* I'm interested in getting sober," she said, annoyed. "So, let the judge know that, okay? If there are AA meetings at the prison, I'll go.

"What's the name of the prison again?"

"Sunstate Women's Correctional Facility. Anything else?"

So, she was on her way to *the* infamous Tent City, which made national news for being one of the worst jails in America. Her new digs would be an Army surplus tent from the Korean War—along with two thousand other inmates. She learned she should bring two towels, a paperback book, up to forty dollars in cash, a flashlight, and reading glasses. No heat and no air conditioning in Arizona jails. Summer temperatures inside the tents could soar to 130 degrees. God help her.

PART II: SURRENDER

Chapter 12

In the cab on the way to the Lower Buckeye Jail on a steamy day in mid-July, Laurel mulled the pathetic state of her life. Her head was filled with noisy voices she couldn't quiet. *I can't believe I left my mother in the lurch. I am such a loser. I can get sober for a while and then,* poof! *Drunk again. Usually over something stupid. That asshole Scott. That fight with Mom.*

Every time she thought of jail and prison her insides twisted.

They arrived at a huge, multi-story complex of white concrete buildings in South Phoenix, surrounded by chain-link fence topped with razor wire. Fighting to control her breathing, she paid the cab driver and walked in.

"I'm surrendering," she said to a uniformed guy behind a glass window. "Laurel Peterson."

Another uniformed man took her elbow. "This way."

They searched her and locked her into a holding cell with twenty other women. At nine in the morning, it was already hot in there. Six women leaned against the scuffed cinder-block walls and the remainder sat on the cold, stained, concrete floor. Most were white or Hispanic.

She wasn't about to sit on that filthy floor. Given how most of the women were dressed, they probably didn't care.

They wore shabby, skin-tight jeans, stretched-out gray sweats . . . Walmart specials. Some wore short-shorts, their flab hanging over the too-tight waists like cake batter overflowing the pan. Several were obese, covered in ugly tats. The distinctive nasty smell of dirty hair filled her nostrils.

Say hello to the ladies you'll be spending the next month and a half with.

No one said a word, the only sound came from an ineffective fan whirring overhead. One by one, someone called a name, and a woman rose to leave with a guard. Whenever a seated woman relinquished her seat, several others scrambled for the vacated chair. At one point, as two women arrived at the chair at the same time, a scuffle broke out.

"Get the fuck off!" a huge Latina with long greasy hair yelled. "I got here first!"

A big busty blonde took her on. "The fuck you did!"

A guard swooped in and grabbed the arm of the blonde who had a smidge less of her fat buttocks on the chair. She started to protest.

The guard glared. "Shut your mouth and stand, or sit on the floor."

Was that why Mickey had told her to make sure she minded her own business, so she wouldn't have to fight? Something else to worry about. She hadn't had a physical altercation since her brothers taught her how to fight off other kids when brawls broke out in her Phoenix neighborhood. Unless you counted the times when she had to defend herself against that asshole boyfriend in New York who threw her down the stairs.

Time dragged. Eventually—it must have been lunchtime—her legs and lower back started to throb. Reluctantly, she sat on the disgusting floor with the others. None of the seated women offered to let someone who stood or sat on the floor take a turn in her chair. Not that kind of women.

By late afternoon, the room sweltered. She covered her nose against the sour smell of sweat, flatulence, and unwashed hair.

Someone asked the guard escorting a woman out, "Can't they make it cooler in here? Get rid of that stink?"

He laughed. "You don't like this? Wait 'til you get to Tent City."

Her stomach rumbled. Finally, a guard called her name. She braced her arm against the wall and stood, her muscles cramped and tense.

A woman with her hand on her chest complained of trouble breathing. The guard held a clipboard and glanced at her, wheezing and struggling to catch her breath. Would he ask if she needed an inhaler or water? Nah, not gonna happen.

Instead, the guard glanced at Laurel.

"Follow me."

He guided her into a small, windowless room and instructed her to complete some paperwork. After what felt like a half an hour he returned to take her to another stale, windowless room. He instructed her to press her fingertips onto some kind of electronic device. Next, she stood up against a white background marked off like a yardstick while a camera popped mug shots—front, left profile, right profile. The flash of bright light momentarily blinded her.

More waiting.

Eventually an officer handcuffed her and escorted her to another holding cell with a different group of women from the ones she'd seen in the morning. After even more waiting, she trudged to a white van that transported her to Tent City.

Geez, that took an entire day. On the other hand, what was the rush?

After a short drive, she arrived at Tent City on Phoenix's northwest side. She clambered out of the van. This was no easy feat with her hands cuffed behind her and her feet chained in shackles. An enormous jail complex, even bigger than Lower Buckeye, loomed in the bleak desert landscape, surrounded by another razor-wire-topped chain-link fence. She'd seen pictures online, but it still shocked her. Rows and rows of khaki canvas tents. The roads were paved, but the rest was dirt. Inmates milled around in black and white striped uniforms like a herd of zebras.

That's gonna be me any minute now.

She waited in line outside a brick building and eventually received her jail ID. Now, she'd been reduced to nothing more than an anonymous number. They issued her a skimpy blanket, a sheet, and a pink towel. No pillow. Then she got her very own zebra jail uniform: a top and bottom made of fabric with four-inch-wide, horizontal black and white stripes, plus pink polyester granny panties. *You can't even wear your own underwear?* She changed in a restroom.

Finally, a male guard escorted her to a large canvas tent, sides rolled up to allow more air to circulate, and gave a five-minute orientation to her and three other women. Twelve double-decker bunks, metal cots really, lined the sides of the tent. They assigned inmates a top or bottom bunk. She got stuck on top. Man, was it filthy, nothing to keep out the blowing desert dust and dirt.

Every three hours, around the clock, they conducted lockdown counts. At midnight, three, six, and nine in the morning; and noon, three, six, and nine in the afternoon; a loud announcement sounded over the staticky PA system telling inmates to sit on their bunks, with their IDs visible, for an identification headcount.

The first night, the announcement awakened her from a fitful sleep at midnight. She had failed to leave her identification visible, so the guard performing the headcount shook her and barked, "Where's your ID?" Trembling, she found her ID.

She tossed and turned for the remainder of the night.

The next morning, the inmate in the neighboring bunk whispered to her to attach her ID with a rubber band to her bunk.

On her second night, a very loud banging woke her. Quavering, she overheard another recent arrival ask about the noise. The men incarcerated in another unit called the Towers, a two-story men's jail just on the other side of the fence, liked to bang things against the metal bars covering the windows to attract the women's attention. They held up signs that read, "Flash." Sometimes the women would accommodate.

Squinting, she glimpsed men masturbating up against the backlit windows, even with no one flashing. She moaned. How disgusting. A knot tightened in her chest. Despite wearing the stupid black and white striped uniform, she felt naked, exposed.

The first few days at Tent City passed in a slow blur, like living in a thick, stifling fog that wouldn't burn off. Unmoored, Laurel did not get up for meals, and slept as much as she could. No one cared, or even noticed. Living in the tents in the extreme heat felt like being in a blast furnace. Between the heat and lockdown counts every three hours, she never slept for long. Even though no one had threatened her—yet—she witnessed some frightening arguments between inmates.

Mickey was right. To survive, she needed to keep her head down. But, staying on constant alert exhausted her. Her heart raced all the time, which kept her striped uniform always drenched in sweat. She stank. She feared someone would hurt her, or she'd break a rule she didn't even know about and get written up.

The jail was mostly empty during the day. Some went out to their jobs on work release, allowed to wear street clothes. They returned to the tents at night and on weekends. Most of the remainder—wearing their zebra uniforms—worked at the jail or as part of one of the chain gangs. The sheriff bused them out in the community for roadside cleanup and landscaping. Others worked inside the jail, delivering meals, or in the kitchen or laundry. She kept waiting for someone to make her work, but it never happened. Would working be better or worse than doing nothing all day?

She didn't intend to withdraw from the other inmates, she just couldn't muster the energy to initiate—or even respond to—conversations with the other women. They baffled her. Some acted friendly with each other, chatting, laughing, even telling jokes. She found nothing about this experience worth laughing about.

On her second weekend, a heavy-set Latina from her tent spoke to her in a Spanish accent. She looked about forty, with slick, messy black hair, covered in gang tats.

"Hey, you gringo bitch. What you lookin' at?"

Laurel looked away. *Don't respond. Just ignore her.*

Another inmate—*Jazmin?*—said, "Leave her alone, Cecilia. She di'nt do nothin' to you."

Cecilia stood with her hands on her hips, glaring at Laurel. "What'sa matter wit' you? You think you're better 'n the rest of us? You can't even answer my fuckin' question?"

In the still, stifling heat, Laurel sat on her bunk, heart pounding, head down. She fingered the coarse texture of her blanket. Probably better to say something, because it didn't seem like she was going to back off. "Sorry, what was your question? I didn't hear you."

"Oh, so you're *not* stuck up. I asked you, how long you in here for?"

"Forty-five days."

Cecilia bent down, getting right into Laurel's face. "What'd ya do?"

Jesus, Laurel could smell the woman's sweat and see her blackheads. Her heart hammered in her ears. She *really* didn't want to get into this. Again, she ignored the question.

But, Cecilia persisted. "Didn't you hear me? I jus' asked you what you did to get in here."

"Cecilia, back off. Leave her alone." Jazmin again.

Laurel covered her face with her hands, dropped her head, and mumbled. "I had a DUI." She looked up and brushed her hair back from her face. "Please leave me alone."

"Now, was that so fuckin' hard?"

Yeah, it was.

She hated the nights, lying in her own sweat, soaked. Sleep refused to come. Sometimes the temperature didn't dip below ninety-five, even with the tent flaps up. And every three hours, the PA system woke her up. Except for the weekends, she was alone in her tent all day long. Fine with her because, with everybody around, tension crackled in the air. It felt so damned unpredictable. Anything could happen. Would there be a fight? New women came and went every day.

Despite all the people around, she'd never felt so completely alone.

She lost count of the days, which all ran together. Had it been more than a week? She felt faint and could barely walk. She couldn't remember when she last ate. *I'm going to have to start eating the crappy jail food.* They served two meals a day, a bagged meal counting as both breakfast and lunch and a hot "dinner" meal. The bagged "brunch" consisted of a piece of fruit, some kind of mystery meat, a roll, and crackers. Or maybe peanut butter and bread.

Better to start with the bag meals, which didn't look too bad. But, sometimes she got so hungry at night she dragged herself over to the cafeteria. Dinner usually consisted of some type of unidentifiable hot slop. Hardly anybody ate there. Curious. She'd read online that the sheriff bragged about these meals costing taxpayers only fifteen to forty cents. Totally believable.

Each time she finished eating, her belly threatened diarrhea. Jail was the last place on earth you wanted to suffer from diarrhea. The only toilets sat completely out in the open—no cover, no door, no privacy. The stench made her queasy. At least, if she didn't eat, she didn't have to use the toilets so often.

One day, Laurel was alone in the tent with Jazmin, a skinny young black lady with processed spiky hair, and asked, "How come there's hardly anybody at the cafeteria?"

Jazmin laughed. "Cause nobody wantsa eat that nasty shit over there. Work-release people eat when they're out, and other folks buy food at Commissary."

"You mean there's more than chips and soda at Commissary?"

"Yeah, they got other stuff, like chili, and burritos, and Lunchables."

Laurel wished she'd brought in enough money so she could've done that. Forty bucks wouldn't last long. Better save it for essentials like deodorant. The other inmates must be bringing more cash in.

One day, a guard announced she had mail. She retrieved the letter, which had already been opened. Oh good, a letter from Caroline!

"Dear Laurel,

Just a short note to tell you that I've been thinking about you. I'm guessing you're on about day 14 at this point, and I'm sure you're counting the days. Since it could have been me, I've been thinking a lot about what it would be like, although I honestly can't imagine it. Please write back and tell me what it's like.

Winston's doing fine so far. I think it's going to work out okay. He hid a lot the first few days, but he's been coming out more and sat on the sofa with me the other night. He hasn't come into my lap yet, but he lets me pet him and he purrs. We're not exactly best buds, but you shouldn't worry. I'm sure he misses you.

It's been too hot (as I'm sure you know only too well) to exercise outside, so I've been working out at the gym. I miss our hikes. It's kind of unbelievable to me that there's no air conditioning there. That should be punishment enough.

Anyhow, that's about it. Please know that I'm praying for you and will be eager for a visit when you get back and before you go to prison.

Hang in there. You're going to survive this and be stronger for it.

Caroline"

Her friend's letter was the first good thing that happened since her arrival at Tent City. Laurel couldn't believe Caroline was praying for her, having completely forgotten about prayer.

Back when she'd returned to daily AA meetings, after the relapse, she'd started to pray for the first time. She asked for forgiveness for what she'd done to hurt others and help in staying sober.

Now, especially, she needed the Serenity Prayer: *God, grant me the serenity to accept the things I cannot change, the courage to change the things I can, and the wisdom to know the difference.* She couldn't remember a time when she'd had to accept so many horrible things, most of which she'd caused herself.

Her sponsor Starr had suggested she start a gratitude list. For a while, she had regularly listed off the things she was grateful for, in spite the turn her life had taken. Otherwise, it was easy to lapse into anger and resentment about everything she'd lost.

So, she vowed to start praying every day and start a gratitude list again. *I've got a ton to be thankful for, like Caroline, who took the trouble to write and that Winston's okay.* And, only about a month remained on her jail sentence. Despite jail, she was healthy. It surprised her to admit it, but Mickey was right: it could be worse, much worse.

She read Caroline's letter over and over, each time despondency set in. When she wrote back to Caroline, she complained about the heat, and the boredom, and the food, and the other inmates, who she described as tough, scary, and sometimes crazy, often getting into fights.

She asked if Caroline could pick her up when she was released at the end of August. She knew that was a long shot because she worked. If not, maybe Starr could do it.

The days passed, each hotter and muggier than the next. Time slithered by like a snail leaving a slimy trail on the floor. The extreme heat made it hard to even walk around. It was too stinking hot to even try to sleep during the day.

Laurel read when she could. She'd finished *The Goldfinch* by Donna Tartt, a long one, a few days back. The book, with its description of a young man's descent into drug addiction, triggered painful memories of her alcoholism. Each time he lied, she thought about her own lies and where drinking had taken her.

The weekends weren't any better than the weekdays, with absolutely nothing to do, unless you considered playing cards with a bunch of drunks, drug addicts, and thieves at picnic tables in the broiling sun something worth doing. She tried not to listen when inmates talked to each other, to shut them out. Every time somebody new came, she watched Cecilia boss them around, jockeying for power, letting newbies know, in their tent, she was boss. Like there was anything to be in charge of. Whatever. She still followed Mickey's advice and kept her head down.

The days crawled by. Sometimes she felt like she was losing her grip. No matter how much she prayed or went over her gratitude list, crazy shit pinballed around in her head. Like, *I'm never gonna get out of here.* Like, *someone's gonna kill me.* Like, *what's the point, when prison's all you have to look forward to anyhow?*

The air simmered, hot and thick with moisture, dead still. Laurel could hardly breathe. She just couldn't seem to suck in enough air. Walking back from dinner she watched the buildup of towering white, fluffy clouds behind the mountains in every direction. The Arizona monsoon was in full force. The pressure built and built, and then *wham!*, a monster storm lowered the temperature to where you could almost breathe. Sweltering, she prayed for a thunderstorm. Maybe her wish would be granted. A monstrous anvil-shaped thunderhead had formed to the east. She heard a low rumble of thunder. The wind kicked up dust devils, columns of dirt whirling into the air.

As she got closer to the tent, the wind strengthened. Dust and dirt blew everywhere, the blowing grit stinging her face. Where could they hide if this turned into a tornado? No basement or protection, and the tents totally exposed. The sky quickly turned black, leaving her with an uneasy feeling. The air almost cracked with electricity. A huge bolt of lightning brightened the sky, immediately followed by a sonic *boom!* That one was close. The sharp, clean, metallic scent of ozone stung her nose.

She ran for the tent. Huge raindrops splattered the hardpan. The temperature had dropped ten degrees.

She heard her tent mates before she saw them. When she reached the tent entrance she caught her first glimpse of the commotion, her hair whipping around, getting soaked.

"Roll the damn tent flaps down!" Chelsea yelled to be heard over the sound of the wind and thunder.

"No way!" Cecilia replied. "I want 'em open so I can feel the breeze."

"Breeze? Are you crazy? That's not a breeze, it's a gale wind. Roll 'em down!"

"Fuck you. Not happening."

Two other bunkmates, Michelle and Brittney, sat on their cots, watching them argue.

Cecilia jumped up and pushed Chelsea hard. She fell back onto the cot.

Chelsea charged toward her attacker. "You fucking bitch! I'm tired of you controlling everything. You are not in charge here!"

But, Cecilia deftly moved out of the way, and Chelsea lost her balance. Both started in on each other, shrieking epithets and curse words, arms flailing, each trying to scratch and bite the other.

Where the hell were the guards?

Rain blew in sideways. Lightning flashed and thunder roared right above them, the wind howling. Cecilia and Chelsea, oblivious, yelled and swore and threw punches while Brittney and Michelle cowered.

Laurel watched, heart racing. Suddenly, she mobilized. Without thinking, she rushed into the tent. "Stop! Stop it, you two! Knock it off!" She insinuated herself between the two and, shoved them apart.

"Cecilia, we have to put the tent flaps down or our beds are going to be soaked. Shit, they might already be soaked. Go outside if you want to get blown away."

Cecilia started to resist, to fight back, but Laurel gave her a menacing look. "Back the fuck off!"

They both retreated.

Wow, she hadn't been sure Cecilia would actually do it.

Laurel gestured to the other women. "Seriously, someone's gonna get hurt. This storm is dangerous. Let's get the flaps down before we're sleeping in puddles tonight. It's miserable enough already."

Chelsea started to untie the flaps.

Laurel glared at the immobile Brittney and Michelle. "Come on, you two. Get moving. Let's get these flaps down."

It took her right back to her childhood, breaking up fights between Lucas and Paul, who went at each other like ferrets. Mom nowhere to be found.

Cecilia came around. "Brittney, Michelle, you heard her. Get moving. Let's get these tent flaps down."

Everyone started laughing, running around like maniacs. They untied the heavy canvas flaps, wet and blowing like crazy in the wind. Afterward, they each climbed onto their bunks to sit in the near darkness, out of the wind, and listen to the rain pelt the canvas tent roof. The roar made it impossible to talk.

That's when the hail started. From her bunk next to the tent entrance, Laurel watched it fall. Soon, hail covered the ground in white. It looked like snow. In short order, the sky cleared as the thunderclouds rolled off to the west. The temperature had plummeted. It was almost chilly.

Laurel slid off her bunk, walked outside, and scanned the sky. *Maybe there'll be a rainbow.*

Cecilia stepped outside and looked at her. "Girl, you are some badass." She bent down and scooped up a handful of the hail. "Is this what snow's like?"

"Yep, pretty much. Not as grainy as this though."

Laurel gazed up at the now blue sky, thunderheads visible only in the distance. She bent to fill her hand with hail, feeling the icy cold pellets melting through her fingers.

No rainbow.

Chapter 13

As her last days at Tent City approached, Laurel grew squirrely. Prison loomed like a dark gray cloud. She paced in the tent and obsessed about what Sunstate would be like. Her emotions twisted into a big gnarly mess, jumping all over the place. Her rational brain had been hijacked.

She hugged herself. *Will prison be harder or easier than jail?* Her chin trembled, she held back tears and, again, cursed her decision to start drinking before that stupid party.

She needed a talk with herself. *Try to remember what you learned in AA about coping, about not getting overwhelmed.* For the hundredth time, she asked herself how she would manage to get through the next fourteen months of being locked up. *Breathe. Stay in the now. Don't get too far ahead of yourself.* She tried to remember the affirmations they talked about.

Oh yeah, you're strong enough to get through this. You'll be even stronger when it's over.

She felt anything but strong. *Laurel, you've got this. You've survived almost a month and a half in jail.*

Her lawyer called one day. "The Maricopa Probation Department is going to interview you and write a report for the judge. Someone will contact you for an assessment, either in jail or by videoconference, in the next week or so. The staff will set it up and let you know the specifics. How're you doing?"

Should she tell him? Scared shitless. Holding on by her fingernails. Nah.

"Fine, looking forward to moving on to the next phase."
Lie.

As Mickey promised, a woman from Maricopa County Probation contacted jail officials and set up a face-to-face meeting.

"My name is Wendy, and I'm your pre-sentence investigator. My job is to write your report that'll go to the judge… an overview of your offense and history. I'll ask you some questions that'll determine your supervision level when you're placed on probation, so your probation officer will have a good understanding of how best to supervise you."

Questions and more questions, about everything from Laurel's health to her employment status, culminating in how she'd pay all the fines and fees she'd be responsible for.

"In the state of Arizona, when you're convicted of DUI there are some pretty hefty fines, fees, and financial obligations imposed by the court. Especially if you go to prison. Once you're released, what are your plans to pay those fines and fees?"

Jesus. She had totally forgotten about those fees. *Fuck, this nightmare just keeps on getting better and better.*

Her voice quavered and she took a deep breath. "Frankly, I have no idea. I had a good job before my DUI but, because of it, I got fired. I have no idea how I'm going to pay them." She squirmed in her seat, staring down at her stupid striped uniform, unable to look at Wendy. Something else to be terrified about after prison.

"Okay."

She pulled herself together. "My lawyer said there're jobs in prison, so I hope I'll be eligible for that. I'm sure they don't pay very much, so I really don't know what I'm going to do."

"Well, if you're placed on probation following your time in prison, your probation officer will work with you to figure out a plan to make those payments on a monthly basis."

If?

"Can you tell me how much those fees are likely to be?"

Wendy sighed. "There's usually a fee that's called a DUI Abatement Fund that's two hundred and fifty dollars. The prison incarceration operations fine amounts to about fifteen hundred dollars. Other fines, fees, and assessments can get up to fifteen hundred as well. Those are all statutory for a DUI conviction. If you're placed on probation after incarceration there's also a monthly probation service fee of sixty-five bucks."

Laurel winced, quickly totaling it up in her head. *Crap, more than three grand.* On top of the four grand she owed her lawyer. She lowered her head and groaned.

"The next questions are about your family background."

You've got to be kidding. That's none of their friggin' business.

Wendy asked all sorts of intrusive, personal questions about Laurel's background, including whether she went to foster care and why, and what kind of relationship she had with her father and siblings.

What father? Did she want to know about the dead sibling, the one in prison, or the one turning tricks?

The investigator asked about past and recent "romantic relationships."

That asshole Scott? Or, the guy who threw me down the stairs? Then, there's Rick, too.

Wendy moved on to her past and recent alcohol and drug use, including whether she'd be willing to complete treatment.

"I would."

"Were you ever the victim of domestic violence in any romantic relationships?"

She didn't answer right away.

"Ms. Peterson?"

"Yes, I was abused by two boyfriends."

"Badly enough to require medical treatment?"

Jesus. "Yes."

"Now we're going to talk about your family growing up. Were you ever the victim or witness to domestic abuse?"

"My mother had a series of boyfriends over the years, and some of them treated her pretty badly, pushed her around and stuff."

My God, when are these questions going to stop? I don't know why I'm even telling her this stuff.

"Okay. Did you ever personally experience any physical or emotional abuse from your mom or her boyfriends when you were growing up?"

"Some of those jerks treated us kids pretty bad. So, yeah, verbal abuse. They weren't too happy having us around. And, we all got hit by mom on a regular basis, the boys worse than my sister and me."

"Would you consider what she did to be physical abuse?"

Come on, enough already. "Sometimes."

"Do you feel these confrontations had any negative effects on you?"

What a stupid question. Of course, they had negative effects!

She found it hard to decide what was worse, these guys slamming Mom around, or her giving it back to them. Or, to us. Laurel took a moment to respond, recalling those years of abuse while growing up that she'd worked so hard to blot out. No wonder she started drinking and smoking pot as a teenager.

In the end, she simply said, "Probably no worse than all the other negative crap that went on in that house over the years."

"Were the police ever called to your house for any type of incidents between your mom and boyfriends?"

"Not between Mom and a boyfriend, but between Mom and my brother, the one who's in prison. They had some pretty bad fights, and the neighbors sometimes called the cops when things got loud and out of control."

Laurel fidgeted in her seat. This interview couldn't be over fast enough. Never had she wanted so badly to get back to her tent. How were they going to use that information? She thought she'd buried those ghosts a long time ago. How long would she be battling those demons?

Laurel's release day arrived at the end of August. Standing outside Tent City, she shifted from foot to foot. Would someone would pick her up? If not, she hoped she had enough cash for the long cab ride to Carefree. Just then, like magic, without ever actually talking to her or writing to her, at eleven ten in the morning, Starr's blue Corolla pulled up outside the jail. Caroline had worked it out.

Thrilled, Laurel stood by the car even before Starr could climb out. "Thank you so much for coming to get me. You have no idea how grateful I am. You are the best!"

Starr, her long wavy gray hair flowing down her back, grinned from ear to ear.

"Hi. Hop in. So, how was it? Obviously, you survived." She frowned. "But, you look even thinner than when you went in."

Laurel described Tent City briefly, including the disgusting food, but didn't want to talk about it. She had two full days before she reported to Sunstate Women's Correctional Facility. She intended to enjoy her last days of freedom as much as she could. Starr would drive her to Caroline's house, where she'd have dinner and visit with Winston. After dinner, Caroline would drive her to her mother's.

Starr changed the subject. "What are your plans for tomorrow? Do you still have stuff to do to get ready to go away?"

"Not sure. I can't drive, so that limits what I can do. I have to see how my mother and her husband have been getting along without my help and see if she's arranged for any professional caregiving yet." She gazed at the Phoenix desert stretched out flat, brown, and barren in the depths of the summer. "We have some time this afternoon, right?"

"A couple hours, at least, before Caroline's home. What'd you have in mind?"

"A stop to get cash for my commissary account in prison. And, then, do you think we could find a meeting? I could really use one. I feel like I need to stock up, 'cause I'm not sure about meetings in Sunstate."

They drove in silence for a while. "Jail gave me lots of time to think . . ."

"How about we talk over lunch?"

Laurel hesitated. "I don't have much cash."

"My treat."

"Really? Okay, I'm not gonna to turn that offer down after the crap I've been eating."

They stopped at Laurel's favorite restaurant, Wildflower Bread Bakery. Starr ordered a chopped salad, while Laurel opted for a chicken, pesto, and feta sandwich on ciabatta bread, with mushrooms and roasted red peppers. Her body craved vegetables. Despite the lunch traffic, they found a quiet booth just being vacated.

Laurel chewed her sandwich, savoring all the flavors, knowing it would be awhile before she got good food again. "I've decided you were right about the counseling. I need it. My lawyer said there'd be counselors in prison. And, I know when I get out, I'm gonna need to enter a treatment program. I guess it's time to acknowledge how badly I've fucked up my life, that I can't do this alone." She thought about the recent interview with the probation lady and all the garbage it brought up about her past. "I've told you I have demons, and there's even more I haven't mentioned."

After the AA meeting, they drove to Caroline's house, which Laurel had never seen. Starr dropped her off, and Laurel thanked her for everything.

Caroline grinned from ear to ear, giving Laurel a big hug as they sat down to catch up. As soon as Laurel started talking, Winston came out.

"Oh my God, he knows your voice," Caroline said.

"Winston, you sweet boy. I've missed you so much," He immediately jumped into Laurel's lap and started purring.

"I know he missed you at least as much as you missed him. And, you were right. He's a nice boy and no trouble at all. Seems to be doing just fine."

Caroline offered some Pellegrino with lime, much appreciated after only plain, lukewarm water in the tents. "So, how was it? Wanna talk about it?"

Laurel sipped on her Pellegrino. Did she really want to get into this? Dredge up all that crap? Not really, but she needed to turn over a new leaf and not keep things bottled up so much. "Yeah, probably be a good idea."

So, they talked for an hour about Tent City—the loneliness, the constant fear, the acute boredom, and how that led to self-reflection, but also obsessing about the future.

Caroline served a crisp salad with salmon and some crusty French bread for dinner.

"So how are you feeling about the prospect of prison?"

"Pretty much all doom and gloom. Shaking in my boots, I guess. By the way, *love* this salad. Really missed fresh vegetables."

"Glad you're enjoying it. Helps me appreciate things I take for granted. So, scared of what exactly?"

"Not sure. It's tempting to say *everything* . . . one thing is how much longer it's going to be than jail was. More than a year. But then, I guess . . . what's next after that is also worrying me. No job to return to, a felony record, and the need to pay off all these fines, and probation and stuff. How am I going to do that?" Tears glistened in her eyes.

"You know, I could give you false reassurance, but I'm not going to." Caroline finished the last bites of her salad. "What I will say is, that's a way's off, and somewhere along the way, you're gonna get help with that. Like from probation."

"I guess you're right. But, it's so hard right now to stay in the day. My mind keeps spinning off into the future, because it's so scary and uncertain." She crossed and uncrossed her legs.

Caroline carried their dishes into the kitchen. "I totally get that. But, what about if every time you catch yourself doing that you just try to bring yourself back to the day, the moment?"

"Any suggestions on how?"

Caroline scooped fruit salad—fresh berries, kiwi, mandarin oranges, and cantaloupe—into beautiful Mexican hand-painted bowls.

"How about if you came up with a special word—a mantra, if you will—or phrase, that would ground you in the present?"

"Sounds like you've had therapy, which my sponsor told me I needed."

"Shit, everybody needs it, as far as I'm concerned. I've had lots."

"Okay, a special word or phrase. Let's see . . . how about . . . how about . . . stay in the now?"

"Sure, whatever works for you. I use, 'be here now.' The trick is to catch yourself when you're spinning off into the future and use the phrase to stop it."

"Be here now. Hmm. Okay, I'll give it a try." She loved the fresh fruit. "I hate to cut this short, but if you don't mind, I think it's time to get on up to my mother's. They go to bed early, so I don't want to show up too late. Would it be all right if I used your phone to let her know I'm on my way?"

She hugged Winston goodbye, trying not to cry, and Caroline drove her to Carefree.

"Thanks a million, Caroline, you have no idea how much this meant to me. And, thanks for setting up the ride with Starr. I'm off to Sunstate the day after tomorrow. Wish me luck."

She walked in the front door and found her mother and Bill in the family room, Bill dozing and Joanne watching TV. She greeted them and explained she'd be in the casita tonight and the next day, and a friend would drive her to Sunstate first thing the following morning.

Joanne didn't ask about Tent City.

Why did that not surprise her? Didn't matter. She'd talked about it enough already. Laurel walked out to the casita. It would be great to go to a meeting tomorrow, but without a car, might not be possible. She found a phone list to see if she could find anyone she knew well enough to ask for a ride to and from the noon meeting the next day, Tuesday. Eventually, she reached a woman named Valerie with whom she'd had breakfast once or twice after another meeting. She felt awkward at first, trying to refresh Valerie's memory of who she was and why she hadn't seen her in a couple months. Laurel explained briefly what had happened, how she'd been in jail, was now on her way to prison. Unfazed, Valerie agreed to pick her up at eleven-thirty and bring her back to her mom's afterwards. What luck!

She looked forward to a blissful—quiet and cool—night's sleep, no loud count announcements or women screaming. That got her brain roiling. What would nights be like at Sun-state? The idea of living with lots more women than in the tents sounded awful. There she was spinning off into the future. She needed to practice her new mantra.

Stay in the now, Laurel. Stay in the now.

After the best night's sleep she'd had in six weeks, she walked into the kitchen in the morning to see what she could scrounge up for breakfast. Her mother already sat at the table with a cup of coffee.

Joanne pointed to the pot on the counter. "Help yourself."

"Thanks. So, I've been wondering how you and Bill were making out without me here." She studied Joanne to see if she could notice any changes. Hard to tell with her sitting down.

"It was pretty bad after you left. I thought we could get by on our own, but . . ."

About as close as she'd get to an acknowledgement of her help. "So, did you hire someone?"

"She comes in twice a week, to clean, run a few errands, buy groceries, and cook a few meals we can have for dinner.

And, I found an outfit that takes you to doctor's appointments. Costs a fortune, but what choice do I have?"

Laurel rummaged in the fridge to find something to eat. She found a peach yogurt and some blueberries. "All right if I have these?"

"Knock yourself out."

"Any chance there's any granola?"

"Whaddya think this is, a health food store?"

Laurel washed the berries and put them into a bowl with the yogurt. "And, how about taking care of Bill?"

"That's the next problem I need to tackle."

Guilt seeped into Laurel like a leak soaking through a ceiling. Somehow her mother always managed to get to her. "I have all day today, except for a noon AA meeting. I could help you look for someone if you want."

"Maybe." Joanne went back to drinking coffee, clearly done talking.

Laurel lingered over her yogurt and berries, finally going back to the casita, unsure what to do. Over the next twenty-four hours, she went to a meeting and spent time with Joanne and Bill and in the casita, staving off the fear that kept bubbling up.

Mickey Lane told her she wouldn't be allowed to bring anything at all into Sunstate with her, so she had no packing to do. The only personal possessions she'd be permitted to have at Sunstate were state-issued clothing, including underwear. She had fifty dollars in cash. Electronic bank transfers could be made to an inmate account. Maybe Caroline or Starr would be willing to do that.

She had so looked forward to this brief time between jail and prison, but she paced in the casita, unable to do anything else, too restless to even read. As she tried to imagine what prison would be like, she had trouble breathing. She tried using her mantra to stay in the current moment, but it didn't work. She turned on the TV to distract herself, but she couldn't focus. Her stomach churned, so eating was not an option, even though it would be her last chance at decent food for more than a year.

Finally, she decided to try to sleep, tossing and turning for what seemed like hours, obsessing over what the next fourteen months would be like and how she would get through it. When she dragged herself out of bed in the morning, she felt like she'd been run over, achy everywhere, an empty feeling in her stomach.

Chapter 14

That morning, Starr drove Laurel to Sunstate Women's Correctional Facility in Buckeye, clear on the other side of the valley. Laurel just gazed out the window, unable to talk. Neither said much in the car.

Starr kept her eyes on the freeway. "I can tell you're scared. Anybody would be. Don't feel like you have to, but if you want to talk, I'm right here."

Laurel couldn't get comfortable. "You're right. I'm beyond scared. Just tell me I'm going to get through it."

"If you could get through Tent City, you're going to be able get through the next year as well. Just try not to get too far ahead of yourself. 'One day at time' will work just as well for getting through prison as it does for staying away from a drink. Try to keep your head parked where your feet are."

Laurel chuckled. "That's pretty much what Caroline said last night—try to stay in the day. Your support means the world to me. Thanks for driving me all the way over here."

Laurel got out of the car and hugged Starr goodbye. Looking around, she saw nothing but barren, windswept dirt with almost nothing growing as far as she could see. Only prison buildings and the interstate. Sheer desolation. On shaky legs, she walked into the lobby, where an armed, uniformed correctional officer, or CO, greeted her—a big burly guy with a beard and slicked-back hair.

"I'm surrendering." Again.

He told her to wait. Shortly afterward, two other COs escorted her from the lobby through the first set of thick, heavy, double metal doors that rattled along rails to open and close. Slow and loud, with a clank.

They entered a small room containing a sliding glass window at a counter. The first set of metal doors slowly rumbled shut with a loud clang. She jumped, her stomach lurching. The glass window slid open, and the COs greeted the guy behind the window. One of them slid through her stack of paperwork. As they waited for him to inspect it, her heart pounded, sweat pouring from her armpits.

Finally, the guy slid the paperwork back. "Here you go. Everything's in order. Shuttle bus is waiting outside." They waited as he opened the next set of heavy metal doors opposite the first set, first sliding it open, then clanking it shut with a loud bang.

Her heart sank. *Here I am, finally, truly in prison, for phase two of my punishment. What will this be like?*

Ninety-five degrees already, and humid. By day's end, it would be beastly. September was still summer in Phoenix. Her first month at Sunstate would probably be as hot and uncomfortable as Tent City. They entered the waiting shuttle bus, on their way to the Reception and Assessment, R & A, center.

"Why are we going on a bus?" Laurel asked.

"Because it's a way's away," he said. "Trust me, you don't want to walk in this heat." The immensity of the Sunstate complex amazed her. You could see it from both Loop 303 and the Interstate 10, surrounded by a razor wire fence and vast fields of dusty brown dirt. She couldn't tell how many buildings there were, but the numerous one-story, gray, concrete-block buildings appeared to go on forever.

The Department of Corrections assigned all newly admitted inmates to the R & A center for five days, during which time no phone calls or visits were permitted. A strip-search, to ensure she was not bringing in any contraband such as drugs or sharp objects, constituted her first indignity.

A female guard, also big and burly, accompanied her to a restroom. "Take your clothes off."

Laurel did as instructed, leaving her bare-ass naked.

"Open your mouth."

Again, Laurel complied.

"I said wide!" She inserted a gloved hand to inspect it carefully, apparently to check for hidden contraband.

"Bend down and flip your hair over." The guard inspected behind her ears and under her hair in the back, while Laurel stood there naked.

For the final humiliation, the CO said, "Squat down on your haunches and spread your butt cheeks." Laurel followed her order. "Okay, now cough three times."

That would apparently discharge anything potentially hidden in her vagina or anus.

This was the second time she had endured a strip search, but it would be far from her last. And, yet, as many times as she went through this exercise in vulnerability and humiliation over the next year, it would never become routine.

"Get dressed." The CO handed her a pile of clothes—the prison-issued bright orange top, oversized and quite baggy, as well as a pair of orange, elastic-waist pants, equally fashionable. Both were well-worn, laundered many times. Concealed between the top and bottom was a pair of panties and bra, who knew what size.

Laurel donned the underwear and orange garments, her uniform for the next fourteen months. How many others had worn these underthings next to their skin?

"Stop your dillydallying!"

During her five days at the R & A, she learned that she would be "classified." This entailed extensive testing and interviewing to determine her security or custody level: minimum, medium, or maximum. This would, in turn, determine where she'd reside within Sunstate, as well as what her health, mental health, and educational needs might be. After that, they'd move her into a permanent housing unit in the general population.

During the orientation period, they also explained the three-phase earned incentive program. Inmates were not automatically awarded privileges such as visits, phone calls, higher paying prison jobs, and recreation. They had to earn these privileges through good behavior and participation in all required program activities and other directives such as substance abuse treatment or education. So, starting out, she'd have few privileges.

I have to earn the right to be outdoors? Or, get a phone call? Not that anyone is likely to be calling me.

She also learned that, to receive phone calls—no cell phones, email, or access to the Internet, obviously—the individual making the call had to be on an approved list. Visitors also had to be approved. The approval process required, among other things, a twenty-five dollar criminal background check, the cost born, of course, by the visitor. It usually took about two months.

Well, that shouldn't be too much of an issue, since I sincerely doubt there's anyone who's going to want to visit me. If I'm lucky, maybe I can talk to Caroline or Starr once in a while.

But, could she really ask them to pay twenty-five dollars to undergo a criminal background check, just to talk to her on the phone? They'd already done so much, she didn't feel she could ask them to do that.

Laurel asked about working. Arizona DOC required all inmates to work once they completed the thirty- to sixty-day segregation period. The types of jobs available depended on classification level and phase in the earned incentive program. Phase II and III inmates got more interesting and better-paying jobs. She learned about the possibilities, surprised to hear the prison had a print shop with jobs similar to what she did as a graphic artist. But, there were no openings, so she'd have to settle for working in the library, which didn't pay as well.

At that point, she thought it'd only be a matter of days until she was moved into the general population. Instead, three boring, agonizing weeks passed in segregation—alone in a cell, twenty-three hours a day, no programming, no work, no contact with other inmates. She felt like she was going cuckoo. When would she get out of there?

Finally, one night in late September, the DOC moved Laurel to San Carlos, a medium-security unit.

Disappointed she'd been assigned to a higher level of security, she complained to the CO who accompanied her to San Carlos. "My lawyer said I'd be assigned to minimum."

A husky young Latino officer answered. "Have no idea why. I don't make those decisions. Get into the bus."

Shit, I finally get the hell out of R&A and they send me to medium.

After exiting the bus, the CO walked her to San Carlos, a dingy gray/beige cinderblock building. Inside, it consisted of a large square, with six-by-eleven-foot, chest high, cubicles—cubes—along the four outside walls, also of block construction, allowing scant privacy in each one. Worn gray vinyl tiles covered the floor.

"How many women live here?" Laurel asked.

"Just sixty in this building. Pretty small. There's another building just like it behind us with the same number."

He walked Laurel over to the "cell" where she'd be staying. Her bunkie laid on her rack. The CO said, "You've got about ten minutes until count and lights out, so you better just toss your stuff into your drawer."

She stared at her new bunkie. "Hi, Laurel Peterson."

The other woman did not look up. "Anjelica Guzman. Angie to my friends, Guzman to you."

Great, just what I need, a roommate with a chip on her shoulder. Laurel dished it right back. "Well, I don't give a fuck what you call me. Which drawer is mine?"

Guzman pointed to one of the two-by-three-foot drawers provided for their belongings. Laurel saw two shelves, one empty.

Laurel sat on the bed. Built out of concrete blocks—who even thinks of building a bed out of cinder blocks?—covered by a three-inch-thick skimpy mattress, it resembled a futon. Didn't smell too bad. A bottom sheet and thin blanket covered the mattress. The thin pillow had the distinctive heady aroma of dirty hair, although the pillowcase appeared clean.

The tiny sink; and a toilet sitting out in the open, no lid, surprised her. No privacy. This should be interesting.

So, she moved in, an overstatement in light of her limited possessions: the prison-issued clothing she wasn't wearing—two more bright orange tops, one pair of orange pants, two more sets of underwear, and two pairs of socks, all stored in a black garbage bag. On her feet, she wore the heavy-duty, prison-issued black vinyl, lace-up boots that constituted her only footwear at the moment. She didn't have a single other possession. She placed her things in her drawer while Guzman watched.

She glanced around and noticed immediately that San Carlos was stifling and very humid, only marginally cooler than the outside. Then she remembered, no air-conditioning. DOC used the much cheaper, old-fashioned Arizona/New Mexico, pre-air-conditioning evaporative coolers. They had earned the nickname "swamp" coolers because, instead of refrigerating the air and removing moisture, they circulated water into the air, which evaporated and cooled it. The system worked reasonably well in low humidity but, once the higher summer humidity arrived, swamp coolers did little good.

To Guzman she observed, "Feels more like a swamp than the desert."

"You'll get used to it."

She sat down on her bed. "Where do we eat?"

"The kitchen, like everybody else."

"How long does it take to get here?"

"Shit, you ask too many questions."

Laurel studied Guzman, lying on her bunk on her side, legs extended, bottom arm bent at the elbow supporting her head, also studying Laurel. About Laurel's age, the Latina looked tiny. Though it was hard to tell how tall with her lying down, she didn't look anything over five feet. Straight dark hair pulled back in a ponytail, dark skin, brown eyes.

"Ten minutes," she said finally.

Ten o'clock arrived, and the PA announced lights out and count. Curious about Guzman, she decided not to ask any more questions, not wanting to annoy her. *Geez, I finally get assigned to a unit, and now I get a bunkie who's already pissed off at me when I haven't even done anything.*

"Are you finally through making noise?"

Laurel considered several snarky comebacks, but decided on a simple, "Yes," followed by, "Goodnight Guzman."

If she'd learned anything so far, it was that there's no point in antagonizing other inmates. Maybe she should try being annoyingly nice. Nah.

Awakened at six the next morning by the sounds of the PA announcing the first count of the day and the other inmates getting up, Laurel prepared for her first full day in the unit where she would live. She sat up, wearing the orange uniform she wore yesterday, that she slept in last night, and that she'd wear today. She needed to find out about laundry.

As the room came to life with women in orange uniforms chattering and laughing, she wandered over to the center of the room to examine the lounge area. Not much to see. A few worn nylon-upholstered sofas in a dirty, dark-rust color. Several small tables covered with pale wood-grained vinyl, surrounded with metal folding chairs. That was it, other than the wall-mounted TV. At the far end, two COs hung out in a station they occupied whenever the inmates were around at night, first thing in the morning, and on weekends.

A woman headed purposefully toward her bed and gave Laurel a big grin. "You must be the newbie. I'm Latisha. That's my bunk over there. Welcome to San Carlos. Who're you?"

Big, black, and busty, Latisha filled out her orange top and pants completely. She wore her hair in cornrows and had dark brown, almost black, eyes, snow white teeth, and cherry-red lipstick.

Finally, someone friendly. "Hi, I'm Laurel. Do you know when and where breakfast is?"

"Started at six-thirty, so we should probably start lining up now. How're you settling in?"

"Have no clue."

Don't reveal too much, she reminded herself. Easier said than done. She wanted to say how tough it was in R&A and how scared she was, but she knew no matter how friendly Latisha might seem, she needed to keep her mouth shut for as long as she could.

"Do you know if you'll be working yet?"

"The library. Haven't started yet."

Latisha headed off to join some other black inmates.

She followed the group and waited in line about thirty minutes before she entered the "kitchen," as everyone called the cafeteria. She looked forward to the cool rush of walking into an air-conditioned room, but of course swamp coolers also "cooled" the kitchen. By then, Laurel and everyone else had large, wet half-moons of sweat under their armpits.

They entered a cafeteria line where inmates with hair-nets served hot food from large, steaming, stainless-steel trays. Today, like most days, it consisted of powdered scrambled eggs, three kinds of cold cereal, white toast, and a thin, gray gruel, allegedly oatmeal. Looked like you could sip it through a straw.

She selected some eggs and Cheerios. When she asked about milk, they directed her to a stainless unit across the way. She sat down at a table with three other women, all white, and mostly older than the typical inmates in their twenties and thirties. Like in Tent City, the inmates kept to their own racial groups. She introduced herself to Nicolette, Joelle, and Danni. Over breakfast, Laurel listened to them chat about prison life and other inmates, keeping her mouth shut, hoping no one would ask her any questions. Both the eggs and the Cheerios tasted blah. The milk had a weird flavor. When she made a face after eating a mouthful of cereal and milk, the others laughed.

"Welcome to powdered reconstituted milk," Danni said. "Nothing is too good for prisoners in Arizona."

"Is there ever orange juice?"

Smirking, Nicolette said, "'Course not. Because, obviously, if there was, we'd be brewing our own hooch with it."

"Hmm, okay," Laurel said. She'd hoped this was going to be at least a little bit better than Tent City. Not so far.

Soon, a CO came by to hurry them out, reminding them of the long line still outside with women waiting to eat so they could get to their prison jobs. So, they returned their trays and walked back to their units.

What was she going to do all day?

Chapter 15

Back at San Carlos, the virtually empty unit surprised her. She lay on her bunk and wondered for the thousandth time what the next year of her life would be like. When would she get the print-shop job, and what would it pay? Did she dare use the fifty dollars in her commissary account to buy food or make phone calls? It would be nice to talk to Starr and Caroline occasionally.

Guzman had already left for the day, her rack neatly made and none of her possessions lying around. Laurel had nothing on her agenda yet, so she sat on her bunk contemplating what she'd do to pass the time.

A CO arrived at the entrance to her cube. "Don't get too comfortable. Your new boss is waiting for you at the library."

Thank goodness, the sooner I get started, the sooner I'll have some money in my commissary account. "Where is it?"

It took ten minutes to walk there in her hot, DOC-issued, made-in-China boots, and she arrived dripping wet. She could already feel blisters forming, despite wearing socks.

But, when she walked into the building blessed air-conditioning encompassed her. She breathed in the cool air and felt herself relax. Who was in charge? Easy to figure out, as the librarian was the only woman not dressed in bright orange.

As Laurel approached her, the woman looked up. "Hi, I'm Mrs. Rogers."

Mrs. R. looked to be in her late fifties, with short, straight graying hair. Her positive manner and upbeat tone surprised Laurel. The cheerful and colorful library stood in sharp contrast to the rest of the prison complex, all drab gray and dirty beige. Healthy green plants lined the windowsills. Numerous colorful posters on the walls advertised books and touted the value of reading.

Being a library aide paid fifty cents an hour, and Laurel could work up to forty hours a week. Although not as much as she hoped, it was better than some of the other jobs she'd heard about that paid less and weren't in air-conditioning.

She might be working less than forty hours per week and, to make matters worse, Mrs. R. reminded her an additional portion of her pay would be removed by DOC for forced savings so she had something—a total of a hundred dollars—when she was released.

Like that hundred bucks is going to get me anything when I walk out of here, Laurel thought bitterly.

That meant, in fact, she would only earn about forty cents an hour for the foreseeable future. Sixteen dollars a week, sixty-four dollars a month. Tears started to sting her eyes as she wondered how she'd afford things like hair conditioner or edible food, or something other than blister-causing vinyl boots to wear during the next couple of warm months.

"Look, I see you're disappointed," Mrs. R. said, "but this is actually a pretty darn good job. It's comfortable in here, you have access to books, which for an educated woman like yourself is wonderful, and access to a computer. When you're not helping me check out books and return them to the shelves, you'll have time to read and do things on the computer."

"Thank you. I'm sorry for reacting so . . . so . . . I don't know, so ungratefully. I *do* know this is a good job, and I'm eager to get started. I really am. Can you tell me what I'll be doing here?"

"Not all that complicated. Basically, the inmates are allowed to come to the library for an hour per week."

Only an hour?

"They can check out two books at a time for a week. It seems very restrictive—cripes, it *is* very restrictive—but it's the only way to accommodate everyone because we're so overcrowded. On most days, the women stand in line for quite a while before they are allowed in for that one hour per week."

"So, what will I be doing?"

"The aides check out books and check them back in when they're returned, help women find books, and make sure no one defaces books or magazines while they're here.

"Let me introduce you to the other two aides. And, by the way," she whispered, "these are exactly the kinds of ladies you want to associate with while you are inside. They're smart, educated, and looking to avoid trouble."

They walked over to a desk where an inmate was checking out books. "Lily, can I interrupt for a second?" Mrs. R. said. "This is Laurel. She'll be joining you and Ashlee as an aide."

Lily stopped and looked up. "Hi, Laurel. Welcome. We can really use the help. Glad you're here." Lily, white, and in her thirties, wore her blonde hair in a ponytail.

Someone was actually glad to see her? "Thanks, I'm eager to get started."

"Okay," Mrs. R. said, "now where's Ashlee?"

The librarian led her to the other side of the room where Ashlee talked with another inmate. The tall, thin, black woman with very short, curly hair—a lot like Caroline's—was maybe in her forties.

Mrs. R. waited until she was done. "Ashlee, our newest aide is here. Welcome Laurel."

Ashlee looked her up and down. "Okay, good. Boy, do we need the help. Welcome to the team."

During the rest of the morning, Mrs. R. showed Laurel the simple system for checking books in and out. She showed her the library collection, consisting mainly of fiction and self-help books.

"Where do the books come from?" Laurel asked. Most looked very worn, especially the paperbacks.

"Mostly donations," Mrs. R. said. "Unfortunately, the library doesn't have a budget, per se. We rely on the generosity of others. Occasionally the librarians can lobby for a little money to acquire a few new things, but rarely. That's why we want the aides to impress upon their fellow inmates how important it is to take good care of the books and return them on time."

Lunchtime arrived, and Laurel left with Lily and Ashlee for the nearby kitchen.

Luckily, the line wasn't too long yet, since it was already hot—though not as hot as it was going to get. While they waited in line, Laurel asked Lily and Ashlee how they liked working as library aides. She knew she should be minding her own business, but she couldn't help it.

Both agreed the job was great. Lily had only ever had the library job since she'd been in Sunstate, two and a half years, whereas Ashlee had had two or three other, more menial jobs, such as kitchen and laundry, while she waited for an aide opening.

Guess I'm lucky I got this right away. Still hoping for that print shop job though.

They served bologna sandwiches on white bread—two if you wanted them—the kind of bread she and her siblings called "foam bread." A few raw carrot and celery sticks completed the menu.

The women didn't hang around the muggy kitchen, instead they returned early to the cool library. This gave Laurel a chance to look over the books so she'd have something to do tonight. By the time the library re-opened at one, she'd found a mystery, and had utilized the computer to create a calendar for herself for the next few months. She wasn't sure she should use the paper in the printer but, since Mrs. R. wasn't around, she decided she'd just do it.

The line started forming at twelve forty-five as women queued up to get inside . . . the air conditioning, no doubt, a big incentive. Once the doors opened, following Mrs. R.'s instructions, Laurel worked closely with Ashlee to learn where different categories of books were kept, as well as the meager selection of magazines available for check-out, such as *Time* and *People*.

Before she knew it, five o'clock had rolled around, time to return to San Carlos. Seemed kind of a waste though, walking all the way back to her unit in the heat, only to turn around a half hour later and return to the kitchen. Maybe after she'd worked there awhile, Mrs. R. would trust her enough to let her stay there to read until dinnertime. Probably best not to ask for special accommodations on the first day though.

Guzman sat on her rack. "By the way, San Carlos is actually not too bad," she said, apropos of nothing. "Most of the women are okay. I've never lived in the dorms, but I hear they can get pretty crazy. Lots of noise and fighting."

"So I've heard."

Guzman seemed a bit more civil than the previous night. "Got visitors coming this weekend?"

"Nope."

"Maybe next week?"

"Doubtful."

"Really? Shit, that's rough. No kids?"

"No kids."

"Well, maybe that's better than kids who make you crazy, like mine," Guzman said. "That's why I was in such a pissy mood last night. I was supposed to see my daughter and grandbaby tomorrow, and she called last minute and said she couldn't come."

Was that an apology? "So, you're footloose and fancy free for the weekend?"

Guzman cracked up. "I guess that's one way to put it."

She might not be so bad after all.

"Ready to walk to dinner?"

Sweat drenched both of them by the time they arrived, followed by a forty-five-minute wait on the steaming black asphalt.

Tonight, the kitchen served some kind of grayish looking meat with gloppy pale brown gravy, mashed potatoes, and canned, also grayish, green beans. Salad, too, if you could call it that: chopped pale green iceberg lettuce, a pink slice of tomato, and two peeled cucumber slices dressed with reddish dressing of some sort. Looked like the Catalina dressing of her childhood.

As Laurel and Guzman retrieved their food and left the cafeteria line, Laurel scanned the room to find a table of white women with an empty seat.

Guzman headed for a table of Latinas. "Okay, see you later."

Laurel noticed some empty tables at the far end of the large room, each accommodating about eight or ten, and walked over to one. That seemed safer than going up to a table of women already seated. Finding a spot, she looked down at the unappetizing food, deciding whether to try anything.

The salad seemed safest, so she started there. Yep, Catalina dressing. Using the side of her spork—no knives, obviously—she tried to cut into the meat, and scraped off the disgusting-looking gravy. It looked like some kind of Salisbury steak, hamburger really. Cautiously, she put a small piece into her mouth with some mashed potatoes. Although the potatoes were the dried, powdered kind, not the kind made from real potatoes, the meat tasted better than it looked, and much better than anything at Tent City. Unfortunately, the overcooked gray-green beans you could mash with the spork. After a few minutes, she'd finished the salad and had eaten about half of the meat and potatoes. No one sat down with her, although most of the rest of the tables had filled up.

Arriving back at San Carlos, she could smell food in the air. Evidently, at least some of these women made dinner for themselves. As she walked toward her bunk, she noticed some women in their cubes worked at preparing a meal, a variety of canned things like soup and chili, as well as packaged foods like the Kraft macaroni and cheese of her childhood. "Cooking" was not the correct term, since they were using one of those immersion coils used to heat water. She hadn't seen one of those since college. She learned later they were colloquially referred to as "stingers."

Where did they get those? And the food? Commissary must sell that kind of stuff.

Contemplating her future, she dozed off briefly, waking about a half-hour later, as Guzman blustered in with her besties, laughing, giggling, and cracking on each other in Spanish. Women she hadn't met, who had nearby bunks, also arrived, and she could hear the TV at the center of the room. Glancing over there, she saw a number of women watching TV, the small tables filled with women playing cards and board games. Hmm, those must come from commissary as well. She didn't feel all that eager to meet these other women. Most of them seemed a lot younger. As she looked around the room, though, she spied women of all ages, some appearing no older than eighteen and a few older than herself. What did women that old do to get in here? The she remembered her own DUI.

As her friends left for their own cubes, Guzman asked Laurel how she was doing.

"Okay, I guess. Trying to get used to this whole setup. Is there anything to do at night besides watching TV and playing cards?"

Guzman snorted. "Not much. Not a resort, you know. Or, hadn't you figured that out yet?"

"Obviously. But, this is totally boring, just lying here."

"You'll get to know some of the others before you know it. Most of 'em aren't that bad, really. Once you start working, you'll get some money in your commissary and can start to buy things. Oh, and sometimes on the weekends they show movies for us. And, I think the library might be open at night for a little while and on weekends. They have magazines over there you can look at, and I think they let you borrow books."

"That's my work assignment. I didn't know they were open at night or on weekends though."

"Maybe I'm wrong."

She spent the night reading a Michael Connelly mystery set in LA, trying to ignore the noise and chaos surrounding her as women chatted, argued, laughed, watched TV, and played cards. Concentrating was a challenge with all that going on, and she hoped, over time, she'd get better at ignoring it. Then the lights went out, things quieted down to some extent, although she still heard loud voices, punctuated by other inmates shouting at the noisy ones to shut up.

By eleven, it had quieted down, but Laurel couldn't sleep. For one thing, she was sweaty. She made a mental note to ask Guzman about laundry. She tossed and turned on the thin, uncomfortable mattress, ruminating about her first full day in the general population. She wondered when the substance abuse program would start so she could get that over and done with. How would she manage with so little money in her account? She got furious every time she thought about what Mrs. R. told her about how DOC took money from her measly wages until she accumulated a hundred dollars. Eventually, despite fighting to stave off feeling totally sorry for herself for causing this unbearable situation, she faced the outside wall and started to cry softly. It built into great choking sobs.

After several minutes of shaking, and sobbing she couldn't control, hands suddenly touched her body. She panicked, preparing herself to be hurt by people she couldn't see, guards or inmates. But, wait, they weren't hurting her, they gently massaged her shoulders, her back, and her legs. It felt good. Surprising, since she knew inmates weren't supposed to have any physical contact.

"Shh, shush…" Was that Guzman's voice. "It's going to be okay. It's all right, really, you're going to be okay."

Laurel managed to stop crying, startled that someone had noticed her misery and cared enough to comfort her. Slowly, she rolled over to face the center of the room. In the semi-darkness, she saw Latisha, Guzman, and three other women of various heights, races, and hairdos. Unaccountably, they all smiled at her. She didn't know what to say, but was filled with gratitude. A million thoughts swirled in her mind, but all she could say was thank you.

Eventually she drifted off into a fitful sleep.

The next day Laurel rose to the sounds of her fellow inmates prepping for their days, and headed over to breakfast herself. She wouldn't rush today. She went directly from the kitchen to her aide job at the library, rather than walking all the way back to the unit and coming back to the library.

When she arrived there at eight, quite a few women already stood in line. Mrs. R. directed her to start working with Ashlee, who helped inmates return and check out books. Meanwhile, Lily helped inmates locate various items. In the afternoon, they'd reverse roles. If no inmates needed an aide's help to find things, that person could read or work on an available computer. The morning passed quickly because of her busyness. It felt good to be working again, being productive in some way.

At lunchtime, she walked to the kitchen with Lily and Ashlee. Ashlee left to sit with her homies, so Lily and Laurel sat together. She felt comfortable with Lily, although she wasn't sure why. Maybe because Mrs. R. told her yesterday these two women were the kind of women she should stick with. Lily asked her about the length of her prison sentence, and Laurel told her. Lily had been at Sunstate for two and a half years, with another year and a half to go. She loved the library job.

"What do you like best about it?" *I thought you were going to mind your own business*, she reminded herself.

"Well, for one thing, Mrs. R. is the best supervisor you could hope for. She treats you like a human being. Actually, she treats *all* the inmates like human beings. Not all the staff are like that. I also like that we sometimes get to read or do things on the computer if we're not too busy. I've always loved to read, so that's a real plus."

"Me, too!"

"Were you in jail before you came here?"

"Yep. Tent City. God-awful. Couldn't do much reading there. No library and no money to buy books. Occasionally, I managed to pick up one that another inmate left behind. Nothing to do. Totally boring. How about you?"

"Came up from Tucson."

"Any tips on coping?"

"Minding your own business, not getting involved in the drama that a lot of the younger women get caught up in all the time. And, staying busy. I do some volunteer work as well as working in the library—"

Laurel raised her eyebrows. "Really, like what?"

"Well, I have a college education, and many of these women haven't even graduated from high school. They're required to get their GED, so they're always looking for people to help teach the GED classes. I enjoy doing that."

"Hmm, sounds interesting. Maybe I'll look into that. Having a lot of time on my hands isn't good for me. It's just going to make me depressed."

"This place is depressing, no doubt about it. I have to work really hard not to get down. Staying busy definitely helps."

"Yikes, it's five of one. We'd better hurry back or Mrs. R. will be on our cases."

So much for keeping my mouth shut.

Laurel walked back to San Carlos after dinner that night, tired and hot, but otherwise okay. It felt good to have done a good day's work. Back on her rack, she asked Guzman about putting in a commissary order, and picked up an order form from the one of the COs. She also asked the all-important question of how one got laundry done. Man, did her clothes stink.

Guzman laughed. "There's a place where we drop it off. All your clothes have your ID number on them. Three days later you can pick them up. I'll show you where."

Going over the list of commissary offerings, Laurel was surprised at how many different things the commissary sold, everything from TVs and other small appliances, to snacks and real food like chili and packets of chicken, salmon, and tuna. But, she worried about depleting her account too soon before she earned better wages.

What did she most need from this list? Shower shoes for sure—they were only sixty-five cents. She'd heard that all manner of disgusting things grew on the floor of the shower room, given the heat and moisture in the dorms. Lip balm, definitely. Her lips had become so chapped over the past couple months. Conditioner, toothbrush, and toothpaste. Some kind of lotion, for sure. A box of tissues would be nice, especially since DOC issued each inmate only one role of toilet paper per week, which would have to double as Kleenex for now.

How bizarre to worry about how much toilet paper she used and whether it would last a full week. She had no clue how much toilet paper she used in a week.

Oh, and sneakers! That'd be her splurge, so she could stop wearing those miserable, hot vinyl boots until it got colder.

By the next day, a routine emerged. Get up early, stand in the breakfast line for twenty minutes or so, eat, and head over to the library. Take a break for lunch, back to the library, back to San Carlos. Hang out for a while, get in line for dinner. While she waited to go to dinner, she heard an announcement for the mail call. Many of the women went outside, hoping for letters from loved ones. Laurel continued to read on her bunk.

Guzman returned, no letter in hand. "Your last name's Peterson, right?"

"Yeah. Why?"

"Well, you got yourself some mail."

"What? That can't be. Must be a mistake. Hardly anybody even knows I'm here. My mother wouldn't write to me with a gun to her head." *Must be Caroline or Starr. That would be awesome.*

"Well, I don't know. They called Laurel Peterson. You should go check it out."

Curious, Laurel hopped off her bunk and went over to the CO station to find out where she could retrieve her mail, which had been returned to the administrative offices.

She had to wait, but she eventually retrieved a real letter. She turned it over in her hands. It was already opened, of course.

Weird. The return address said California Institute of Technology, Pasadena, CA. No name.

Chapter 16

Finally, back on her bunk, she removed the letter from its envelope. She opened the brief, typed letter and gasped. Her hands shook so much she could barely hold the piece of paper.

> *"Dear Laurel,*
>
> *I'm not even sure if this letter will reach you. I'm writing to find out if you are the Laurel Peterson who was in a relationship with my father, Rick Murphy, in 1995.*
>
> *If so, please write back and let me know if you are my mother and why you left me.*
>
> *Sincerely,*
>
> *Ryan Murphy*
>
> *P.S. And, why are you at Sunstate Women's Correctional Facility?"*

Holy shit! Her whole body started to shake. She read the letter again. And again. She couldn't stop trembling.

Oh my God, my son Ryan has found me in prison.

Surreal. She couldn't believe this was happening. Memories flooded in from that time in her life, a miserable time when she drank all the time, overwhelmed and fighting with Rick constantly. Suddenly, a drink flashed into her mind. Good thing there was no booze in there, because she'd be sorely tempted.

Again, she re-read the letter. *"Dear Laurel,"* not mom. Of course, not mom. Was she ever really a mom to him? Maybe for a few months before her drinking got the best of her. Somehow it never occurred to her that her leaving actually hurt Ryan. She was such a friggin' mess at the time, she thought Ryan would be better off with Rick, even though it tore her heart out. Part of her wanted to be in Ryan's life, to be his mother, but at the same time, she knew she wasn't equipped, certainly not then, to be a mother. She wanted a drink so badly she could actually taste it. Vodka, rocks, with a twist.

What did he want? Was he angry? Could he possibly want a relationship after all this time? Did Rick put him up to this?

Should she write back? How could she not write back? What should she write?

She had to think this through. She'd better find an AA meeting. Maybe Guzman would know. Or surely the COs would.

What would she say to him? She didn't even have any paper or pen to write with yet. So, she had to get some paper, stamps, and an envelope next week from commissary.

Jumping down from her bunk, she walked over to the CO station. "Do you know where and when the AA meetings are held?"

The CO consulted a binder. "They're only once a month, but you're in luck. Tomorrow night. Classroom 201."

On Thursday night, Laurel attended her first AA meeting inside Sunstate. Despite having attended hundreds of AA meetings on the outside, she was all jitters walking into the room. The classroom was bright and colorful, and air-conditioned. Much to her surprise, only eleven women showed up, spanning all ages and ethnicities.

A woman named Ava led the group. Slight, almost fragile looking, she appeared to be in her seventies, with short white hair and steel-blue eyes. She had come from the outside and brought a speaker with her, who introduced herself as "Kristina, alcoholic and addict."

Ava began, as AA meetings usually do, by reading the Preamble. It comforted Laurel to hear those words, something familiar in an otherwise frightening and alien environment. She felt herself relax a bit, eager to hear the speaker.

Kristina's story had many similarities Laurel's—a difficult childhood with a single mom and a chaotic adolescence when she started to drink and use drugs in junior high. But, Kristina got into serious drug use later on. A daily drinker by high school, she also used pot and cocaine when she could find them. She described her twenties as a period of homelessness, hooking up with bad men, occasional prostitution, and ultimately using heroin. Brushes with the law got her sent to rehab multiple times, but she managed to avoid serious jail time or prison.

Laurel scanned the room as Kristina spoke, noticing nods of acknowledgement. Finally, Kristina said, by her early thirties, she managed to stop using. She attended a long-term program that provided housing, insisting that all clients go to multiple twelve-step meetings every week. She tried NA in the beginning, but ultimately found that the AA meetings offered more people with long-term recovery. She said she had to be around those people, the people who kept coming back with years of sobriety under their belts, to believe that the program would work for her. With the support of AA and the treatment program, Kristina attended community college. Currently she worked in a halfway house for recovering women with mental health issues and attended college part-time. Still, she attended multiple meetings a week.

She ended by saying, "I know it's got to be tough in here. This could have been my story. Somehow, I just got lucky and never got more than an overnight in jail and probation, despite my years of using. If you're here tonight, it's because you have a problem with alcohol or drugs. I hope you'll take advantage of whatever programming and meetings they have at Sunstate so when you're released you have a chance of staying clean and sober. When you get out of here, run as fast as you can to a meeting. It's your best hope. Thanks for listening."

The women clapped quietly and murmured thank yous. It was only six twenty-five in the evening—thirty-five more minutes remained—so Ava asked if they'd like to go around the room, introduce themselves, and say a few words. Heads nodded agreement.

A few women just said their first names, omitting "alcoholic" or "addict." One of them, who seemed no older than nineteen or twenty, appeared depressed, speaking in barely a whisper. Laurel noticed cut marks and scars all along the inside of both arms. She shuddered. Other women introduced themselves and said a couple sentences about their struggles with drugs and booze.

Before walking in there, Laurel had intended to talk about Ryan's letter, but she changed her mind. No one had said anything personal, unlike AA meetings on the outside where women often shared extremely personal things with a reasonable expectation of confidentiality. Many meetings included an opening statement reminding people that what was said should not to be shared outside.

Instead she just introduced herself as "Laurel, alcoholic," and thanked Kristina and Ava for going to the trouble to bring the meeting here. She said she related to Kristina's story and admired that she had been able to overcome her past. "I really hope I can finally do that, too."

The meeting ended. Laurel nervously wondered whether they'd hold hands in a circle the way most AA meetings ended, knowing that DOC policy prohibited inmates from having physical contact with each other. To her surprise, they did, and one of the women who knew Ava went up to her after the meeting to chat, after which they hugged.

As Laurel made her way back to her bunk she wondered whether the meetings would be as helpful as she had hoped. Maybe.

Over the next few days, while awaiting her writing supplies, Laurel obsessed over what to write back to Ryan. Using scrap paper pilfered from the library, she went so far as to write a few drafts of the letter, but tossed them into the trash.

She wanted to be honest—Ryan deserved that after all this time. On the other hand, she feared if she was honest and leveled with him about what a mess her life had been since Rick kicked her out, and now, he wouldn't want to write back. She remembered her conversation with Starr about her character defects, lying in particular. She had no idea what Ryan wanted, though. Did he want to connect, to have some kind of relationship? If so, she desperately didn't want to blow it, to turn him off, to scare him away.

What if he just wanted to vent, to tell her how fucked up she was?

Discarding the drafts she didn't like and heaving a big sigh, Laurel made a decision. Time to bite the bullet and see a counselor. She walked to the CO station and filled out a formal request form, berating herself for not having done it sooner. She hoped an appointment would be quickly scheduled, because she hated obsessing over this. With the weekend approaching and little to do, she feared she'd spend the whole weekend agonizing. Once Monday rolled around she knew she'd be okay, because she'd be too busy to obsess. But, the weekend? That would be tough.

She spent an uneventful first weekend on the unit in San Carlos, having been in Sunstate five weeks. October arrived, still too hot to spend time outside, except to hike over to the kitchen for meals. She slept a bit during the day, tried to catch up on sleep lost during nights of tossing, turning, and trying to figure out what to say to Ryan. Even though most inmates were not at their jobs, the unit was peaceful. Some had visitors. The rest played cards or other board games, watched TV, or chatted in small groups. Some slept or read on their bunks, pretty much like her. Good thing she had checked a couple books out of the library to occupy her time.

She'd thought a bit more about what to say to Ryan, but felt proud of herself that she wasn't obsessing. She focused on compartmentalizing it until she could see her counselor on Friday. After all, no big rush. Better to think through what she wanted to say, rather than impulsively write something she couldn't take back.

She'd heard that the kitchen prepared a special breakfast Sunday mornings. She realized how much she'd been looking forward to it when her hopes were dashed by the super high carb fare they served. A biscuit and sausage gravy, which really looked nasty. A cinnamon roll, though not too bad, seemed more like dessert. A fried egg—a real one, not powdered—but cold. Fried potatoes, more Cheerios, and canned pineapple which, at least, was actual fruit. Oh well.

The highlight of Sunday brunch was not the food, but rather bumping into Lily. They sat together and talked. Because Lily lived on another yard, they couldn't visit each other, but they could talk outside, at work, or at meals. They found a picnic table outside to chat.

Laurel wondered what Lily did to get into Sunstate, but had picked up that you shouldn't ask direct questions about that. She'd decided, despite the advice to keep to herself, to take a big risk and share some personal information.

"I went to my first AA meeting here last Thursday night. Have you ever gone to one?"

"Nah. Drugs were my issue more than booze. I heard the occasional NA meetings in here are pretty dysfunctional. But, the main drawback, from what I've been told, is there's no confidentiality. The other inmates just blab whatever you've said in there. So, no, I don't need that."

"Good to know. This was a speaker meeting, and she was pretty good. But, I did notice when it was time to share, nobody said much of anything personal. So, this is kind of awkward, but here goes. I like you and kind of, uh, hope we can be friends since we'll be working together, at least for a while. If you feel the same way, uh, can we agree to keep what we say to each other to ourselves?"

"Sure. It'd be nice to have a friend in here. I've made a few, like the woman who just left the library… she was released, so that's how you got the aide job. When inmates are released they always say they are going to keep in touch. But, they never do."

"I have to go to the substance abuse program. Do you know anything about it?

"Yeah, already completed that. Big waste of time, but you have to do it regardless. I've been to a few rehabs that always do an educational piece—"

"Me, too."

"But, education was not really what I needed. Actually, I'm not sure what I need, but it isn't education. Pills were my thing, opiates like Oxy and Vicodin."

"How did you get started on that, if I'm not being too pushy to ask?"

"Started with some surgeries I had after a car accident. This was about seven years ago. Back then, the doctors were very generous, so to speak, with pain pills. I had three surgeries over a couple of years before I got straightened out, but by then I was popping those pills like there was no tomorrow.

"They kept prescribing, but the legal prescriptions were just not enough once I got hooked. So, I started looking around on the street for other ways to get them. They're out there, but very pricey. That's why a bunch of people turn to heroin, which is actually cheaper. Thank God I didn't go that route—injecting drugs is absolutely not for me—but I got so desperate I stole prescription pads from a couple of docs and got caught."

Lily moved to shade her eyes from the sun. "Luckily, it was my first offense, but it's still a Class A felony. So, here I sit for two and half years. I'm about halfway through. Then, three to five years of probation. One thing I can tell you, for sure, is getting off those things cold turkey sucks big time!"

Laurel started thinking about Caroline. Similar story, but with a very different outcome. Wonder why Caroline essentially got off and poor Lily got stuck in here?

Chapter 17

Having survived her first weekend in San Carlos, Laurel sleep-walked through Monday and Tuesday, dragging herself out of her bunk in the morning after tossing and turning at night, getting almost no sleep. Despite swearing she wouldn't obsess about what to write to Ryan, she couldn't stop thinking about it. She walked over to get her meals, spent two uneventful days working at the library, and tried to watch TV at night so she wouldn't think about what to write to her son. The appointment with that counselor couldn't come fast enough.

"I hate you! How could you leave me?" A sandy-haired little boy pounded her with his tiny fists. "What's wrong with me? Why couldn't you love me and take care of me? What happened to you?"

Thoughts caromed around in her head. Should she run away? Protect herself? Put her arms around him? What should she do?

"Wait, wait!" she yelled. "Ryan, stop hitting me. Let me explain. Hold on for a minute!"

The little boy kept pummeling her, totally out of control. Finally, she put both arms around him, holding him until he stopped hitting and squirming, and dissolved into tears. Crying herself, she rocked and rocked him until he stopped crying.

She woke up with a start. It was still dark. Her heart hammered inside her chest. Sweat soaked her orange uniform. Disoriented. Where the hell was she?

Shit, Sunstate.

Finally, Friday arrived, the day she met with her new counselor. Thank God. This Ryan thing was driving her crazy. She walked the short distance from the library to the counselor's office in the Correctional Health building, arriving just before two o'clock. She found room 127 and after a quick knock on the door, opened it into a small office. Startled, she saw another inmate in the chair, facing a woman sitting behind a desk. Hearing the door open, the inmate's head whipped around.

She glared as Laurel said, "I am so sorry."

The other inmate jumped up to face the counselor. "Thanks, Ms. Lane." Her voice dripped with sarcasm.

Laurel's face reddened, and she backed out the door.

"That's. Okay. I. Was. Just. Leaving." The inmate added a scowl to her emphasized words.

While waiting for her to depart, Laurel apologized again and took the chair in the small waiting area.

After the other inmate left with a frown, the counselor introduced herself as Autumn Lane.

"I'm so sorry," Laurel said. "I just needed to talk to you so badly!"

"I can see you're agitated. Let's start by having you try to relax for a minute. Sit down and close your eyes. Take a few deep breaths."

Laurel sat down. She closed her eyes and inhaled deeply several times, becoming aware of how fast her heart beat and how sweat trickled down her temples and along her sides. Damn menopause!

After a couple of minutes, Autumn cleared her throat gently. "Okay, that's better. Let's begin. So, what brings you here? The referral says a combination of anxiety and depression."

Laurel exhaled and stared into Autumn's smiling pale-blue eyes. "I just said that to make sure I got to see you."

She whipped out Ryan's letter, carefully folded into her pocket. "Twenty years ago, I had a baby with a man who I lived with, Rick, and he kicked me out when the baby was about a year old. I haven't seen him since—the baby I mean. This letter is from him, from Ryan. He's now nineteen years—"

"Whoa, hold on. I think you're going to need to back up. When I reviewed your record, I thought it said you didn't have any children."

"Probably does say that. Generally, if I'm asked if I have children I say no, because really, I don't. I mean I did, but only in a technical sense. And, now I'm totally freaked out." She leaned forward in her chair. "So, I got this letter, and he wants to know, what did I do to get in here, and why did I leave him."

She handed the one-page letter to Autumn, who took a few seconds to read it.

Autumn looked up. "Sounds like you didn't see this coming."

"Absolutely not. I never expected to see or hear from Ryan again, and now I'm completely panicked. I have no idea what to write back to him. I've been totally obsessing over it. Can you help me?"

She didn't let Autumn answer though. "The first thing I thought of after I read the letter was that I wanted a drink. I mean, really, really, wanted a drink. Thank God there's no booze in here. Haven't had a drink since my DUI, about three months ago. *Really* don't want to drink. I want to—need to—get sober once and for all." She paused, searching the counselor's eyes. "Can you help me?"

Her gaze flitted nervously around the office for the first time. Tiny and quiet with white walls. But, somehow Autumn had made it seem almost airy, with cheerful posters of nature scenes, and plants that somehow thrived on the fluorescent lighting.

"Yes, I think we can work on this together. But, I'd like to spend some time getting some background on you before we get into that specific issue. Okay?"

Laurel nodded.

"So, the record says you're in for a third DUI, correct?"

Avoiding Autumn's gaze, Laurel stared at the stained carpet the counselor had managed to disguise with a colorful throw rug.

Laurel spent a few minutes filling her in on her background as a chronic alcoholic, who despite several rehabs had managed to avoid any kind of one-on-one counseling. "My sponsor says I have issues—and I agree—that it's high time I got to the bottom of. But, if you could first try to help me with the letter, I'd be grateful. How does that sound?"

"Okay, but I think what I need for you to do first is to start at the beginning. Can you tell me what was happening when Rick kicked you out, as you put it?"

"I was in my early thirties and living with him, but things weren't going well. Rick had anger issues, in fact was, uh, pretty abusive. I seem to have a knack for choosing bad relationships."

She looked up to make sure that registered with Autumn. "I was drinking. A lot. Then I got pregnant. I wanted to have an abortion, but Rick said no. He *really* wanted me to have the baby. In fact, he insisted. I just was, um, too much of a hot mess to fight back. Certainly in no condition to become a mom."

She stopped and took a breath, hoping her queasy stomach would settle down. This was harder than she'd bargained for. "I drank through most of the first trimester, before I knew I was pregnant. When I found out, Rick insisted I quit and watched me like a hawk."

Laurel crossed her arms over her chest. "He actually became a little nicer to me when I was pregnant and, for a while, I thought he might have changed, that maybe becoming a father would make him a better person."

She shifted in her seat, trying to get comfortable. "It was a miracle that Ryan was born okay. No effects from my early drinking, which was a huge relief. I wasn't working at the time—had lost my job—so Rick was supporting us all. At first, I thought it might be okay. I snuck drinks, because Rick was monitoring my drinking, but not every day. Then Ryan got colic and cried all the time, no matter what I did. I was exhausted and feeling like a total failure as a mother. Rick would come home from work tired, wanting dinner and peace and quiet. But I just couldn't get Ryan to calm down and sleep."

"How was Rick as a father?"

"Crappy! For someone who wanted this baby so badly, once we had him, Rick found out it wasn't all that easy or fun. He let me know every day what a lousy mother I was. We fought all the time, just like before I got pregnant . . . I mean, I had the mother from hell. I was clueless about how to care for an infant, completely freaked out by the whole experience. It terrified me having this helpless creature totally dependent on me, and not being able to comfort him, no matter what I did. I felt trapped and incompetent and scared."

"So, what happened?"

"In the beginning, I hid my drinking. By the time Ryan was about a year old, though, it became daily. I was a mess—depressed, isolated, drinking every chance I got. One day, when Rick got home from work, he found me passed out on the sofa with Ryan screaming in his crib, hungry and with a messy diaper. He flipped out on me, screaming and yelling for me to get out. No amount of begging on my part, or promises to stop drinking made any difference. I left the next day."

She let that sit there a minute. Autumn waited. Eventually, she gestured with a questioning hand. "What happened after that?"

"I kinda pulled myself together enough to move in with my sister for a while. She made it clear I couldn't stay there for long, so I frantically began to look for a job. She kicked me out after a couple months and I found an apartment with a roommate. It was tough. Once I was on my own again, the drinking got pretty bad. It didn't take long . . . That job sent me to my second rehab."

"Do you remember anything about your feelings during this time?"

"I pretty much stuffed my feelings about losing Ryan right into the bottle. Looking back on it, I'd say I was pissed off, for sure. Frustrated, and really sad. Sure, I wasn't the best mother in the world—I know I wasn't—but I still loved that kid."

"And so," Autumn observed, "you had a major loss, which you never had any opportunity to grieve?"

Laurel sat, quiet, head down, hands fidgeting in her lap, tears filling her eyes. Loss? Grief? "No, I really never even thought about grieving when I left Ryan . . . And, now this letter comes, demanding an explanation. Why did I leave him?"

"Do you think that little boy, now almost a man, deserves to know the truth?"

Laurel thought about that for a minute, finally answering, "Yes, I do. But, I'm terrified of what might happen if I tell the truth."

"What are you afraid of?"

"That knowing the truth about why I left and why I'm here will end any shot at having any kind of relationship with Ryan."

"Yes, I suppose that's the risk, but what's the alternative? Not responding at all? Obviously, you're not going to lie to him. What would be your goal in responding to him?" She handed Laurel a tissue.

Laurel stopped crying, wiped her eyes, and blew her nose. "Well, I guess my goal, or at least my hope, would be to write a letter that made him want to write back, so we could have a dialogue through these letters. Maybe I would even get to see him again, as a young man, when I get out of here . . . probably a long shot. I'd still like to try to work toward that. Does that seem like even a remote possibility?"

"Well, I suppose anything is possible. Is it likely? I agree that it's a long shot. But, having said that, I'd also encourage you to consider it. I think it'd be worth trying. It'd give you the chance to make amends to Ryan. It might open the door to that process."

Laurel nodded.

"So, let's talk about what you might say in this first letter in the time we have left this afternoon. Then you can go back to your yard and work on a draft."

"Okay."

"What are the messages you'd like Ryan to hear about why you left and why you're here?"

"First of all, I'd like him to know that I didn't leave voluntarily, that Rick made me leave."

"Oka-a-ay. But, don't you think he should know why Rick made you leave?"

"I guess. So, he needs to know I am an alcoholic, that I drank during that first year of his life. Also, that Rick found me drunk and that's why he made me leave. But, I think he deserves to know how I begged Rick to give me a second chance, promised to get help, and he refused."

"All true, but I'd caution you about making Rick out to be a bad guy."

"Point taken. I know Rick was being protective of Ryan. I understand that. I was a bad mother at the time, I was a mess, and I should cop to that."

Autumn stared intently at Laurel with those piercing blue eyes. "Okay, what else do you want Ryan to know?"

"Well, let's see. That my drinking continued on and off over the years, but I never stopped trying to get sober."

"What else?"

"I guess that brings us to how I got in here. Probably the hardest part of the letter."

"Okay, so how're you going to approach it?"

"Well, for starters, I think I have to be completely honest and take responsibility for what I did. I got drunk, and got a third DUI." Laurel groaned. "This is going to be so friggin' hard!"

"Yes, it is. But, you can do this. Those things need to be said, but what about some more positive messages that are also true?"

"Like what?"

"How about how surprised and happy you are to get this letter from him? And, how much you hope this can lead to some kind of a relationship with him after all these years?"

"Yeah, right, all that is true. Thanks. I do need to tell him that."

"Okay, we're out of time for today. Are you ready to tackle this letter?"

Over the next week Laurel wrote and re-wrote her first letter to Ryan. In a way it helped her adjust to prison, because the chaos around her became background noise as she tried to focus on drafting the letter well.

She went to her job, ate her meals, read books, talked to other inmates, most notably her cubemate Guzman, and Lily, her co-worker at the library. Other than that, she kept her head down, stayed out of trouble, and reworked the letter.

Finally, Friday came around again… time for her next appointment with Autumn. She brought her draft, got some feedback, made some more changes, and finalized the message. Autumn cautioned her about including lengthy explanations of why she left Ryan, and why she was in prison in this first letter. Better to wait and see if—and how—Ryan would respond before getting into that.

About two weeks after receiving her first letter from Ryan, with shaking hands, she put the following letter in the mail.

> *"Dear Ryan,*
>
> *Yes, I am your mother and I am in prison. Why I'm in prison is a long story, one I'm willing to tell.*
>
> *I can't tell you how surprised and thrilled I was to get your letter. After what happened when you were a baby, I never expected to hear from you again. Yes, I did leave you and owe you a full explanation for that, and I'll do my best to be as honest as possible about what happened.*
>
> *Ryan, I have never stopped loving you and am eager to hear more about your life.*
>
> *Laurel Peterson"*

Chapter 18

She felt good about her brief first letter, but had trepidations about whether Ryan would respond. She'd kept a copy, and in the ensuing weeks re-read it many times, wishing she had also invited him to ask any additional questions he might have.

Every day for two weeks she went to mail call and waited for her name to be called. Nothing. As two weeks passed with no response, then three, she began to fear she'd never hear from Ryan again. Maybe she'd scared him away. Over and over, she nearly drove herself crazy with questions, wondering whether he'd write back. Would he condemn her for being an alcoholic and not getting sober? Would he be open to any kind of a relationship in the future?

Her spirits plummeted. Each day dragged, more gloomy and monotonous than the next. Finally, she decided to tell Lily about Ryan and the letter. She had to have someone to talk to about it other than Autumn. She worried she should keep to herself, but needed someone to talk to about the memories of that time flooding her brain.

Lily turned out to be sympathetic and understanding, saying all the things a really supportive friend should say. Plus, Laurel saw Autumn a couple more times. She recommended patience.

Easier said than done.

She had adjusted to Sunstate, or so Autumn thought, and settled into the colorless, tedious boredom of incarceration. She went to work; ate tasteless and sometimes downright disgusting meals; took her three showers a week with prison-issued soap and shampoo, drying herself with skimpy towels; and endured the still-hot Phoenix days.

She enrolled in the substance abuse class that met on weekends. As she suspected, it wasn't very useful. Mostly educational and focused on the illegal drugs most of her fellow inmates were addicted to: heroin and methamphetamine, as well as prescription drugs like OxyContin.

Thank God she'd only smoked pot and had never gotten into those other drugs. Booze had caused enough harm for a lifetime.

After she'd given up hope, in early November, another letter arrived.

"Dear Laurel,

Dad told me I could start to look for you when I was 18 if I still wanted to. I'm 19 now, almost 20, and it has taken me a year to track you down. On the off chance you even care to know about me after all this time, or even remember me, here goes.

I'm in my third year at California Institute of Technology in Pasadena, CA (Cal Tech). I'm pretty good in math, just like Dad, so when I started I thought it was going to be engineering for me. After a couple of years here, I'm not so sure. It's a great school, and I love California, but I just don't know if engineering is for me.

I've had to take liberal arts courses, and I've enjoyed them a lot more than my boring engineering courses. Dad keeps telling me the job market is good for engineers, but I'm having a hard time imagining myself doing engineering full time if it's anything like these courses. And then, there're the guys (and it is mostly guys) who I take courses with. REALLY boring. So, I don't know. I'm kind of stressed out by the whole thing, because I have to make a decision pretty soon about a major or I'm going to lose credits and have to go another year. Cal Tech is private and very expensive, so I don't want to waste any time. I have a tuition scholarship. Right now, the deal Dad and I have is that he's paying half of room and board. I'm paying for the other half and for everything else, like books. So, I have to work a lot of hours.

If you're wondering what I look like, I enclosed a photo of myself. That's my dog, Rusty (not very original, I know, but I was only 10 when we got her as a puppy, and Dad let me name her). We lost her last year. I have to tell you, that was really tough.

I've been wondering a lot about you. What your life has been like. What you did to end up in prison. How long you are going to be there? I used to ask Dad about you all the time. Where is she? Why did she leave us? Do you think she loves me? Is she ever going to come back?

At first, Dad was kind of patient and tried to give me answers. Like, he told me you did love me. But, then I kept asking, if she loves me, why isn't she coming back?

Eventually he got mad, sick and tired of my questions, so I just stopped asking. But, I still have all those questions. Why did you leave? How come you never came back?
Your son,
Ryan

A photograph of a young man and a golden retriever fell out of the envelope. A knot formed in her chest. After reading the letter she studied the photo. Ryan had an unmistakable resemblance to Rick. The picture showed an almost grown-up Ryan with a dog by his side, a russet golden retriever. The young man stood tall, with sandy hair, cut pretty short, and Rick's nose, dressed in jeans and a plaid shirt. He looked like a typical high school or college student. Handsome, though, and clean cut. Looked like a nice kid.

After talking it over with Autumn she wrote back.

"Dear Ryan,
As I'm sure your dad told you, I'm an alcoholic. I have struggled my whole adult life to get sober and have succeeded in doing so for some pretty long periods. But, right before I got pregnant with you, things between your dad and me were not going very well, and I was drinking heavily. When I found out I was about two and half months pregnant, I stopped drinking and you were born without any problems. What a blessing!
Unfortunately, your arrival did not improve things between your dad and me. Ryan, I had a very prob-lematic upbringing and honestly knew nothing about

being a mother. To complicate matters further, you had a bad case of colic, which meant you cried and fussed all the time. It seemed like no matter what I did, you were miserable. I felt like a total failure as a mother. No matter how much I loved you, I just couldn't seem to comfort you.

Your dad was working long hours, coming home too exhausted to help much with you, and I just fell apart, returning to drinking secretly a couple months after you were born. I felt scared and trapped, and my drinking worsened. When you were about a year old, your dad came home from work and found me passed out and drunk while you cried in your crib. That was the last straw for him. He told me I had to leave. I begged him to let me have a second chance and promised to get help, but he was understandably concerned for your safety and said no.

I moved out and tried to put my life back together, missing you terribly. When I found a job and an apartment, I got back in touch with your dad to ask if I could be a part of your life, but he adamantly said no. I had no choice but accept his decision. After that, I decided it was best not to try to interrupt your life and gave up on ever seeing you again. BUT, I HAVE ALWAYS LOVED YOU.

My life since leaving you has been intermittently okay, but often difficult because of my drinking. I graduated from college before you were born and became a graphic artist, which has enabled me to find jobs pretty easily, jobs I sometimes lost because of my drinking.

Most recently I ended up back in Arizona, where I grew up, at a job in Scottsdale near where my mother lives. She has Parkinson's and really needs my help. I had been going to Alcoholics Anonymous and was sober for almost two years, when things in my life started to unravel. I drank again and got arrested for DUI, not my first. That led to a month and a half in jail and ultimately to a prison term of a little over a year. I had only been here a month when your letter arrived.

As much as I hate being here, I understand that I have to pay the price for my actions. I have not had a drink since that night, will be attending a substance abuse program here, and will be on probation for two years after I am released. I hope they will help me find housing and a treatment program, because I am determined to stay sober once and for all. I have tried to be completely honest with you.

Ryan, you sound like a wonderful young man. It's obvious your dad did a great job in raising you on his own. I hope this can be the beginning of at least a correspondence between us, if not a relationship after I am released. You deserve much more than my apology for being an irresponsible mother, and leaving instead of fighting for you.

Your letter has given me renewed hope. Thank you so much for writing to me.
Love,
Your mother Laurel"

Two weeks passed and another letter from Ryan arrived.

"Dear Laurel,

I'm sorry it's taken me so long to respond to your letter. The fall semester has been super busy.

It does sound like you were honest in your letter, and I appreciate that. Dad had told me some about what happened—that you were drinking and not a good mother—but I didn't know you tried later to see me and that he said no.

It sounds like drinking has taken a big toll on your life. Just so that you know, I pretty much don't drink. That's kind of weird for a college student, since most of my peers are big drinkers. They smoke a lot of weed as well. First, based on what Dad said about you, I know that drinking could be risky for me. And, even if I didn't have that history, I see what it does to the other students, and I don't like it. They act very stupid, for one thing. Plus, a bunch of them get drunk and hung over on weeknights and don't make it to class the next day. They're always asking me for my notes, and I'm like, no way.

It also sounds like you're paying a big price for your drinking and what you did when you were drunk. I'd be interested in hearing more about what prison is like.

The other thing I'd like to know about is your family. Dad told me nothing, other than the name of your mother. That's how I found you, by the way. I actually paid a private detective to track her down after I couldn't find you. She was very surprised to hear from me, said she didn't know she even had a grandson. You should know (you probably already do) that she's very, very pissed off at you. I don't know what I expected, but she wasn't very nice to me. She did at least tell me where you were, and I was able to go online and find your inmate number and address.

It may take a while, but I'll try to write back.
Ryan"

Oh my God, he wrote back, and he says he'll keep writing! She read the letter three times and couldn't wait to take the letter to Autumn at her next appointment. It sounded like he accepted what she did, both leaving him and the drinking, without too much judgment.

I feel so lucky. Now I just have to work at earning his respect and making amends.

So, her mom did know about Ryan now. Wonder how come she never let on.

She wrote back quickly, trying to respond to all his questions. She told him about her family—her brothers and sister, as well as her difficult mother and how baffling she was, how hard it was to figure out why she had been such a bad parent. She also talked about her stint in foster care—how the kids were separated, how traumatic it was, and that she was the last one reunited with her mother. She also mentioned her mother's drinking, and that she had been able, unlike Laurel, to stop on her own. That left her unable to understand why Laurel had had so much trouble getting sober.

The letter continued:

"My brothers and Betsy did not fare as well as I did. Lucas died in a bar fight, and Paul has been in

prison for dealing drugs, according to Mom. I lost touch with both of them when I left for college. I'm not in touch with Betsy now either. Mom is furious that we all turned out so badly, none of us in any kind of shape to take care of her, but what kind of chance did we have for it to be any different? As badly as I turned out, my siblings probably ended up worse. Certainly, dead is worse.

Still, I'm determined to break that pattern. I'm working with a therapist here, and I plan to continue to get professional help when I'm released. Plus, I know I need to attend AA.

Ryan, I could hear how busy you are from your last letter. The opposite is true in prison: The challenge is filling the time, which is boring and monotonous, and passes very slowly, probably because most of us are not very busy.

Please, continue to write back. I love hearing about your life. I'll let you know about what prison life is like in my next letter.

Love,
Your mom Laurel"

Prison life had fallen into a predictable, if boring, rhythm. Weekdays were easier to take: up early, work at the library, lunch, back to the library, dinner, an evening of reading on her bunk. Weekends were tough, with no structure, and many inmates enjoying visits. The substance abuse classes, despite being useless, helped fill the time. She'd tried another AA meeting, but found it to be largely a waste of time, too.

She'd figured out how to survive in prison, though, and began to see a light at the end of the tunnel, despite it being many months away.

Many of the women in her unit were younger, in their twenties, covered in ink, yelling all the time, and itching for a fight. Many of them, especially the Latinas, had been in gangs before prison, accustomed to stealing, drugs, and violence. Not surprisingly, that often spilled over into their prison lives . . . getting written up and carted off to isolation. So, drama swirled all around her—chaos, yelling, fighting—but she managed to avoid it.

Finally, having kept a clean record, Laurel advanced to Level II of the Earned Incentive Program, making her eligible for the Print Shop job. Still no openings though.

Laurel instantly relaxed and felt safe as she settled into the chair in Autumn's office. Although the sessions with Autumn had decreased to every other week, she still looked forward to them.

Autumn got down to business. "Since things seem to be pretty stable, it's time to talk about the events leading up to your relapse and the DUI that got you in here."

Laurel nodded her agreement.

"So, bring me up to speed. I remember you saying you'd been sober a couple years before that day… working, going to meetings. You've had months to think about it. So, what happened, why did you get so drunk?"

"I've realized that relapse was very much like most of my other relapses, other than the fact that I was going to AA, although my meeting attendance had dropped off."

"In what way—are you seeing a pattern?"

"Definitely a pattern. Several negative things converge, I isolate, keep things inside and, before you know it, I'm feeling overwhelmed and I just drink."

"What were those negative things in this case?"

"First, I had a terrible cold. I'd felt like shit for days and still had to work."

She explained about Scott dumping her, the pressure at her job, and the unsuccessful attempt to make amends to her mother.

"She was a real bitch about it, and I didn't handle it well. It really pissed me off. Made me feel even more resentful."

"Okay, that's a lot. I can see how you must have felt overwhelmed. And angry."

Laurel went on to discuss the actual day of the relapse—starting to drink before the party, which she couldn't face sober, then at the party, and driving home drunk when the cops stopped her.

"So, you got dumped, you got angry, you were overwhelmed, you were resentful. Is that the pattern?"

"Pretty much. When I get dumped, I get scared, angry, hurt, and overwhelmed by my feelings. Add being sick, the fight with Mom, and having to go to that stupid party, and I resorted to what has reliably made me numb over the years, alcohol. Preferably in large quantities."

"Okay, we've established what happened that day, including the catastrophic consequences of your drinking. What I'd like you to do now is to rewind the video on that day, now that you know what happened, and figure out a solution to the problem of your overwhelming negative emotions, to lead to a different outcome. Can you do that?"

"Maybe, hopefully, but I need more time to think about it. Can you elaborate on what you mean?"

"Sure. If you could relive that last week, when all those challenges came down on you, how would you do it differently so you didn't end up drinking?"

"Dear Laurel,

I haven't been able to stop thinking about your letter since I got it. I had no idea you had had such a rough childhood. Dad never said anything about it. Sometimes, I've felt sorry for myself, not growing up with a mother, so I understand some of what you went through. I always wished I had at least one brother or sister. Being an only child was kind of tough. At least we weren't poor, and Dad never had women around. It's hard though, having only one parent, as you well know. And, despite what little Dad told me about your leaving, I always felt somehow it was my fault that you left. I mean, who has a mother who leaves? I've had plenty of friends whose fathers haven't been around or available, but I never knew anyone who didn't have a mother. So, it was helpful hearing your side of why you left and what your family was like.

The end of this semester is crazy busy. I'm taking 18 credits, which is 3–6 credits more than most other kids are taking. Plus, I have a work-study job at an engineering lab. About half of my hours are on weekends, and sometimes when it's not too busy I get to do homework, so it's not too bad. But, I don't have much free time.

I'd still like to hear about prison life. I can't imagine what it would be like to be locked up in a

*boring, horrible place with very little to do. Actually,
sometimes the idea of very little to do sounds appealing
(just kidding!).*
Ryan"

Laurel sat with the letter, stewing about its contents. She felt shitty realizing what she'd put Ryan through growing up. Not just not having a mother, but feeling like it was his fault in some way, no matter what his father told—or didn't tell—him. She'd never really thought about how different, and unusual, it would be to grow up without a mother as opposed to a father. She'd always thought having a really crappy mother and no father was as bad as it could be, but maybe not having a mother was worse. At least Rick was apparently a good father. She couldn't decide how to respond, although describing day-to-day prison life should be a breeze.

Finally, she learned that a print-shop job opened up. She couldn't wait to tell Guzman, but dreaded telling Mrs. R., Lily, and Ashlee that she'd be leaving the library. She'd enjoyed working there, having the opportunity of first dibs on books as they came in, and using the computers sometimes.

"Guzman, I start at the print shop in a few days!" Laurel practically danced around the cube.

"How come you're so excited? I thought you liked the library."

"I do. I did. But, the print shop pays more. I'd love to fatten my commissary account a bit so I can buy some warmer clothes and eat a halfway decent meal once in a while."

"I hear you, girl. Good for you, Peterson."

Chapter 19

"I've been thinking all week about what you asked last session. You know, about how I could have avoided my relapse. It's not rocket science. Bottom line is, I should have been talking to someone about what was going on. But, I didn't. Instead, I did my usual thing . . . isolated and panicked."

"Who could you have talked to about it?" Autumn asked.

"I had two people, really, both women and both new in my life. My sponsor and a new friend named Caroline. I have such trouble trusting people, I kinda didn't even think of them."

"Okay, so lesson learned there. And, we'll get to that trust issue later. What else could you have done?"

"Well, the obvious thing would have been to get to a meeting, more meetings in general. What I inevitably do after a while is stop going." She stared at her lap, fiddling with the zipper on her hoodie. "Life gets in the way."

"Okay, lesson number two." Autumn leaned forward. "So, what's the take-home point? Was what happened inevitable? Was it unavoidable?"

Laurel's face flushed. "Of course not. It sounds like I'm making excuses. It's obvious—now—I should have gone to any lengths to avoid drinking. I had things I could have done, and I guess I didn't, or I wouldn't have gotten drunk. Clearly, if I'd been able to foresee what actually happened, I'd have done that."

"I guess what I'm saying is that, moving forward, with your history, any time you *decide*, you *choose,* to pick up a drink, you're running the risk that you won't be able to stop, and disaster will ensue."

Head down, Laurel quietly sat and pondered that. "Of course, you're right. Those were bad choices I made that Saturday, and in the past, too. Like drinking when Ryan was a baby. I have to stop doing that, once and for all." She shifted her position and looked directly at Autumn. "But how? I think my best shot is to get into treatment as soon as I'm released from here and stay involved with AA long-term. What do you think?"

"I agree. That is your best option. How about the AA meetings here? Have you gone to any?"

"There aren't many, first of all, but yes, a couple. No one really shares, though. I guess the word in the yards is that there's no real confidentiality. From what I've been told, you can pretty much assume what you share will be blabbed around. So, for somebody like me with trust issues . . . Plus, in the two meetings I went to, it was a different set of women each time. Bottom line? Not very helpful."

Before Thanksgiving, she wrote Ryan with her news about getting the print shop job. She also described life in prison—its tediousness, the noise, the lack of privacy, the miserable and combative young inmates, and her strategy of trying to mind her own business as much as possible.

A week later, a short note arrived from Ryan, telling Laurel some life news.

"My big news is that I met a girl in my PoliSci class. We've gone out twice for coffee. Her name is Madison, and she's very pretty (red hair and the cutest freckles, although she doesn't think so) and easy to talk to. I'll keep you posted on how things are proceeding (ha, ha!). Keep your fingers crossed."

Well good for him. She hoped it would go well.

As the first day of her new job in the print shop approached, Laurel had lots of questions. Would the supervisor be okay? How many other inmates would she work with? What would they be like? What exactly would she be doing?

She'd work different hours from the library job, reporting to work at five o'clock in the morning and done by one, giving her afternoons to do something else. She'd started volunteering with the GED classes to stay busy. Having a lot of time on her hands invited trouble.

She walked the thirty minutes to the print shop, a huge gray, one-story concrete block building. There she met Mr. Martinez, the supervisor.

He ushered her into his office. "I looked over your file and it looks like you've had experience in graphic arts."

"Yes, a degree in graphic arts and a number of jobs in the field."

Mr. Martinez, with his square, stocky body and slicked-back hair, described the operation. He explained the shop was part of Arizona Correctional Industries, a for-profit business operated by the DOC using exclusively inmate employees. It covered all the printing needs of the state as well as some private businesses.

They arrived at a large, very warm—despite the air conditioning—warehouse-sized room with high ceilings, filled with large, bulky, complex machines. Most of them noisily crunched away: copying, making three-hole punches, printing brochures and flyers, and so forth. Fifteen women in orange tee shirts and baggy drawstring pants staffed the behemoths.

Once Mr. Martinez learned about Laurel's work experience, he involved her immediately in the design and administrative aspects of the operation rather than running machines.

Fantastic! This was more than she could have hoped for.

Over the next week, Laurel dragged her butt out of bed at four-thirty. She reported early each morning to the print shop where the inmate supervisor, McNeil, showed her the current print jobs.

At the end of her first full day on the job, as she and several other inmates were leaving, Laurel discovered they strip-searched each inmate as they left. Really? Every day? McNeil explained it was because there were so many dangerous things like paper clips and staples—*Seriously?*—that could be snagged and fashioned into weapons. Or, just valuable things like staplers that could be stolen. After all, you never knew when an inmate might insert a stapler into a body cavity like her vagina.

Would she ever get used to those strip searches?

By the end of the week, she had the lay of the land and figured out how things worked.

During her time there, Laurel designed or helped design a wide variety of printed materials for both Arizona state agencies and outside organizations, including brochures and flyers, letterhead stationery, calendars, booklets, and spiral-bound reports. Some were boring and routine, like business cards, but other projects were more complicated and interesting, not unlike her previous jobs. She enjoyed helping a client design a new newsletter, and Mr. Martinez praised her work.

Her volunteer job with the GED classes took up three afternoons a week. She also got to talk to Lily. It amazed her how little education those women had. Having taken her own education for granted, she began to appreciate her good fortune. Most of those women could barely read or write, or do simple arithmetic. No wonder they couldn't find jobs, and ended up pursuing illegal activities.

The other two afternoons she'd go to the library, visiting with Mrs. R., Lily, and Ashlee, and taking out a couple books. Sometimes—surreptitiously—she'd read books sent from the outside to other inmates, even though both knew that sharing of this nature violated DOC policy. What a dumb policy... but, she didn't want to get caught and written up for it either.

She spent evenings at San Carlos reading and watching the occasional TV show worth seeing. Prison wasn't exactly PBS land. Sometimes, someone talked her into a card game or board game with a few other inmates. But, for the most part, she kept to herself and avoided conflict or trouble, doing her best to follow the rules.

After she had reached the required savings DOC mandated for each inmate, her commissary account grew. She could afford to buy occasional luxuries, like a sweatshirt for when the mornings started to get chilly. Sometimes she even treated herself to some edible food—popcorn, canned soup, or chili. The latter entailed borrowing another inmate's "stinger" to heat it, another no-no that risked getting her written up.

Then another letter arrived from Ryan came.

"Dear Mom,

Sorry it's been so long again since my last letter. Thanks for your recommendation to go slow with Madison. We have actually. And, you were right—we're both so busy with school and jobs (she has a part-time job, too)—that we don't get to see each other all that much. But, things are going well between us. I can't afford to fly back East for Thanksgiving, and Madison's invited me to her home in northern California for the long weekend. I'm actually kind of stressing about it. I'm not sure I want to go. I don't feel ready to meet her family yet. Somehow that seems like something that should only happen if the relationship is getting serious, and I didn't think it was. What I've told her so far is that I'm not sure I can get away for the weekend with school projects due right afterward. Plus, if I stay here, I can put in some extra hours for work and make a little extra money.

"Enjoyed" isn't the right word, but I found it interesting to hear about what prison is like. It does sound boring. I was glad to hear about your jobs, the library one and the new one. I didn't realize prisoners had to work. Seems like a good idea though.

That's about all the news. The semester ends December 8th, so I should have more time after that. I'm flying back to Boston for about ten days to see Dad for Christmas.

I don't know if the prison does anything special for the holidays, but I hope so.

Best, Ryan"

She read the brief letter several times, noticing the *Dear Mom* right away. She couldn't believe it! Those were the best two words she'd seen since she got to Sunstate. She couldn't wait to tell Autumn. Maybe, just maybe, she'd have a shot at a relationship with Ryan.

Chapter 20

Right before Thanksgiving, Autumn suggested a final session to end their work together. Though things inside were going as smoothly as they could, Laurel felt unsure if she was ready to quit counseling. They spent their last session reviewing her progress. As they wrapped up, Autumn asked if Laurel had any contact with her mother in the three months she'd been at Sunstate.

"None at all, but I didn't expect to. First of all, we've never been close and, second, things between us were very raggedy, to say the least, when I came in here. After all, my last relapse really messed things up with my help to take care of her and Bill. So, I can understand her being really pissed off at me."

"Have you thought at all about contacting her… trying to make amends, for example?"

"Tried that already at the urging of my sponsor. Blew up in my face. So, no." She absolutely didn't want to repeat that fiasco.

"Well, how about just a letter? You could ask her how she and her husband are doing, for starters. And, she might be interested in how you're doing in here."

"Doubtful. I don't believe she cares a damn about how I'm doing."

"Let's examine that for a second. Are you saying there's *no* evidence at all that she cares even the least little bit about you?"

Like what? "Not that I can think of."

"What about the fact that she let you store your stuff at her house and let you live in their casita?"

"Okay, you're right. She did some things to help me out when I was really in bad shape, which *might* suggest on some level she cares."

"I think so. So, my parting suggestion to you is that you at least write to her once to find out how she's doing and let her know how you're doing. You don't have much to lose. If she writes back, fine. If not, at least you tried. How about it?"

Laurel shrugged. "Okay."

Autumn had forgotten all about the trust issue. Should she bring it up? Better to let sleeping dogs lie.

Laurel did write to her mother, telling her about where she was and how much longer she had to serve, letting her know she was likely be out in mid-September. She told her about the library and print shop jobs and that she'd been sober since the DUI.

After inquiring about her health and Bill, she encouraged her mom to write back. She also reassured her mother she wouldn't be expecting a place to live when she was released, that she would try to find a slot in a treatment program.

In the previous months, Laurel had kept pretty busy, having to attend the substance abuse classes on weekends. When they ended, she agonized over how she'd fill her time on weekends. Maybe she should look into other classes or programs she could attend. All she had to do this weekend was read. Thank goodness for books.

When she arrived back at San Carlos on Saturday after breakfast, rather than going to her bunk, she headed over to the lounge area in the center of the unit where she saw some women hanging out. She introduced herself to several of them.

As they chatted and played cards, Laurel sat and listened. Three of them discussed some kind of program. It sounded like they all had drug or alcohol problems, because the program seemed to have addiction treatment. Curious, Laurel considered asking them about it, but wondered whether it was too personal. What's the worst that could happen… that they tell her to shut the fuck up and mind her own business? Women in prison had no problem telling you that.

"So, it sounds like you guys are in some kind of special program for people with drug and alcohol issues, which I've got. What's it like?"

They continued to play cards. Finally, the black woman called Tameeka spoke. "What was your name again . . . Peterson?"

"Yeah, Laurel Peterson."

The one called Kat started without looking up. "It's a new program for women in medium units with drug and alcohol problems. It's called 'pre-release and post-release.'" She shuffled the deck and dealt a new hand.

"Which means what?"

"Well, it starts when you're still in here, three to six months before your release date, and continues after you're out," Tameeka said. "I don't know how long afterwards."

"How do you qualify for it?"

The three women looked at each other.

"Anybody know?" Nicole asked.

The other two shook their heads, returning to their cards.

Kat threw a card on the table. "Um, I think you have to be released onto probation. Are you two doing probation?" she asked the others. Both nodded.

"And, what's it like when you get out?"

"So many questions!" Tameeka said, finally looking up. "Go ask a C.O. or a counselor, Peterson."

After the boring weekend with nothing to do, Laurel welcomed work on Monday. After work, she laid on her rack in the late afternoon, reading.

Guzman came in. "I think I heard them call your name at mail call a little while ago."

"Thanks, I'll check it out."

Hmm, way too soon for Ryan to be writing back.

After waiting in a long line, they handed over a letter, postmarked "Carefree, AZ."

Well, I'll be. Mom wrote back. Pretty amazing.

Her mother had to put Bill into assisted living after he kept confusing her with his ex-wife, and became incontinent. She had had someone come in to help, but Bill didn't respond well, and the woman quit. His adult children had gotten involved, pressuring her to keep Bill at home to save money, but it didn't work. By the time she moved him into assisted living, Mom was losing it. They told her to wait a month before she visited to let him get settled, but then he had no idea who she was.

The Parkinson's medication had ceased working and she struggled to care for herself. And yet, she had to take care of

Bill's affairs as well. She finally concluded the house was too much to manage. She sounded overwhelmed and depressed, worried about whether Bill had any assets other than the house, and concerned about how she'd manage on just her Social Security and minuscule pension.

Once again, guilt reared its ugly head as Laurel considered how the DUI and its consequences prevented her from being able to help her mother. Toward the end of the week, she wrote back to her mom, telling her how sorry she was about her circumstances. At least Joanne had a place to live for the time being. Since her mother had Bill's power of attorney, Laurel suggested contacting his lawyer about how to proceed with the house and Bill's assets.

Laurel made another appointment with Autumn right before Christmas to discuss her eligibility for the new program she'd heard about. The counselor promised to check into it.

She also apprised Autumn on what had been happening, including her new print shop job, and gave her an update on her family issues. Specifically, she described the letter she'd drafted to her mother, and the response, and the fact that Ryan had addressed his most recent letter "Dear Mom." Autumn complimented her on what a good job she'd done on the letter to her mom as well as her willingness to take the risk of corresponding with Ryan, of opening herself up and making herself vulnerable to getting hurt.

After the appointment, it was all about waiting to see if she was eligible for the program.

Finally, Laurel received a letter back from Ryan. She'd been dying to know if he'd gone home with his new girlfriend for Thanksgiving or what he decided to do. It had been awhile since she'd heard from him.

He wrote that Thanksgiving with Madison's family had turned out okay. Her parents were very welcoming, but he found all the family members overwhelming in comparison to the kind of small, quiet holiday celebrations he was accustomed to with his dad. He also expressed his concern that the relationship was moving too quickly for him, although he also looked forward to spending time with Madison over the holiday break. He'd be spending a couple weeks back in Boston with this father for Christmas.

Before she knew it, Christmas was just days away. Despite being locked up, most of the women looked forward to the approaching holiday. Many had made clever decorations using arts and crafts materials bought at commissary and displayed them around their cubes. Laurel was surprised at how festive it felt. The high spirits cheered her. She wondered if the prison would make Christmas inside more bearable.

Laurel reclined on her rack. "Guzman, how many Christmases have you spent inside?"

"Why don't you start calling me Angie, like my friends do." Guzman sat on her bunk reading a magazine.

Laurel beamed.

"This'll be my sixth Christmas behind bars."

"Wow… Angie, what's it like? Does the kitchen do anything special?"

"They try, but it's not all that great. What *is* great is what the women manage to do for themselves, using their commissary accounts and their creativity."

"Like what?"

"Oh, they'll make desserts and casseroles and things. And, everything gets shared no matter how much or little people can afford to contribute. It's actually pretty cool."

"Sounds nice."

"And," Angie said, "the women get super creative about making gifts for their families. Even for their friends inside, though that's strictly forbidden."

Of course, it was. Wasn't anything that made this experience more bearable strictly forbidden?

Even though Christmas on the outside had never been a big deal for her, Laurel moped, envying everyone's visitors the weekend before Christmas. Having none herself made her feel shitty.

In the days leading up to Christmas, she watched women surreptitiously exchanging little gifts they'd made or purchased for each other—strictly against the rules—and started to pout. Reminding herself that she'd vowed, coming in, to mind her own business, provided little consolation. Although she enjoyed getting to know Lily from the library and Guzman—Angie—she had mostly kept to herself. As a result, no gift exchanges for her. Feeling sorry for herself, she recalled the expression she often heard in the rooms of AA about the dangers of self-pity: "poor me, poor me, pour me a drink." It made her realize, once again, how fortunate it was not to have any alcohol available. As she thought about that, she realized it had been a long time since she'd thought about drinking. What a blessing!

It took two long weeks to get in to see Autumn. Laurel was dying to learn what she'd found out about the new program.

The counselor sat across her desk from Laurel with her hands steepled. "Here's what I've learned. The program's being run by a consortium of community agencies. Sounds really good. It's called Women in Recovery Can Make It. The initials are WIRCMI, which they pronounce 'Work Me.' The goal of the program is to reduce recidivism, because more than sixty percent of the women incarcerated here end up back in prison. So, the program is targeted toward high-risk inmates."

"What do they mean by high risk?"

"High risk for committing another crime and ending up back in prison."

Laurel didn't like the sound of that. "Do I qualify as high risk?"

"If I understand their criteria correctly, you probably do."

"What are their criteria?"

"First of all, substance abuse, and you've got a history of chronic relapse. Secondly, mental health issues, which will be an easy case to make."

Laurel sat on the edge of her seat, listening intently, head down, nodding.

"Another high-risk factor for you is social isolation—you have no family support and few close friends on the outside."

Laurel didn't want to look at her.

"The last thing is not having anywhere to go when you're released and no source of income unless you can find work. Ex-offenders, even with your education and work history, typically have a hard time finding work right after they've gotten out. So, high risk? Yeah, I'd say you can be considered high risk."

Laurel sat quietly, thinking. *Jesus, I'm going to be an ex-offender? High risk for recidivism.* The words set off alarms in her head.

There is no fucking way I'm ever coming back here!

On the one hand, this was good news. This is what she wanted to hear, right? She might be eligible for the program. On the other hand, it made her feel like such a loser. She remained bent over in her chair with her head in her hands.

"Laurel, what's going through your mind right now?" Autumn's voice sounded caring.

The knot in her chest and the lump in her throat made it hard to talk. "I'm really scared. I feel so . . . I don't know . . . vulnerable. Even though what you've told me is probably good in the sense that I might qualify for the program, hearing about all the factors that make me 'high risk' is terrifying. But, dammit," she said defiantly, "I'm not coming back here! Ever!"

"Okay, I understand your feeling terrified. But, you've got a good chance to be accepted into the program. I'll definitely give you a strong recommendation. Plus, I'm sure they're also going to assess motivation, and you're *very* motivated. I admire your determination to not come back here. That's what they want. Women who are going to commit to the program and work hard to make it on the outside. I think that's you, Laurel."

By this point, tears streamed down Laurel's face. "Thanks. What happens next?"

"You'll have a screening interview in March. They have a new cohort starting the eight-week pre-release portion of the program in April or May. They'll give you the details at the interview."

Autumn confirmed that Work Me helped clients find housing and offered treatment for both substance abuse and mental health.

"In my recommendation, I'll indicate you're a strong candidate for therapy. I think you can really benefit. You've demonstrated that with me." Autumn paused. "Start to make a list of the questions you have about the program so you can ask them in the screening interview next month. That'll indicate your interest and motivation for the program."

"How many women are they taking?"

"I think fifteen."

Laurel groaned. How many were applying? Did she really have a chance?

Autumn offered some final words of encouragement. But, Laurel left feeling like her emotions were jerked all over the place. Hearing about why she was considered "high risk" had been hard. But, ironically, that's apparently what would make her a good candidate for the program. They were taking so few women, though.

Okay, Laurel, just put one foot in front of the next and keep moving forward.

Chapter 21

Laurel thought about Ryan and wondered how he was, how his Christmas went. She hadn't written back since before Christmas.

They exchanged letters. Laurel told him about the Work Me program and asked about Christmas in Boston, and how things were with Madison.

He wrote back that Christmas had not gone well. He and his father had argued a lot, especially about his relationship with Madison. Rick disapproved of it, fearing it would tie Ryan down despite his son's obvious happiness with the relationship. Ryan had even assured his dad it wasn't a long-term commitment. They also argued about Ryan getting in touch with Laurel. Rick couldn't understand why his son would want to connect with her, and grew angry when he heard Laurel was in prison. He feared Ryan would be hurt by the relationship, as minimal as it was. Ryan ended up feeling unsupported by his father, so he committed to staying in LA to find work the following summer rather than returning to Boston as he had during previous summers.

Her heart ached when she read her son's letter, especially the part about Rick being so angry with him for writing to her. Why would Ryan even tell her that? Was he trying to make her feel guilty about it? Because that's not how she felt. All she felt was gratitude that, at this stage of life, Ryan chose to be in touch with the mother who abandoned him nineteen years ago. *I guess this must be what it is like to be a parent, to love your child and hurt as you see them struggling with difficult things you can't help them with.*

She tried to understand how Rick must feel about Ryan's relationship with Madison. Rick didn't want him to get tied down, to close certain doors on his career. But, Ryan was a great kid, a thoughtful kid, a serious student who worked hard to help pay for his expensive education… an education he appreciated. Didn't he also deserve to have a girlfriend? Laurel thought so, but she tried to understand it from Rick's point of view. Ryan had not asked for her advice, nor was she going to give it. She'd hardly earned the right to weigh in. Still, it bothered her.

Laurel interviewed with Sarah Pelham from the Work Me program in early March. They sat in a small, windowless room used by lawyers off the huge visiting room. Laurel had never had occasion to visit it before.

Sarah began by explaining the program to Laurel, prefacing her explanation with the observation that many incarcerated women found it difficult to transition to life on the outside. The pre-release part of the program consisted of twenty-five "lessons" offered to small groups of women, covering social skills, problem solving, and self-change. Each lesson would include instruction, as well as role-playing and homework assignments. They would discuss things like how thinking affects behavior, and appropriate ways to respond to anger. In addition, each participant would be assigned a mentor from the outside, with whom they could connect before release.

The post-release part of the program provided transitional housing, help finding a job, and counseling, confirming what Laurel had heard, all at no cost. The program expected participants to commit to a full year in the program post-release.

Hearing all that, Laurel breathed a huge sigh of relief as they moved on to the assessment phase of the interview. Sarah asked a lot of the same questions the probation officer asked in Tent City, like about her use of alcohol and drugs. But, she also asked specific questions about Laurel's motivation to quit drinking and stay out of prison in the future.

Laurel decided to be honest about her history—troubled childhood, drinking, DUIs, domestic violence. After all, she was high risk, right? She also emphasized the jobs she'd done in prison and her clean record—no fights or infractions of any kind. She did her best to convince the interviewer of her motivation to end, once and for all, her history of chronic relapse.

As they wrapped up, Laurel looked directly at Sarah. "I know I need help getting back on my feet. I want a place of my own and a job. I want a normal life. I know I need to stick close to AA and get a sponsor. With some help and support I think—I know—I can make it… stay sober."

Oh, Work Me sounded so good. But, will they let me in?
Fingers crossed.

After Ryan's upsetting letter after Christmas, Laurel wrote back, letting him know how badly she felt about the arguments he had with his father, especially about her. She told him she felt kind of guilty about that, but that their correspondence had been the best part of her life since she'd entered prison, and helped motivate her to clean up her act once and for all.

She described the Work Me program and all it offered… the answer to her prayers about what she'd do post-release. Finally, she told him about her mother—his grandmother, at least in name—and the challenges she faced with her husband and her worsening Parkinson's. Writing the letter made Laurel realize that, given her age—fifteen years to retirement—she needed to get serious about getting her life back on track. Otherwise, she could end up like her mother, poor and dependent on someone else.

She ended her letter by saying:

> *"For what it's worth, I think you are an outstanding young man. I've been so impressed by how mature and serious you are, how thoughtful. Despite how your dad may have behaved over Christmas, I'm sure he thinks the same thing. I'm guessing he's just scared that you might get sidetracked and compromise your education (Madison) or get hurt (me). I'm sure he's acting that way out of concern for you, even if it's coming across like he's being really negative.*
> *Love, Mom"*

The end of March came and went with no word about Work Me. The first week in April, Autumn summoned Laurel to her office. Her stomach churned as she awaited the verdict.

Autumn started by saying, "I know it's not what you hoped."

Shit! She didn't get in. What was she going to do? She slumped in her chair, head down. She looked up at Autumn, fighting tears.

"I'm sorry to have to tell you that you didn't get into Work Me. I know how disappointed you must be. But, it's not necessarily over yet."

Finally, Laurel was able to muster, "What does that mean?"

"Well, here's what they told me. You were a pretty good fit on all their criteria except two: the length of your sentence and having a college degree. Apparently, they were looking for women who are even more high risk than you based on those two factors."

Great, so now she wasn't high risk enough.

"But, here's the good news. You're first on their waiting list. If someone turns down the program before they start the pre-release portion at the end of the month, you're next in line."

Laurel let that linger. She grabbed a tissue from the box on Autumn's desk, wiped her eyes, and twisted the tissue into a knot in her lap. The thought of a drink flitted through her mind. It happened in an instant. An ice-cold vodka, straight from the freezer, icy and burning at the same time as it slid down her throat. Then, a few minutes later, the relaxation and numbing that predictably followed. She considered the idea for a second, then shook her head.

You're frustrated, you're pissed off. But, don't let those things get the better of you.

"What're you thinking right now?" Autumn asked.

Should she tell her? Should she be honest? "Well, like you said, I'm really disappointed, but also angry—it seems so unfair! I'm also scared, really scared of what'll happen to me when I leave here if I don't get some help. Then, right after that, I thought about drinking an ice-cold glass of Stoli, right from the freezer. It rocketed through my mind. I thought about it, even though I know I can't do it. That it wouldn't get me anywhere."

She fidgeted in her chair. "I'm wishing there was a really good AA meeting or sponsor in here that I could talk to right now. I need to speak to someone who understands how 'normal,'" she used air quotes, "it is to think about a drink at times like this, even knowing where drinking took me less than a year ago."

Autumn's sparkling blue eyes fixed on her face. "I know I'm not your sponsor or even an AA member, but you can talk to me about this. You *should* talk to me about this. I'm not in recovery, but I do understand something about addiction. I *know* it's normal for an addict or alcoholic to think about using right away after a big disappointment like the one you just had. But, let's talk about what you can do instead, okay?"

"Okay . . . well, for starters, I can think through what would happen if I drank again, even in here."

"Good. And, what could happen?"

"I'd get written up if the COs found out. I might blow off my print shop job and get in trouble there. If I got drunk, I could get so pissed off I might get into a fight with somebody, and get written up or even thrown into solitary." She paused. "All of which would jeopardize my early release status and make me stay in here longer."

"All true. And, none of which you want. Would any of it increase your chances of getting into Work Me? Because remember, you're first on the waiting list."

"Right. None of that increases my chances. Any idea how likely it is that someone who gets in says no?"

"I honestly don't. But, I really hope you don't do anything to jeopardize that chance. I'm pulling for you."

Chapter 22

As the end of April passed, and May rolled in like a dust storm in Phoenix, Laurel sat on her bunk and stewed. With her release just over three months away, she agonized about what she would do when she left Sunstate. She had so counted on getting into the Work Me program. January, February, and March almost flew by, but the past few weeks, since she'd learned she was not admitted to the program, was like waiting for Christmas when you're six. Life turned colorless. In the beginning, she looked forward to getting out all the time, but now the prospect gave her an upset stomach.

Who would hire her as an ex-offender? Where would she live? Even if her mother would let her stay there again, the house might be sold any day now. Plus, even if it wasn't, she couldn't live way out there without a driver's license. Her mother shouldn't be driving either, so maybe she'd find a less-expensive place in Scottsdale or Phoenix on a bus line. Maybe. But could she really ask her mom to get a bigger place to accommodate her daughter? And, would she, even if she was asked nicely?

A zillion questions zinged like pinballs off the sides her skull. She tossed and turned all night long, night after night, envying other inmates like Angie who had families to return to, families to embrace them, and be thrilled to have them home.

As worry overtook her harried brain, things that previously provided satisfaction, like her job, and accumulating a little money in her commissary account for occasional little luxuries, no longer afforded her pleasure. She worked, ate her meals, returned to her cube, volunteered with the GED classes, and tried to read—things she'd been doing all along and enjoying. But now, she just sleepwalked through them, enduring each day, wanting to be anywhere else, but not knowing where that would be or how she'd even get there.

In early May, another letter from Ryan arrived. He said things with his dad were better, that he didn't seem angry anymore. His relationship with Madison was going well. He also acknowledged the difficulties his grandmother was experiencing, and said he hoped Laurel would get into her program.

After reading Ryan's letter, which reminded her about not getting into Work Me, Laurel paced in her cube, agitated, unable to focus. She could feel herself spiraling down into despair, and she worried about that, too. So, she made another appointment with Autumn.

"I underestimated how much I had riding on getting into Work Me, because not getting in has thrown me for loop."

"How so?"

Laurel talked about feeling hopeless and overwhelmed, fearful about the future, and unable to stay in the day, not experiencing any joy or satisfaction with work or volunteering or reading, all triggered by not getting into the program and worrying about what she'd do when she was released.

"Have you been thinking about drinking?"

"I guess not. I've made peace with that, sort of. For the moment at least."

"Well good for you. And, guess what?"

Laurel rolled her eyes. *I am* so *not up for surprises.* "What?"

Autumn could not hide her huge grin. "Turns out you got into Work Me, after all. Someone wasn't interested. I was just about to contact you about it. I assume you're still interested, based on what you just said."

"You're kidding! I thought it had already started. Yes, I'm absolutely still interested!"

"It starts pretty quick. Next week. Guess they got off to a late start."

"Do you have any kind of schedule for the classes?"

"I don't, but I have the name of the person you need to contact. I believe it's two or three evenings a week, so it doesn't interfere with people's work schedules. You need to reach this person right away and let her know you're interested so they don't go to the next person on the list. I told her I was pretty sure you'd take it." She wrote down a name and phone number on a piece of paper and handed it to Laurel.

"Sarah Pelham, same person who interviewed me. Okay, I'll call her right away."

"So, are there other things we need to discuss?"

"I guess not. I was upset about what I was going to do when I'm released. It's been keeping me up at night. So, I wasn't sleeping very well and feeling exhausted, which was making me feel even more depressed and anxious, a vicious circle. But, I guess, now, if I'm really starting the program next week, maybe I can relax a bit."

Laurel spoke to Sarah Pelham, who told her she needed to select a mentor from the roster of volunteers.

Laurel blinked. "Oh, I totally forgot about the mentors. How do I go about it?"

In the first meeting, a video showed the available mentors' brief presentations, in which they described themselves to participants. Laurel already knew she wasn't interested in a faith-based mentor, and she was skeptical about whether there would be an appropriate professional or business woman she could connect with. Maybe a peer mentor?

After the evening's lesson ended, she and four other group members stayed to watch the video where volunteers talked about themselves and why they wanted to help participants on the cusp of being released from prison. Laurel listened to the other group members—mostly black and Latina—comment, joke, and cynically consider whether any of these white women could understand them enough to be helpful.

Laurel had had a few AA sponsors, most recently Starr, so she felt if she connected with the right woman, it might be beneficial. But, it had to be the right one. One after another, women's faces appeared on the screen, but none of them resonated.

Then an older woman named Victoria introduced herself as a recovering alcoholic who'd served time in county jail for a DUI. She mentioned being involved in twelve-step work in addition to her work as an artist… a painter. She looked older than Laurel, easily in her sixties, with short, curly salt-and-pepper hair, pale freckled skin, and a kind face. Victoria—not Vicky, Laurel liked that—mentioned that, although she had never been to prison, she could have ended up there if she hadn't gotten sober after her DUI.

She's the one. A certain humility about Victoria appeals to me. I can't wait to meet her.

As June unfolded, time began to speed up again as Laurel moved into the full swing of the program, along with work and volunteering. Then another letter arrived. Walking over to pick it up, she wondered whether it was from Ryan or her mom. The return address, though, was Phoenix. When she took the letter out of the opened envelope, she learned it was from Victoria, her new mentor.

Laurel read the letter twice. Sarah must have told Victoria that Laurel wanted her as a mentor, and she'd already written back. She must be pretty motivated to do this mentoring thing. Sounded like they had a lot in common. Unlike Ryan's letters, which he wrote on his computer, this letter was penned long-hand, in beautiful handwriting.

Now, it's my turn.

It took Laurel a couple of days to craft a letter back to Victoria—sometimes having a lot of time on your hands was not a good thing. Eventually, though, she wrote a satisfactory letter and mailed it. She didn't want to wait too long to reply and risk Victoria thinking she wasn't interested.

A couple more weeks passed before she remembered it was her turn to write back to Ryan. Nice to have good news to report.

She wanted to tell him how hard she was working on getting her life back on track.

> *"Dear Ryan,*
>
> *I got into the new program I mentioned, Women in Recovery Can Make It. We're well into the swing of the pre-release portion. I've been attending classes two nights a week in a segment of the program called Thinking for a Change. I was skeptical about it at first, but it turns out that it's been helpful. The focus is on how our thinking affects our emotions and our behavior. Most of the lesson consists of role-plays where we try out new skills. Because I have a lot more education than most of the women, I assumed I wasn't going to get much out of it. Boy, was I wrong!*
>
> *For example, we had a lesson on knowing your feelings. I thought I was pretty good with that, especially having had a pretty good counselor here in Sunstate. But, I realized that, often, I don't really identify my feelings until after I feel them, rather than when I am actually feeling them. They teach you to start by tuning into what is going on in your body when you are feeling something, and then try to figure out what happened to make you feel that way. The last step is to put a label on the feeling. It sounds really basic, and maybe most people do that naturally or automatically, but I didn't grow up learning that.*
>
> *Growing up in a really chaotic household, with three brothers and sisters and an absentee mother, feelings were really dangerous. It was better to just not tune into what your body was feeling or put a label on it. Absolutely, you wouldn't want to talk about feelings!*

My brothers were pretty impulsive. I know now what that means, but I didn't know it then. They had feelings all right, like fear that transformed into anger—I was angry all the time, too—and then that anger morphed into problem behaviors that got them into trouble all the time once they were teenagers. Like running away, not going to school, and violence.

And, Mom was pretty much the same way, impulsive like that. Drinking, leaving us alone, hitting us when we did something wrong, yelling all the time at the top of her lungs. That's what I saw growing up. It was the only way I knew to be. It was normal. And, once I started drinking and getting drunk, I had no chance, really, to make sense of my feelings. If I felt lonely or scared or sad, I didn't call it loneliness or fear, I would just try to grab onto the first guy that came along so I wasn't lonely or sad anymore, hoping he would save me, no matter what a jerk he might be, or how he might treat me. I did that over and over. And, when it didn't work, I self-medicated my feelings with booze. I can't afford to do that anymore, and I probably shouldn't be sharing this with you.

Hope things are going well for you, that you're not too overwhelmed with school and work. Take care.

Love, Mom"

Chapter 23

As time raced by, another letter from Ryan arrived in mid-July.

"Dear Mom,

I was happy to hear you got into that program and got a mentor. Really great. I've also been thinking about what you said about feelings in your family growing up. My situation couldn't have been more different. It was just me and Dad, for starters, no brothers or sisters. And, Dad was a good parent, pretty much always there for me even though he worked really hard. Looking back on it now, I realize the sacrifices he must have made for me to make sure I was taken care of—the costs, both financial and emotional for him. Like he never really had much chance for a girlfriend. It was of kind lonely for me, with no siblings or other family around, and only one parent, but now I realize it must have been pretty lonely for him as well. Things at home were orderly, I'd say, organized, certainly not chaotic as you described. I took all that for granted. Hearing more about your childhood, I can see that now. But, interestingly, as different as our families were growing up, I don't think I ever learned how to deal with feelings either. Dad and I just never talked about that. Looking back on it, I recognized that I had feelings, like loneliness and disappointment, but it never occurred to me to talk about them.

This issue of feelings has come up with Madison. It seems like she wants to talk about feelings all the time, but she says I never do. She says I "brood," and maybe I do. She wants me to tell her about what I'm brooding about, but I just don't want to. Sometimes I know and just don't want to share it with her. Like I came back from Christmas vacation in a pretty bad mood because of the arguments with Dad about her and about you. But, no way was I going to talk to her about that. In fact, I haven't told her anything about you yet. Meanwhile, she came back from Christmas all cheery and full of stories about how much fun she had with her family. I just didn't want to hear it. Then, other times, when I'm in kind of a bad mood, I just don't know why. So, it's not that I won't tell her, it's that I can't, because I just don't know what I'm feeling.

I've discovered that relationships can be hard work when they go beyond the getting to know you and having fun stages, yet I really care about Madison. She says she's in love with me and expects me to say that in return. So far, I haven't, and it's clear she's feeling hurt about that. I haven't been in love before, so I don't know what that feels like. But, I'm worried if I don't say it, I'm going to lose her.

Sorry to go on and on, but I can't talk to Dad about it. Recently, Madison and I had our first big argument. The issue was where I was going to live this summer after the semester ended. I'd already told Dad at Christmas I wasn't coming back to Boston this summer because my lab job asked me to stay full-time over the summer with a small pay raise. I couldn't stay in the dorm. Madison told me if I'd get an apartment with her, she'd stay for the summer in Pasadena rather than going home. Of course, I wanted her to stay here so I can see her over the summer, but I didn't feel ready to move in together. Plus, it would have been really expensive, just the two of us. She wants us to live together next fall, too, for my final year. She's looking for a commitment—living together to me is a BIG commitment—but I guess I'm just not there.

I'm not too worried yet about what's going to happen after graduation (Madison doesn't graduate until the year after I do), but I agree with Dad that I should be free to relocate if the right job comes along. I might find something in LA, but obviously I increase my chances of finding something good if I can move. In the end, I told Madison I wouldn't live with her this summer and probably not next year either. She was very disappointed. I took an apartment with three other guys, which is more economical, so she just moved back home for the summer. Things were pretty tense between us when we said goodbye. I've only seen her once since then, although we call and text, of course. I'm afraid it might mean the end of the relationship, but maybe that's what needs to happen. I feel like I'm just not ready to be tied down at age 20. But I'm torn.

I guess that's it for now, Mom. BTW, when do you get out? I seem to remember it's fairly soon.

Ryan"

As Laurel read and re-read the letter, her heart ached for this youngster struggling with the lessons of becoming a man. Maybe having his heart broken by his first real love. Feeling the tension between committing himself to a relationship he knew he wasn't ready for, and knowing he'd worked really hard for a promising career he wanted to leave the door open to. Wanting to have Madison with him for the summer, but knowing he wasn't ready for a living-together arrangement that might stretch into his senior year, complicating his job search. His maturity and willingness to share his struggle with her again impressed Laurel. What a gift. If you'd told her a year ago she'd get a letter like this from the son she abandoned years earlier, she wouldn't have thought it possible. She felt so blessed. But, would she ever get to meet him?

She wasn't sure what to make of the fact that he had chosen not to tell Madison about her—and that he'd let her know that. Of course, she got it. On the one hand, Madison seemed to come from a nice, intact family. It was bad enough growing up just with your father, much less having a mother in prison after her third DUI. She wondered what, if anything, he'd told her about what happened to his mother. But, on the other hand . . . Well, maybe there was no other hand. The story of his mother was a long, painful one, and perhaps not worth telling unless he intended to commit to this person. It was his story to tell, if and when he was ready. So, she decided to let that one go and not take it personally.

Before she even knew it, in the blast furnace of the Arizona summer, August arrived and Laurel was "counting days," with a month left on her sentence at Sunstate. It pleased her to learn that she could take any accumulated commissary funds with her when she left. Not that there was much, but she knew she'd need every penny when she got out with no income. Although she'd splurged on a few things from her account, she'd been frugal all along, not knowing when something might come along that she needed. So, she'd have a few hundred dollars to take with her when she walked out the door on September fifteenth.

She next received a letter from Victoria saying she would pick her up upon release, and drive her to the halfway house.

At a meeting with Sarah Pelham, Laurel learned what would come next upon release. First, she'd live in a sober living house in Phoenix with seven other recovering ex-offenders for at least three months. She'd be enrolled in Medicaid upon leaving the facility, which would cover the cost of the program and be her health insurance until she could find a job.

An agency called Women Recovering from Alcohol and Drugs, WRAD, operated the treatment program on the outside. She'd be enrolled in intensive outpatient treatment three mornings a week. Meanwhile, a vocational counselor would help her find a job.

Victoria would meet her at Sunstate and take her to her new home. Also, the program arranged for each woman, upon release, to receive a "goodie bag" when they left the facility, courtesy of the Junior League. Inside, she'd find hygiene products of all kinds. In addition, Victoria would take her to a storage facility where she'd be allowed to select donated clothes, shoes, and purses. She felt such gratitude upon hearing about the thoughtful gestures of volunteers to help her transition back into the community. Concerns she had agonized over for months had been addressed by this organization.

Right before she left, she wrote her last letter to Ryan from Sunstate, giving him details about what awaited her on the outside—the halfway house and the treatment program. She also told him her heart was breaking for him as he struggled with his issues with Madison. She closed with how much she looked forward to having more contact with him—perhaps by phone—after she was released.

PART III: REDEMPTION

"What would it be like if I could accept life—accept this moment—exactly as it is?"

– Tara Brach, Radical Acceptance: Embracing Your Life With the Heart of a Buddha

Chapter 24

It seemed like she'd been waiting for this day, forever. Now that it was here, her brain and heart raced with apprehension. She'd barely slept the past few nights. A year and half of intermittent terror. Wondering how she'd survive. And yet, she *had* survived, both jail and prison. But, outside, would she finally be able to stop drinking once and for all?

She'd had plenty of time to think about what she wanted from her life. Work, a decent job, hopefully in graphic arts. A decent place of her own. And, friends. She wanted sober friends, something she lacked in the years leading up to her most recent relapse. Caroline was a start, but she wanted more women—and maybe men—whom she could connect with, who understood her struggle. She'd had a taste of that in jail and prison, but she wasn't long enough in either place to develop the kind of deep relationships she thought might be possible. She saw other women experiencing them, though she never had—or even wanted—them herself. She looked at the black garbage bag next to her and shook her head. Age fifty-two and carting around her possessions in a garbage bag.

A CO startled her out of her reverie. "Peterson, someone here for you."

She looked up and saw a small woman with curly black hair laced with silver. She approached smiling, her blue eyes twinkling.

"Victoria?"

"Yes!" Victoria dashed over and gave Laurel a big hug. "I'm so happy to finally meet you."

"Thanks so much for coming to get me and agreeing to mentor me." The words rushed out.

As Victoria pulled out of the parking lot in her silver Prius, and drove over to the Interstate 10 freeway entrance, Laurel felt unsure what to say. Finally, she asked, "Are we headed to the halfway house where I'm going to live?"

"Yes, exactly."

"Have you been there before?"

"Nope. We'll both be seeing it for the first time. Actually, I think they call it a sober living house."

"Okay, a sober living house then."

Victoria broke the awkward silence. "Do you have any idea what your living situation will be like?"

Laurel fidgeted. "Not really. I'm just relieved I got into the program and have some place to go."

They exited the I-10 at I-17 and headed north, eventually moving onto surface streets. After a few more minutes, making a couple more turns, Victoria turned to Laurel. "Keep an eye out for number 14352."

Laurel spotted it. "There it is, I think, although I don't see a sign or anything."

Victoria pulled into the double driveway of a large, single story home with beige stucco exterior walls and terra cotta roof tiles.

Getting out of the car, Laurel's stomach twisted into knots.

"How're you doing?" Victoria asked.

"Kind of nervous, actually." She'd waited for this day forever, so how come she wasn't feeling thrilled?

When they rang the bell, a woman eventually came to the door, rubbing her eyes, her hair disheveled. "Sorry, I was sleeping and didn't hear the bell right away."

"Hi, I'm supposed to move in today. I'm Laurel and this is Victoria."

"I'm Nikki. Heard we were getting a new resident. Come on in. Everyone's pretty much gone during the day.

"I think there's only one empty bed," Nikki said, "so I assume that'll be yours, but maybe you should wait until staff gets here at four or so, before moving your stuff in. Meanwhile, I'll show you around."

What stuff?

Victoria and Laurel nodded. Nikki gave a brief tour, pointing out the living room, dining room, and kitchen. In the living room, two oversized couches and two lounge chairs provided seating facing a big-screen TV. The dining room contained a huge dining table in the center. Then they headed into a roomy, bright kitchen with lemon-yellow walls. It looked clean. Laurel was surprised at how homey it was, not at all institutional. Plants lined the sills of the picture windows.

Nikki lifted a wooden dowel from the bottom of a double sliding door, and they stepped outside onto a covered patio. Laurel shielded her eyes from the bright sun. Walking out to the grass, she surveyed the yard, surrounded by a six-foot block wall. Two huge mesquite trees and a Palo Verde provided shade. Birds twittered all around her. She closed her eyes and breathed it all in, smelling the fresh scent of just-mown grass.

Better than I imagined. Didn't realize how much I missed grass and green and birds and trees.

Following Nikki back in, Victoria whispered, "You doing okay?"

Laurel simply nodded yes, with a lump in her throat and tears stinging her eyes.

They followed Nikki inside and Laurel saw four bedrooms, each with two single beds and dressers. Nikki pointed to one of the beds. "This is where I assume you'll be staying. The woman who lived here before has moved into her own apartment."

"How long do people usually stay?" Laurel asked.

"Depends. I've been here four months and it'll be probably a couple more before I'm ready to move out. Still don't have a job, but I'm working on that with the vocational counselor at WRAD. Hopefully it won't be too much longer.

"Okay, just a couple of other things," Nikki said. "Only two bathrooms for eight women, so things get busy in the morning when we're getting ready, and at night before bed. That's probably the most common thing we argue about. Last thing is a laundry room back here with a washer and dryer. That's about it."

"Thanks for the tour," Laurel said. She glanced around again and looked at Victoria. What time is it?"

"Quarter to two. I'm starved. Since staff aren't back until four, I was thinking I could take you out to lunch, Laurel. What do you think about that? Could you eat?"

Laurel didn't respond. Could she eat? Probably a horse.

"Are you hesitating because you're not hungry or because you're worrying about how you're going to pay me back?" Victoria asked. "If it's the latter, forget about it. The program will reimburse me. It's a special treat for women just coming out. What do you say? I know a great little place not far from here. Then we can come back, and you can get settled in."

"I'm starved, too. You're right, I was worrying about paying you back. But, if it's really okay, I'd *absolutely love* to go to a restaurant for real food."

Victoria drove to the Coronado Café, an older adobe home converted into a restaurant. The lunch crowd had departed, and Laurel welcomed the privacy. The waitress delivered menus and two waters, with a wedge of lemon perched on the edge of each glass. Lemon! Laurel smiled as she squeezed the lemon wedge into her water.

The waitress came back to take their orders.

Laurel hadn't even read through half of the menu, and she intended to study every word. "Could we have a couple minutes? I'm still deciding."

"Must be hard after having only prison food for so long," Victoria said. "I've forgotten how long were you in there."

Laurel glanced around to ensure no one was nearby. "Fourteen months, counting jail and Sunstate."

When the waitress headed back over, Laurel decided on the spinach salad with chicken, bacon, mandarin oranges, strawberries, and almonds.

"Okay. Well, I'm having the Southwest chopped salad," Victoria said. When the waitress left, she asked, "How was the food in prison?"

"Pretty much as bad as you'd expect. Virtually no fruit and very few fresh vegetables. When we had vegetables, it was usually things like canned green beans."

"I'm a big fan of fresh produce myself. I'd find it very hard to eat a diet that lacked fresh fruits and veggies."

Laurel sat in silence for a few minutes, listening to the mellow New Age music in the background. Iced teas arrived, along with a basket of coarse whole-grain bread, still warm. Laurel helped herself to a slice, slathering it with butter. Taking a bite, she closed her eyes as she savored the nuttiness.

Watching her, Victoria laughed. "I'm guessing from the look on your face that it's pretty good."

Shortly, the waitress delivered two beautiful salads. Laurel's stomach growled. The salad looked so luscious, she wanted to wolf it down. Instead, she forced herself to eat slowly, relishing each mouthful, enjoying the crispness of the greens and the sweet tanginess of the orange sections and sliced strawberries.

Victoria smiled. "I'm so glad you're enjoying this. And it's fun *watching* you enjoy it."

"It's so yummy. Thanks for thinking of this."

After they started eating, Laurel asked, "What made you decide to become a mentor?"

"You know, I was so lucky when I got sober. I lost hardly anything. I used to go to these meetings in South Phoenix—"

"That's where I grew up."

"Yeah, it's a poor neighborhood. The women in those meetings talked about how hard it was for them to get sober, how little they had, how much they'd lost. Most of them weren't working, couldn't find jobs, no education . . . Anyhow, their voices haunted me, and I vowed that once I got on my feet I'd figure out how I could give back. More than just sponsoring."

Laurel nodded. "I'm so grateful you decided to help."

They finished eating, each savoring her meal. Finally, Laurel declared she was stuffed and couldn't eat another bite. Victoria paid the bill. At three-thirty they headed back to the sober living house.

They grabbed Laurel's belongings from the car and went inside. A staff member had already arrived. Victoria wrote down her phone number and gave Laurel a quick hug goodbye.

"Thanks so much for everything—coming to get me, and for lunch, especially."

Okay, now the hard part.

After four o'clock, the women started trickling home. Lorena, a Latina in her fifties with kind eyes who appeared to be in charge, confirmed Laurel's bed. She explained that most nights residents ate together at the common table in the dining room. If they weren't going to be there, they had to give a reason and let someone know in advance. Everyone signed up for chores, like food shopping, cooking, and cleaning. Tonight, spaghetti and meatballs, and salad at six-thirty.

"How will I get connected to the program?" Laurel asked.

"The van arrives at eight tomorrow morning to take you and the other women over to the WRAD offices. You see your counselor at eight-thirty. She'll explain everything to you about the program: when group meets, when your individual appointments are, when you meet with the vocational counselor, and so forth.

"After dinner, I'll sit down with you and go over the rules of the house. There's some paperwork for you to sign verifying your understanding of the rules, and that you jeopardize your place here if you violate them."

"Okay." Suddenly, Laurel had trouble breathing.

It's going to be fine. You've survived jail and prison, you've got this.

Chapter 25

Laurel was up at seven her first morning. "How does breakfast work?" she asked. "Everybody just fends for themselves?"

"Pretty much," replied the woman with long black hair. "I'm Kristi. Bread in this drawer here, peanut butter up in that cupboard, jelly and butter in the fridge. If you want cereal, there's three or four kinds up there," she said, pointing to another cupboard. "Milk and OJ in the fridge."

Laurel learned that they called it Hope House. She dressed in the same clothes she had on yesterday, a tee shirt and a pair of baggy black yoga pants, the only pair of pants she had. She studied herself in a full-length mirror in the hallway, shocked by her appearance. She'd lost some weight, her face pallid, haggard, almost gaunt. Her hair hung in strings, with shocking amounts of grey. Her pants just hung off her, hipbones poking out below her waist. Hard to believe that a mere fourteen months jail and prison could do this to a person.

Wondering what she should bring with her to the morning meeting, she realized she had nothing to carry anything in except the garbage bag and a pillowcase, not even pockets. The van showed up at five minutes after eight. They shuffled outside and climbed in. She shuddered. *Moving right along.*

After the short ride to the WRAD offices, Laurel checked in, mentioning it was her first day. The receptionist told her the counselor would be with her shortly. The waiting area bustled with talking and laughing women of all races, shapes, sizes, and ages—even a baby! All the seats on three shabby sofas were taken, so she stood. A couple of women sat on the laps of other women. Colorful posters hung on the walls, a few plants struggled to survive, and piles of well-worn magazines littered the tables.

A staff member entered the room. "Okay, ladies. Who's ready for group?"

A bunch of women followed her out, like ducklings. Laurel grabbed a seat and a magazine to pass the time while she waited. She felt surprisingly relaxed.

A woman showed up at the door. "Laurel Peterson?"

Laurel jumped up. "That's me."

A tall, thin woman with wispy blonde hair cut into a medium-length bob extended a hand to her. "Hi, I'm Krisha, your counselor. Welcome to WRAD."

They spent the next hour in a whirlwind of paperwork and assessment, and a million questions about Laurel's history of drinking, relapsing, treatment, health, work, relationships, and family. Krisha reiterated that Laurel must apply for Medicaid and call her probation officer within twenty-four hours. She'd be in a group session for two hours Monday, Wednesday and Friday—Intensive Outpatient Treatment, IOP—and counseling every week with Krisha. She'd also work with the vocational counselor to find a job. AA meetings in the community were mandatory, and she needed to learn how to take the bus.

Laurel's head spun. *Whew! Remember to breathe.* Could she really do all this? She'd gone from having too much time on her hands in prison to a jam-packed schedule in a matter of two days. She jetted from relaxed to completely inundated in just an hour. Was this how you got sober, 'cause it seemed pretty friggin' overwhelming. Well, she could freak out about it, or call Victoria.

"Glad you called. I was thinking about reaching out to you. How was your first morning in treatment?"

Laurel explained it all—the groups, therapy, getting back on Medicaid, probation, vocational appointment.

"Sounds like you're going to be quite busy."

"I hope it's going to be okay. I mean, I want to be busy. Less time to think about drinking."

"Have you been thinking about drinking?"

"Not really. Not yet. I'm sure I will eventually though, based on my history. Prison was easy in that sense, 'cause there was no booze around. Well, there probably was, but I wasn't looking for it. On the outside, though, it's everywhere. Billboards, magazines, the grocery store, Walgreen's. You can't escape it."

"You're right. I'm remembering back to my first year sober. It's daunting, when you want to drink all the time. At least you've got over a year under your belt without alcohol, so the worst of the physical cravings are gone."

"It's not about physical cravings anymore. It's more about what happens in my brain when I'm feeling certain things. And, for me, feeling overwhelmed by life is one of my triggers. One of the things I learned from my prison counselor was, when I'm feeling swamped, I need to talk about it, so I don't end up so messed up that I drink over it."

By four-thirty most of the women were back at Hope House from their various activities. Laurel sat in the living room, listening as several women talked about their days.

One of them asked, "Laurel, right?"

She nodded.

"How'd your first day go?"

"I'm sorry, but I've forgotten your name."

"Kristi."

"Oh yes. It went okay, I guess . . . Kinda feels like it's, uh, too much," Laurel said tentatively.

Feeling tearful caught her by surprise. Why wasn't she overjoyed to be out of prison?

Kristi came over and sat down close to Laurel. "You know, we've all been where you are. It *does* feel overwhelming at first. Seems weird, because it's good, but it's still, like you said, almost too much."

"Exactly. Right before you said that, when I felt myself starting to cry I was thinking I should feel totally happy about finally being out, but instead I feel . . . I don't know . . ."

Another short, heavyset woman with too much eye makeup had been observing them. "It'll get better, it will." Laurel looked over to the new speaker. "Cindy," the woman repeated from their previous introductions, running her hand through her messy brown hair.

"Sure hope so." Laurel looked up from picking at her ragged fingernails. So, how do I get into the chores rotation?"

"Chores!" Nicole shouted from the kitchen. "The lady wants to do chores. Let's show her how it's done."

After helping with dinner cleanup, Laurel called her mom at seven-thirty. It rang a zillion times. No answering machine. Just as she was about to hang up, relieved—but also disappointed because she wanted to get this over with—her mom answered.

"Hi, Mom. I'm finally out of Sunstate—"

Joanne's peevish response proved why Laurel always dreaded these calls. "I already told you, you can't live here!"

Exasperated already, Laurel sighed. "Mom, I'm not calling to ask if I can live there. I have a place to live. I'm calling to see how you are and when I can come get my stuff."

"Oh, okay. This damned Parkinson's has gotten worse and I feel like crap. Bill is still in that home and doesn't know who I am when I visit, so I stopped visiting. I'm still living in his house, but I did meet with his lawyer about selling it."

"What'd he say?"

"Well, it's a good thing Bill signed papers giving me power of attorney before I moved him into that place, because my name isn't on the deed. So, I wouldn't have been able to sell it. I met with a Realtor a few days ago. She told me a whole bunch of stuff I need to do to sell it. 'Make it marketable,' was how she put it."

Oh boy. "What kind of stuff?"

"Some small repairs, cleaning up the clutter, getting the windows washed, clearing out the garage, that kind of thing."

Could Mom handle that? "Mom, I'd be willing to help if I can get there. I'm living in Phoenix, at a sober living house, but I can't drive and can't get there on public transportation. If I can find someone to come get me, I could help you clean up. What do you think?"

Silence on the other end. "Mom?"

"I'm thinking. Could you come this weekend?"

"If I can find someone to drive me. Does Saturday morning work?"

After she got off the phone with her mother, Laurel sat on her bed and called Caroline. "I just got out of Sunstate a few days ago. I survived!"

Laurel gave her an abbreviated version of her last year, explaining that she was living in Hope House and in the WRAD program, promising more details when they got together. She asked about Winston.

"He's doing just great."

"I know it's a lot to ask, since I just got out, but I was wondering if there was any chance you could pick me up here and drive me to my mother's in Carefree this Saturday or next." She explained the plan, that she'd stay overnight at her mother's, help her out for the weekend, and come back on Sunday. If Caroline couldn't do it, she'd try to find someone else to pick her up and bring her back. Starr, maybe? Or Victoria?

"I don't have much planned this weekend, so yeah, I can do it. I'd love to see you and I know someone else who would, too," she said, clearly petting Winston, judging from the purring coming through the phone. "I'm sure your boy would love to see his mommy."

Chapter 26

They had fun on the ride to her mother's on Saturday morning. Laurel loved hearing about what had happened in Caroline's life during the stay in Sunstate. She had a new relationship going on with a guy she met at the animal shelter.

"Good for you. I'm happy for you. It's nice to hear about something positive going on in somebody's life. How's your job?"

They were almost to Carefree. Laurel had dished about prison and the program she was in. She might be starting to get the hang of this friendship business. She'd given Caroline the short version of her relationship with her mother, including the episode in foster care, but not the worst thing about that.

"So, do you see why I was so reluctant to talk about all that when you were asking about my childhood on that hike?"

"Sorta, but not really. You're not embarrassed about it, are you?"

"Of course, I am."

The closer they got to Carefree, the more squirrely Laurel grew. As they pulled onto her mother's street, she squirmed in her seat.

"You're all over the place, just sitting there. Why so twitchy?"

"Not looking forward to this. Here's the thing about my mom. She's . . . unpredictable. Mostly she's miserable, needy, snarky, and self-centered."

"Whoa, Laurel, that is harsh."

"I suppose, but she's really tough to deal with. I mean, I love her, of course, and I'm trying to help her—"

"Didn't she help you out a lot, before you went away?"

"Yeah . . . she did. Storing my stuff, and letting me live in the casita, but . . ."

"But, what?"

"Well, you'll see eventually. You can just drop me off. Thanks for the ride and I'll call tonight about tomorrow."

"You know, I could come get you tonight and you could stay with me if it really gets hairy."

Laurel rang the bell. Eventually her mother let her in. "Hi, Mom."

"Hi, Laurel, you finally got here. I thought you were gonna be here an hour ago."

Please, God, don't let it be that kind of day. Why does she have to be such a crankypants? Laurel waited for her mom to congratulate her about getting out of prison, or even ask how she was. Didn't happen.

She decided she'd just talk, and if her mother didn't like it she could tell her to just shut up. So, she told her about the Work Me program, Hope House, the counseling, help finding a job.

"Sounds good." Okay, so she was listening at least.

"I want to get sober once and for all, and to work as soon as I can and get my own place. I'm sick of being dependent on other people."

"Well, you should. You're fifty-two years old. You should be taking care of me for a change."

Laurel could feel her body tensing. She reached up and massaged her neck. *Like you took care of me when I was a kid?* She just bit her tongue, kept her mouth shut, and let it go. They went into the kitchen. "Do you have a list of things you need help with to get the house ready to show? Oh, Mom, I forgot to ask you. When you talked to Bill's lawyer, what did you find out about Bill's will? Did he make any provisions for you?"

"The good news is that he did leave me something in the will. Although who knows whether there'll be anything left after he finishes paying for the nursing home. The bad news is I can't really access that money now. So, all I really have is my Social Security and a tiny pension from when I worked at the Four Seasons."

"What about when the house is sold?"

"That's not gonna help, because whatever's left after paying off the mortgage will go into his investment account. I won't have access to any of it."

Laurel considered that. "Sounds to me like you're best off dragging your feet on selling the house, because that way you at least have a place to live and can pay the bills from Bill's assets. Right?"

"I guess . . . you're right."

"Is anyone pressuring you to put the house on the market, like the lawyer, or Bill's kids?"

"His kids, yeah. I don't think there's anything they can do, though. The lawyer didn't say too much about what Bill's will says about the kids, but they don't get anything until he dies either."

"So, selling the house doesn't help them. They're in the same position you are. No money until Bill is gone."

"Then why're they pestering me?" She had trouble catching her breath. "I'm exhausted, I'm going to rest."

"Wait, Mom. If you could just give me some direction, I can get started on things while you're resting. Actually, wait a sec. If you're not in a rush to sell the house, do we even need to be doing all these things?"

Heaving a huge sigh, Joanne sat down at the kitchen table. "Lemme think . . . Well, some things might need to get done even if I'm not selling." She sat there, considering. "You know what, I don't think so. I have that lady coming in three times a week, so no, I don't think I need you after all. I'm gonna go take a nap."

Crap, she'd made all these arrangements to get there and now Joanne didn't even need her. What could she do to recoup this day? "Okay, Mom. Then I'm gonna get my stuff ready to take back with me tomorrow." It didn't even make sense for her to stay there tonight.

At one o'clock she stopped for lunch, not finding much around to eat. Wasn't the helper lady supposed to buy groceries? She wished she could take the car and go buy food. She hated not being able to drive. And, there was no public transportation nearby. She could kick herself for suggesting Joanne take her time selling the house. Plus, Joanne obviously couldn't manage a place this big alone. The more she thought about it, the less sure she felt about the best thing to do.

She walked to the casita to see about what to bring back to Hope House. It looked basically unchanged from a year ago, although dusty. She tried to locate her AA phone lists, hoping to find someone she might tap for a ride to a meeting, but came up short. So far, she hadn't thought about drinking, but that could change in a heartbeat.

Then she remembered she hadn't written back to Ryan since she'd been out, and she wished she had his last letter to read. She found a pen and paper, and wrote to him about getting out and living in Hope House, as well as being in the Work Me program. She closed with her new address and phone number.

Laurel awakened the next morning in the casita. While her mother still slept, she went over to the kitchen, relieved to find coffee. *Boy, does this taste good, I really missed good coffee in prison.* She rummaged around to find something for breakfast, pleased to discover a package of English muffins in the freezer. While she waited for her mother to wake up, she enjoyed her coffee and buttered muffin with strawberry jam, something else she hadn't had for the past year.

Finally, her mom shuffled into the kitchen. "I smell coffee."
"Morning, Mom."

Joanne poured herself a cup of coffee. She looked like crap, tangled hair, scrunched up face, walking like she hurt all over.

"Want me to toast you an English muffin?"
"Sure."

At ten sharp, an older Hispanic woman drove into the driveway. Mrs. Hernandez agreed to have Laurel accompany her to the Safeway. Laurel had some cash with her and decided she'd splurge on a bit of makeup—lipstick, blush, eyeliner—as well as hair dye. She was sick of looking at all the gray in her now mousy auburn hair. She'd have loved to go to a real salon and get a good cut and highlights, but wouldn't have the cash for that for a while. She could, at least, get rid of the gray.

As they headed out the front door, her mother said, "Laurel, if there are some things you need, go ahead and charge them on my card."

Really? "Are you sure? I thought your money was really tight right now."

"It is, but you really need to do something about that hair. Plus, your face looks pretty awful. You could do with a bit of makeup."

Laurel burst out laughing. Mrs. Hernandez cracked up, too.

"I know. It looks like shit, doesn't it? I was actually thinking about picking up something to get rid of the gray. So, if you're sure, I'll take you up on your offer. What's your limit, just so I don't go overboard?"

"Oh, fifty bucks, I guess."

"Thanks, I don't think it'll be that much. And, I'll pick up some makeup, too."

Laurel and Mrs. Hernandez made small talk in the car, and Laurel wondered what it was like to work for her mother. She shuddered.

The minute they entered the store, Laurel felt weird. As she looked around, she became light-headed, a little woozy, and instantly had the sense of being overwhelmed—with color, with sounds, with light, with choices. *Is this what agoraphobia is like?* She put her head down, dizzy, took a few deep breaths, and grabbed a shopping cart, as much for something to hold onto as to collect her purchases.

Once she got moving, she started to feel better. Prison had a lot fewer choices. She wended her way over to the Health and Beauty Aids section to pick up hair coloring and makeup. *I wonder if there's someone at the house who would help with my hair, or who could give me a trim. Maybe it'd help me feel better if I looked a little more presentable. Not to mention having to go on job interviews.*

Finally, she found Mrs. Hernandez and they checked out, loading the groceries into the car.

Because her old sponsor Starr couldn't give her a ride on Sunday, Laurel called Caroline, and at about noon they packed Caroline's Audi with as much of her stuff as would fit into her shared room at Hope House. Most of the clothes she tried on were too big, so she took only some shoes and underwear. She hoped, with access to better food, she'd regain the weight she lost, and clothing she'd left in the casita would fit again.

Caroline commented wryly, "Now that's a problem I wish I had. So, how did the weekend go?"

"Not too bad. No big fights. I realized if Mom was going to stay in the house for a while, rather than sell it, most of the things she wanted me to help with didn't need doing. When I started to get bummed about making a wasted trip, I realized I could still get some things I needed to take back."

She told Caroline about her mother's offer to pay for hair dye and makeup—a first—and her weird reaction in the Safeway.

"I know I'm never going to have a great relationship with my mom but, if we could achieve some kind of peaceful coexistence, that would be good."

Caroline nodded as she drove. "Mothers are tough. I already told you about mine. I should probably call her 'smother' rather than mother. The opposite of yours. I really have to live on the opposite side of the country to coexist with her. She'd control every aspect of my life, still, if she could."

Laurel worried about her mother's future, considering whether to bring it up with Caroline. She decided to broach it. "One thing I'm kind of afraid of is that, down the road, if Bill lives another couple of years, I might have to somehow take my mom in. I mean, assuming I get my act together enough to live on my own."

"Oh boy, that'd be tough. What makes you think that might happen?"

"Well, if she had to sell the house and try to live just on her tiny pension and Social Security, without any help from Bill's assets, I don't think she could make it."

Could she and her mom possibly live together without killing each other, or another relapse?

When they arrived at Caroline's door, Laurel pressed her hands together. "I'm so excited about seeing Winston again. Do you think he'll remember me?"

"Are you kidding? Of course, he will. He's your favorite boy."

He did, and after a short visit, Caroline drove Laurel back to Hope House. She thanked her friend for everything, including keeping Winston for a bit longer, as no pets were allowed at Hope House. She hoped the old boy would live long enough for her to get him back into her own apartment.

Sunday night at eight, she attended the mandatory Hope House meeting, a lively affair. The residents hammered out issues, put together the chores schedule, and discussed the upcoming week. A staff member named Sara, who "graduated" from WRAD, served as moderator. They discussed access to the washer and dryer, remembered to put things on the shopping list, and handled other mundane issues of shared daily living.

Laurel listened, not saying much other than to agree to her chore assignment: dusting and vacuuming next Saturday. She hoped she'd remember, without any kind of calendar to keep track of appointments, of which she now had quite a few.

If she didn't start writing things down, it'd only be a matter of time before she forgot something important.

When she got back to her room, she reread her letter to Ryan, and noticed something missing. She'd forgotten to add her new online contact info. She couldn't wait to start talking to him on the phone, too.

Chapter 27

Monday morning Laurel awoke to her first full week out of Sunstate and in the Work Me program. After group that morning, she had an appointment at two-thirty with Jessica, the vocational counselor. She either had to take the bus back and forth to Hope House, squeezing lunch there in between, or shell out her own paltry funds for lunch somewhere else. Should have brought a sandwich. She decided to try the bus.

Big mistake. She had to walk two blocks to the bus stop and wait in the mid-September heat. Then she rode the blissfully air-conditioned bus for about forty-five minutes and had a five-block walk to Hope House at the other end. By the time she got home, totally drenched, it was already after one. Fearing she might be late getting back, she called WRAD and explained the situation to the receptionist.

After a quick change into a clean shirt, Laurel choked down a sandwich and ran back to the bus stop. Then she realized she didn't know how to get the bus going in the other direction. She finally figured it out, but the bus didn't come until after two. So, she arrived back at WRAD at almost three o'clock, out of breath, and with sweat stains the size of watermelons below her arms. Knocking on Jessica's door, Laurel burst in, embarrassed and apologetic. A perky looking, freckled, pony-tailed redhead sat behind the desk. Could this kid help her get a job?

"Hi. Laurel Peterson. Sorry for being late."

"Jessica Stanfield. No big deal. So, let's get started. I don't have much information on you yet, so what can you tell me about yourself in terms of your education and employment history?"

They spent the next half hour reviewing Laurel's education and work history. Her felony conviction would be a problem, but not insurmountable. Jessica assured her she could find her work fairly quickly, but not a graphics job. That would take a more time.

"I want to get to work as soon as I can."

Jessica said she could get Laurel minimum wage work within a few weeks that wouldn't jeopardize her Medicaid status. She'd help her find a graphic arts job, while Laurel did something else to at least earn a paycheck.

"I'll be in touch when I find something."

On Tuesday afternoon, Laurel met with her probation officer for the first time, entering through a metal detector and other security at the entrance. An armed guard directed her to a waiting room where the receptionist sat behind a bulletproof glass window. Signs warned about no guns. It reminded her of Sunstate.

Her new PO, a buff, young, bearded guy named Trevor, reviewed the terms of her probation: sixty-five dollars for each visit, plus fees from the DUI, amounting to almost three thousand dollars. The color drained from her face. On the positive side, Trevor smiled upon hearing she lived in Hope House and had enrolled in a treatment program.

"So, how are you planning to pay off these fees?"

Her breathing shallow, Laurel fidgeted in her chair. "Um, I have no idea. I came of out Sunstate with a couple hundred dollars to my name, which won't last long. The vocational counselor at WRAD thinks I can find a good job in my area, but not immediately. Meantime, I told her I'd take pretty much any job, but I don't have one yet. Sounded like she'd have something for me soon. But, until then . . ." She looked up at Trevor with a furrowed brow. Could they throw her back in prison? Or jail?

"Okay. I'll take sixty-five dollars for today. That's enough of a plan until our meeting next month, when we'll work out a payment plan. But, by next month, you need to begin to making payments on a schedule we set up, even if they're small. Sound doable?"

"Not really." She dropped her head. "I don't have sixty-five dollars with me. Let's see," she said, pulling out her wallet, "I have about thirteen dollars."

"Okay, I'll take that, assuming you have bus fare home."

Laurel exhaled. "Yes, hopefully I'll be working by then. I won't be making much, but it's not costing me anything for the sober living house, so even with a minimum wage job I'll able to start making payments. Here's the thirteen dollars."

Laurel left the building, grateful her probation meeting was over. How could she come up with at least one-hundred and seventeen dollars for next month's appointment? On the way home on the bus she agonized over how she'd handle this and, for the first time since she left Sunstate, the thought of a drink crossed her mind. *Oh no, you don't! Don't even go there. A drink isn't going to make anything better. You know that.* She resolved, when she got back, she'd find someone, anyone, at the house to talk to.

But, when she got back to Hope House, no one was home. She called Victoria, but had to leave a message. Embarrassment kept her from trying anyone else.

She read until four-thirty when the other women started returning. Victoria still hadn't called back. Darn. So, she forced herself to talk to her roommate.

"Karina, do you have a few minutes to talk?"

"Sure, what's up?'

"You know I just got out of Sunstate last week, right?"

"Yeah, me too. Got out about six months ago. What a shithole."

"You got that right. So, I just had my first probation appointment and I'm feeling kind of, um, I don't know, freaked out, I guess. Are you on probation?"

"Yep. What happened?"

"Nothing happened, I guess. Other than my PO informed me about how much each appointment would cost, and the fines I owe. It's a shitload of money that I don't have right now. Thousands of dollars. I got out of prison with, like, two hundred from my commissary account. That's it!"

"I know, me too. That's tough. But probation's gonna work with you on that. They work out a payment plan based on your income—"

"But, that's just it. I don't have any income right now."

"You will, soon. Are you working with Jessica?"

"Just met with her."

"Well, you should be getting a job real soon."

The house phone rang and someone yelled, "Laurel?"

Victoria said, "Hey, how's it going?"

Laurel explained what happened at her probation appointment, lamenting how much money she owed, and about her meeting with the vocational person. She paced in the hall, back and forth, phone in hand.

"Okay, you're probably not going to want to hear this," Victoria said, "but my advice is to try to be patient. It'll all unfold just the way it is supposed to."

"You're right. I *don't* want to hear that. I've gone from being really happy to get out of prison—that lasted about a minute—to just freaking out about everything."

"How about I pick you up tonight and we go to a meeting?"

Laurel breathed a sigh of relief. "Perfect. What time?"

In the car, returning from the meeting, Victoria asked, "Feeling any better?"

"You know, I actually am. The meeting was good, and talking to my roommate Karina helped when I couldn't reach you. Then your call. That all really helped."

"I was impressed at the meeting, when they asked if anyone was thinking about a drink, you raised your hand and talked about what was going on. That was brave. But, why didn't you mention wanting to drink on the phone?"

"I don't know . . . shame, I guess . . . embarrassment? It's just hard to believe that after all I've been through, after what drinking did to me, that the thought of a drink would even cross my mind."

"You're an alcoholic. I'd say it's pretty normal. For one thing, you're not all that far away from your last drink. And, you're in some challenging circumstances. That probation appointment would be tough for anyone. And, not having any money, while owing a bunch. I've never had to face that, so I can only imagine how hard it would be. That's a lot to deal with."

They stopped at a red light and Victoria looked over at Laurel. "Try not to beat yourself up for thinking about drinking. You did exactly the right thing, you talked to people, you went to a meeting. That's how it works."

Laurel listened to Victoria's wisdom. She whispered, "Thanks for saying that. I *was* beating myself up, even though I know that's not going to get me anywhere. Sometimes when I get stuck in my head, when anxiety and fear get the best of me, it just seems like it's never going to get any better, like I'm never going to have a normal life again."

"But, you will. It's just going to take time, and you're going to have to be patient."

Being patient sucked.

Friday, after group, Laurel had her first therapy appointment with her counselor Krisha. The three days that had passed since her freak-out following the probation appointment had gone okay. She'd attended group, went to another AA meeting with some women from the house after dinner, and managed to fill her time with reading. But, still no word from Jessica regarding a job.

Krisha wore a black dress with some interesting African-looking jewelry. "So, how're you feeling now?" Her gray eyes peered at Laurel.

"I wish I could say great, but not so great. Since I've been out of Sunstate it's been like . . . I don't know, um, it's like I'm at the ocean where huge waves of different emotions are crashing. First, I'm on top of the world, then I'm terrified, then I'm frustrated. I'm all over the place." She twirled a lock of her hair. "Seems like most of the time I'm stressing out about something. My first weekend out, I went to my mother's to help her out. I probably need to explain in detail about my relationship with her, but the short version is she was a lousy mom, all of us kids turned out terribly—I mean, I'm probably the most highly functional, so what does that tell you?"

The words rushed out at seventy miles an hour. "And now she's got Parkinson's and is going downhill fast. I offered to help her, because she has a house that's not even hers that she needs to get ready to sell. Which is going to leave her with no place to live and very little income. So, added to my list of worries is that I'm going to have to support her at some point in the not too distant—"

"Whoa, slow down, let's take it down a notch. Sounds like you've had a tough time since you got out, and not that this helps much, but I'd say that's pretty normal. Most women have high expectations for how great it's going to be after they're released, and real life turns out to be disappointing. So, I'm frankly not surprised you're having a hard time. But you're doing all the things you're supposed to be doing, putting one foot in front of the next. It was nice of you to offer to help your mother."

"It *was* nice of me. My last sponsor encouraged me to make amends to my mom, which I tried, but it went horribly. I guess, by helping her, I'm doing what AA calls 'living amends,' changing my behavior toward her to make up for some harm I caused her in the past."

"Have you gone to any meetings since you've been out?"

"Two actually. One with my mentor Victoria, and another with the women from the house last night."

"And, what about a sponsor?"

"My sponsor from before is still willing to sponsor me, although she lives in Scottsdale."

So, how come, after all that support, I still feel like shit?

Chapter 28

So far, being out of prison had been disappointing. Krisha nailed it: huge gap between her expectations and the reality—being in treatment, trying to stay sober, having no money, and getting her life back on track.

By the end of September, Laurel still had no job and less than one hundred dollars to her name. She talked regularly to the women in Hope House, to Victoria, in her group, and in individual therapy sessions.

I'm sick of talking.

Starr offered to come by on the weekend and take her to another meeting, which meant three a week.

Walking into group on Friday morning, the receptionist told her Jessica wanted to see her after group. Maybe she finally had a job. She could hardly pay attention in group, fantasizing about what kind of job might be available, and what she'd to do with her earnings.

After group ended, she walked over to Jessica's office, who sat behind her desk.

Laurel looked out her window where a thunderstorm brewed to the west. "The receptionist said you wanted to see me?"

"I think I finally have a job for you."

Laurel's heart quickened. "Fantastic!"

Jessica leaned forward. "First of all, lower your expectations."

Shit.

"Okay, expectations lowered. What are we talking about?"

She should have known it was a mistake thinking about how great this was going to be.

"All I can come up with right now is a commercial cleaning job, obviously way below your skill level. It just pays minimum wage—eight dollars and five cents per hour—and, to make matters worse, it's not full time."

Frowning, Laurel dropped her head.

"I know you're disappointed—I am, too—but it's the best I can come up with right now. Something better will turn up. The hours are five p.m. to eleven p.m., Monday through Friday, thirty hours a week. So, it won't interfere with your program here, and that's good."

Laurel quickly did the math in her head—about two-hundred fifty dollars per week, just over a thousand dollars per month—crappy, but better than nothing. And, she'd lose some of that in taxes.

She would meet with her PO again this Tuesday, and at least she could say she had something, and could start paying on her fines.

She crossed and uncrossed her legs. "Okay, you're right, I'm disappointed, but I'm not in a position to turn it down. Do I have an interview? Can I get there by bus?"

After eating the sandwich she'd brought from Hope House, Laurel had another appointment with Krisha. In previous sessions she'd shared some of her history—the relapse and what led up to it, the abrupt breakup with Scott, and the son she gave up as an infant who now corresponded with her.

"We haven't talked at all yet about your childhood. Were there things about it that you think are related to your drinking?"

She dreaded going there and didn't answer right away. "My childhood really sucked." Sighing, Laurel talked about her mother's poor parenting and drinking, the absent fathers, her three siblings, the chaos and abuse, and the house fire that led to foster care.

"What was that like? How long were you there?"

"Horrible. Almost two years. The other kids were with different families." She was so reluctant to open the box she'd managed to keep closed for so long.

When she didn't continue, Krisha probed. "What in particular was horrible about it?"

She wrestled with whether to share what had happened. She *so* didn't want to get into it after working so hard to keep it under wraps.

Bite the bullet, Laurel. It's gotta come out!

"Okay here goes. I've never talked about this before. To anyone. In fact, only a couple people even know I was in foster care. I know it wasn't my fault, but I still feel, um, ashamed and embarrassed about it."

She sat with both arms folded around herself, unable to look at Krisha. After exhaling a long sigh, she said, "I was sexually abused by the family's older son, Michael."

Krisha let it sit there until Laurel's tears subsided. "Are you ready to talk more about it?"

"Just give me a minute."

"Take all the time you need."

We're in some kind of shed at the far end of the yard. It's dark inside. There's only one window, but it's so coated with dust and

dirt, and covered with cobwebs that hardly any light comes in. I can see the dust motes floating lazily in the sun streaming in through the open door. Dirty old tools are scattered everywhere, a pitchfork, old rusted machinery, a lawnmower, broken terra cotta flowerpots, bags of fertilizer. Dusty folding chairs lean against the plywood walls. The dirt floor smells of earth and rot. Creepy little bugs crawl all over. I begin to worry about spiders, which terrify me. It's much cooler inside the shed than outdoors, where it's hot and muggy. A bird chirps nearby.

"Come over here."

I don't move a muscle.

"I said, com'ere."

My heart beats really fast. "Where are the kittens?"

"What kittens?"

"You said you were going to show me some kittens."

He snickers. "You believed that? There aren't no stupid kittens, you friggin' little cunt. I said get over here. And, pull down your pants."

I still don't move. He takes two steps toward me and grabs my arm.

"Stop, Michael, you're hurting me!" I whine.

"Stop, Michael, you're hurting me," he mocks.

"Let go of me. Please!" He's so much bigger and stronger than I am. A huge, sloppy, overweight, pimply-faced, greasy-haired teenager, and I'm a scrawny eight-year-old. Suddenly, I'm terrified. He pulls down my shorts as I struggle to keep my underpants on.

Summoning what little courage I can muster I burst out with, "If you don't let me go I'm going to tell Mama Janet."

"And, I'll just say you made it up. Everybody knows foster kids lie all the time. So, if you know what's good for you you'll keep your stupid mouth shut."

He lets me go, but I am frozen in place. I will my legs to move, to leave through the open doorway, but am paralyzed. My shorts are still down around my ankles. He unzips the fly to his blue jeans and takes out an enlarged red organ the likes of which I've never seen, despite having two older brothers. He begins to massage it with his hands.

He grabs my right hand and growls "Your turn." I try to pull away, but he grabs me again with one hand and, with the other, takes my hand and puts it on his swollen appendage. I'm aware of my hand shaking as I touch this warm, firm, but frightening organ. My whole body starts shaking. Suddenly, I'm freezing cold even though it's the dead of summer. As he rubs my hand up and down his organ, I have the weirdest sensation. It's as though I am floating above, on the ceiling of the shed, watching the whole scene below, completely detached. The next thing I know, he's making moaning noises and a warm, wet, slippery liquid pools on my underpants and slowly dribbles down my bare legs onto my sandals.

Michael throws a greasy rag my way, mumbling, "Clean yourself up," and saunters out the door. My face is red and hot with shame, as tears wash down my face, but I am flooded with relief as he leaves. I finally stop shaking enough to use the rag to get that slippery, sticky stuff off my underpants and legs, pull up my shorts, and leave.

I'm awakened out of a sound sleep by someone touching me. I am lying on my back and someone's arm is under the covers and touching my private parts underneath my nightgown. Where is Jason, the other foster kid I share this room with? I remember he's gone to visit his mom this weekend. I'm utterly alone in this bedroom. Except for this person who is touching me.

"Don't make a sound and you won't get hurt. Besides, you're really gonna thank me for this later."

Michael. Again. Why is this happening to me? I am so frightened I can't move a muscle, much less cry out. He crawls next to me in bed and pulls the covers over both of us. His hand is on my private parts and he is on his side, up against me. I can feel him rubbing against me with something hard, rubbing and rubbing, and moaning. A single cry of "ohhh," and he rolls away from me, just lying there next to me for a minute. My heart thumps.

"Keep your mouth shut, or else." And, he's gone.

I lie there for the rest of the night, tossing and turning, until I begin to see streaks of orange and pink through the bedroom window. I finally get up and go downstairs to breakfast, like nothing has happened. Did it really happen? I am relieved to see Michael is not up yet. Mama Janet is in the sunny kitchen. I can smell coffee.

"Did you have a good sleep, Laurel?"

Silence.

"Laurel, I just asked you a question."

"Fine."

By the time Laurel finished, choking sobs wracked her shaking body.

Krisha just let her cry for a few minutes, offering her tissues. Finally, she said, "Laurel, that took tremendous courage. How long have you been walking around with that secret festering inside of you?"

"I was eight, so forty-four years. Almost my entire life. I've tried so hard not to think about it . . ."

When she didn't say anything more, Krisha asked, "Did you tell anyone when you finally went home?"

"I tried to tell my mother, but she just didn't want to hear it. That's a big part of why I have so much trouble dealing with her. I *resent* her so much."

"Can you say more about that resentment?"

Laurel stared at her lap, twisting a tissue. "First, it was about how she neglected us, how her drinking that night led to the fire. Then it was because we ended up in foster care." She started crying again, sobbing, with her nose running.

Krisha handed her more tissues.

When she was able to speak again, Laurel choked her words out. "And then, dammit, she just didn't want to hear it. She told me I was lying, making it up."

By that time, she was sobbing so hard again she couldn't talk any more.

"It's good to get in touch with that anger, to get it out," Krisha said. "We'll talk more about that next session. But, I think that's enough for today. I want you to make sure you're gentle with yourself after this, and that you have support. If there's someone you trust enough, I would urge you to talk to that person, if only to say that you talked about your abuse for the first time today in session. Are you okay?"

All Laurel could do was nod.

"For next time, I'd like you to think about the possible impact of the abuse on your life, beyond the resentment toward your mother. Can you do that?"

She nodded.

Leaving, Laurel felt a headache coming on. Her whole body felt wobbly, drained. But a profound sense of relief settled over her, too. She might finally be able to get this dark canker out in the open and get to the bottom of what it did to her.

So, why was she also terrified? She wanted a drink as badly as she ever had.

She returned to Hope House, on the bus, her whole body feeling bruised. She was stuck up in her head, back in that shed, hating that asshole Michael. All she wanted was something to make these feelings disappear, to make her numb. Despite being wiped out, she forced herself to call Starr.

"I had a rough therapy session today." She took a big breath. "I told Krisha about being sexually abused when I was in foster care."

"Oh my God, Laurel. I had no idea you'd been abused—or in foster care. Do you want to talk about it anymore?"

"Not really, not now. But, I will admit that I *really* want to drink right now. To blot out those feelings, the shame, the anger . . ."

"But, you know that drinking won't make anything better, right? That when you finally sober up, that abuse is still going to be there."

"I know, I just needed to hear that."

"The only way to the other side is right straight through the pain. And, you've already taken the first step today. Where are you?"

"At Hope House."

"So, I'd suggest either getting to a meeting, or at least letting one of the other women know you've have a rough day and you've been thinking about drinking. To tell on yourself, in other words. Can you do that, or do you need me to come there?"

"No, you don't have to come. If there isn't a meeting nearby I'll talk to one of the ladies. I will. Thanks, Starr."

But, she didn't. Instead, she went into her room, crawled into bed, and cried some more.

Chapter 29

The next day, she received another email from Ryan. After sending him her first letter post-release from Sunstate providing her new email address, Ryan responded very quickly online. Since then, she'd received a couple more emails, shorter than the letters, but more frequent. She hoped to work up to a phone call, but hadn't proposed it yet. As she read his latest response, she wondered whether she'd ever have any more of a relationship with him than emails.

She interviewed, got the cleaning job, and went Wednesday night for the first time. The work was not all that different from what she'd been doing at her mother's, but on a larger scale. She went through the motions of dusting and vacuuming the offices and cleaning the restrooms, following their checklist. It didn't seem like it would take her until eleven to finish but, since this was the first night, she stayed that long.

She rode the bus to see Krisha with an empty feeling in her stomach. In the first session since her big revelation, what would it be like to talk about what happened? She couldn't afford to crave a drink all the time.

Her counselor began with Laurel's desire to drink and what she'd done about it.

"I'm not at all surprised," Krisha said. "I'd be more surprised if you *hadn't* thought about drinking."

Really?

Then Krisha praised her for how she'd dealt with it and asked if she'd thought about how it affected her life.

"I did, and I wrote down some things about the potential effects. The list is long."

"Good, let's hear what you thought."

Some things were obvious: the resentment she'd already mentioned, the anger at her mother for not protecting her, the shame, her drinking starting in adolescence. But, also how she lost herself in school, in art, how she'd learned while she was good at art, and received attention from teachers for it. While was drawing and creating things, she got completely immersed in the activity.

In the course of the discussion, Krisha probed more about her relationships, the abuse she experienced from men. Did she think it could be related to the sexual abuse?

"Maybe. I never thought about it before. I'm not sure I see the connection."

"Do you think it was a coincidence that you ended up in two abusive relationships?"

"I'm not sure." *Why am I feeling defensive?* "What're you getting at?"

"I wonder whether the unworthiness and shame you felt because of the abuse led you to choose men who mistreated you."

Hmm. Made sense.

How come she never figured that out before?

The weekend arrived, and she and Starr went to a meeting, followed by talking afterwards to catch up and continue her work on the twelve steps. Starr was very pleased to hear how Laurel decided to help her mother out and raised the issue of taking another stab at making amends to her.

"I think that's a good idea. But, let's give it a little time. Give me a chance to hang in there with her for a while, so she can see I've, in fact, changed. I think what's more important to me than making amends is that we seem to be getting along okay. Plus, I am making living amends, right? We seem to have made peace with each other, at least for now. And, given our history, that's the best it's ever going to be."

"Then let's talk some about some other amends I think you need to make. Ryan and his dad."

A whoosh of air escaped from Laurel's mouth. "Okay, wow, didn't see that coming. First, let me say I feel like I've already started that process with Ryan. I'm not sure I've apologized per se, but I've certainly explained what happened, why I was forced to abandon him, and have taken responsibility for it. I also explained how I ended up in prison. So, I'm not saying I don't have work to do there, but I've started."

"Great, good for you. What about his dad? What was his name?"

"Rick Murphy. And, that one . . . I'm going to have to think about that. On the one hand, you're probably right. I fucked up back then, and I've never acknowledged that to him. But, opening that can of worms? I don't know . . . He's already argued with Ryan about his having a relationship with me, such as it is."

"That may be true. But let me remind you that these amends are not about what the other person did to you.

They're about you acknowledging the harm *you* did and trying to make up for it if you can. So, if all you can do is write a letter, then that's okay."

"I don't know . . . There's a lot of baggage between us because of how abusive he was to me—"

"And, it's going to be challenging to put that aside and just focus on your part. Which is what you tried to do with your mom before your DUI. It may not have worked out like you hoped, but in terms of your communication to her, I think you got it right. So, I'd like you to work on it."

God, she dreaded it.

Chapter 30

"So, why do you think you're having so much trouble writing this amends letter to Rick?" Krisha asked.

"I know exactly why. First, because he doesn't want me to have any kind of relationship with Ryan. And, second, because of his abuse toward me. To be honest, we were pretty abusive to each other, mostly emotional, but also physical. That was my part. I was drinking a lot, a hot mess at that point in my life. He was a real shit, and I guess I haven't been able to let go of my anger toward him after all these years."

"What exactly is that anger all about?"

"Well, the abuse, obviously." She paused to reflect. "Actually, the anger is about other things, too. He pressured me into having the baby when I was pregnant, knowing full well I absolutely did not want one. And, when I turned out to be just as bad a parent as I knew I would be, he threw me out. He had no concept of what I was going through in that apartment all day with a crying baby I couldn't console . . . totally isolated, not having a clue about how to be a mother. He didn't want to hear about how frustrated I felt about not being able to be a good mom. Also, he wasn't much interested in being a good dad. He was more intrigued with the idea of being a parent than the reality."

"Yet, from what you've said about Ryan, it sounds like he must have turned into a good parent."

"Yes, I guess he did. That part's so confusing to me. Anyhow, that is what I'm most angry about from the past."

"From the past. Is there also something from the present."

"Yep. In the course of struggling with that stupid amends letter, I've realized I'm also really pissed off that he's now trying to punish Ryan, or at least interfere with him having a relationship with me after all these years. I'm furious about that." She almost whispered, "And it keeps seeping into the letter."

"How?"

"I keep wanting to trot out how well I'm doing now, so he'll back off and feel okay about Ryan having a relationship with me."

"It sounds like you want his forgiveness."

"Of course, I want his forgiveness! I deserve to be forgiven."

"Yet, have you forgiven him?"

"What? Does he deserve to be forgiven? Based on how angry I still am, obviously I have *not* forgiven him. Or myself, for that matter."

"So, maybe that's what we need to work on now. Forgiveness of yourself and Rick."

Laurel groaned.

"Let's think about it in terms of radical acceptance. Have you heard of that?"

"Hmm, radical acceptance? Uh-uh."

"Radical acceptance is when you choose to accept something you don't really like—similar to what AA calls 'life on life's terms'—by not resisting something negative you can't change. Everybody has to deal with a bunch of bad stuff not under their control. We can choose to fight it, and make ourselves miserable, or decide to accept it, even though we may hate it. The people who subscribe to the concept say, 'pain is inevitable, but suffering is optional.' In other words, suffering occurs when we refuse to accept that pain is part of life."

She let that simmer for a minute, giving Laurel a chance to think about it.

Finally, Laurel said, "I'm not sure I understand. Aren't pain and suffering the same thing?"

"Not really. What I'm trying to say is that it doesn't help to fight things, painful things, we can't change. But, if we can accept things, we can avoid unnecessary suffering."

"Maybe, but what does forgiveness have to do with radical acceptance?"

"Well, let's talk it through. It seems to me there are a lot of aspects of this situation with Rick that you have absolutely no control over. For example, your past history with him. The bad things you did to each other. Those things can't be changed, but how you *think* about them can."

Laurel leaned forward, elbows on her knees, listening.

"You can *decide* to let them go rather than holding onto that anger at him for what he did, or at yourself for staying in that abusive situation. Or, because you couldn't be a good mother. You did the best you could at the time, given that you were deep in your disease."

Laurel looked up at Krisha. "Okay, I see that."

"What other aspects of the situation do you not have control over that you might just have to accept, even though you don't like them?"

Laurel sat back and thought about that. "Well, for one thing, I have no control over the fact that he doesn't want Ryan to have a relationship with me. I mean, over time, I might affect that in a small way if I can show him I'm staying sober and getting my life back on track. But, I have to admit, even then, Rick's opinion might not change for the better."

"Absolutely right. So, you can drive yourself crazy obsessing over that and trying to change something you really have no control over, or you can decide to accept it and focus instead on the marvelous fact that despite his father's objections, Ryan seems interested in having some kind of relationship with his mother."

"You're right. That *is* marvelous that he got in touch with me at all, while I was in prison, no less. Plus, he's continued to correspond with me and share some parts of his life."

"That's a tribute to *you*, Laurel. Somehow, in the letters you wrote from prison, you made him want to get to know you and to share his life with you. Despite taking responsibility for what happened when he was a baby. Don't you think that's kind of a miracle?"

Laurel reflected. "It *is* a miracle! Of course, it is. You're right."

"So, try to let that be enough. At least for now."

"Okay, I'm going to work on that, and think about it. Forgiveness, too."

Finally, Laurel reworked her amends letter to Rick. In it she acknowledged her drinking and the heavy price she paid for it. She told him about the sober living house and being in treatment. She acknowledged the harm she did to him and their baby Ryan with her drinking, and admitted being abusive to Rick. She apologized for it all, sincerely.

Later, she showed the letter to Starr.

"Wow, big change. Nice job. How did you get from your last version to this one?"

"Well, as I talked, in group, about what happened, and listened to the other mothers, the more I began to forgive myself. The more I forgave myself, the less angry I felt at Rick, and the more I was able to forgive him. Krisha helped a lot. Radical acceptance," she said.

So, she sent the letter off to Boston, acknowledging she had no control over whether Rick would accept her amends, or respond in any way at all. The universe had it now, but she felt better.

One warm day in early November, Laurel got word that Jessica wanted to speak to her. As she'd been hoping, Jessica heard about a job in graphic arts. Laurel still worked at the cleaning job, slowly beginning to accumulate a little cash while also paying off her fines and fees through probation. It felt good to finally have a little money in her pocket so she could have an occasional meal out with friends, buy a prepaid phone, and so forth. A "real" job would be wonderful, though.

Jessica gave her the contact info, and they discussed the application process and interview, agreeing that Laurel should take the lead. Laurel contacted the HR person, and set up an interview for the following week. She sat on pins and needles the whole time she awaited the interview date.

Finally, the day arrived. She rehearsed in her mind possible interview questions. The Hope House women helped with advice on what she should wear for the interview: a crisp new white blouse and black slacks. She was ready.

The day didn't go as she'd hoped, however. Several other people on-site also interviewed for the job, all a lot younger. It unnerved her. No one looked like they just got out of prison a few months ago. By the time they called her name, she almost trembled. When the interviewer asked her what she'd been doing in her most recent jobs, she became tongue-tied and stumbled, talking in vagaries rather than the specifics she knew he wanted. She had no idea whether the interviewer, or the company, knew about her incarceration history. All she knew for certain—or *thought* she knew—was that having a felony conviction didn't eliminate her from the pool of applicants. Finally, it ended.

She dragged herself to the bus stop. When she arrived at Hope House she called Jessica.

"How'd it go?"

"Horrible! I completely messed it up."

"What do you mean?"

They talked about it for a while.

"Next time you'll be better prepared," Jessica said. "Try not to beat yourself up over it."

Two weeks passed, and she heard nothing about the job. She hadn't expected to get it, but a letter thanking her for applying and letting her know for sure would have been nice.

She mentioned it to her roommate Karina, who said, "Don't stew over it. Go to a meeting and let it go."

Why hadn't she thought of that?

It had been weeks since she'd spoken to her mother, so Laurel finally she called her.

"Your sister Betsy . . . is dead," Joanne blurted out.

"What? How? What happened Mom? How did you find out? Where was she?"

"I got a call from the police in Philadelphia. I'm not sure I even knew she lived there," Joanne said, her voice a low moan. "I have no idea how they found me."

"What did they say?" Laurel asked.

"She was found dead in her apartment. They think she might've been murdered. Murdered!" Joanne wailed. "They said it didn't look like an accident, but she might have committed suicide."

Laurel struggled to get any useful information out of her now nearly hysterical mother.

"Was she shot, or stabbed or what?"

"No, no, I don't think so. I don't know!" Joanne started sobbing. "I just can't deal with this. Two kids in prison and two kids murdered. What the hell did I do to deserve this?"

Laurel said nothing. What could she say? "Mom, try to calm down. Do you want me to come over there?" Could she even get there? Should she call Victoria? She closed her eyes and let out a sigh of relief when her mother said no.

What a fucked-up family.

Somehow, she'd have to figure out how to go see Mom. She could feel guilt's slippery hands clawing at her neck.

Chapter 31

By mid-November, fall had finally arrived. The nights and mornings were cool, the afternoons warm, as Laurel waited for the bus to her cleaning job. The mindlessness of it had become routine, but she'd hoped to have a "real" job in graphics by now.

Since her mother told her about her sister's death the previous week, she felt like she'd been sleepwalking through her life: group, work, dinner with the other residents, AA meetings. Regret gnawed at her. She should have done more to connect with Betsy. Instead, she'd left her in the lurch. Her Friday appointment with Krisha couldn't come fast enough.

In response to Krisha's question about how things had been going, Laurel admitted to a very tough past couple of weeks.

"I called my mom last week and she told me she just heard from the police in Philadelphia that my younger sister Betsy was just found dead, probably murdered."

"Gosh, that's terrible. Tell me more about her and what might have happened."

"Well, for starters, Betsy and I were never close. I did feel somewhat responsible for her because she was my younger sister and, in some ways, got the worst of what happened during our dysfunctional childhood. She did help me, after

Rick kicked me out, by letting me live with her for a while 'til I found work and got back on my feet."

Laurel played with her zipper. "I thought what she was doing back then was pretty dodgy—probably prostitution—but I wasn't really sure what was going on and didn't really want to. In retrospect, the guy living with her was probably some kind of pimp. Mom said she was, quote, 'turning tricks.' In any event, didn't stay in touch with her after that. In fact, when Mom told me it what happened in Philly, I'm not even sure I knew that's where she lived. That's how bad our relationship grew. I guess Mom wasn't in touch with her either." She ran her fingers through her hair. "So, I'm kind of confused about Mom's reaction."

"What do you mean?"

"She was super upset. I mean, so hysterical on the phone I could barely even get her to tell me what had happened. What confuses me is why she was so upset when she had virtually no relationship with Betsy."

"How are you feeling about what happened, Laurel?"

"Not sure. When Mom told me, I was so taken aback by her reaction I think I was more concerned about her than anything. I offered to go to her house, but admit I was relieved when she told me no. Plus, although I feel like I *should* try to comfort her or something, I'm not sure how to go about it. I'm kind of afraid if I start talking to her about it, then I'll get upset."

"Are you saying you're feeling kind of numb about it?"

"Guess so. Like I know how you *should* respond to hearing your sister is dead, and might have been murdered . . . like really sad, upset. For whatever reasons, though, that's not how I feel."

"I wonder whether you might be feeling like you have to hold it together because your mother is falling apart."

"Mm-hmm. I think you're right. I'm going to try to get there this weekend. Dreading that."

"You remember how we've talked about forgiveness in the past?"

Laurel nodded.

"Do you think you might be starting to forgive your mother, even though you were quite resistant to the idea when I brought it up?"

That thought hung in the air. Was she starting to forgive her mom? "Not much point in holding onto a resentment under the circumstances, right?"

Krisha smiled. "Not from my perspective, no. But, then again, from where I'm coming from, there are virtually *no* circumstances where holding onto a resentment makes sense."

"Yeah, okay, I hear you. Don't know if I'll get there."

On the bus back to Hope House, Laurel thought about Ryan. Wouldn't it be great to have an actual conversation with him on the phone? She'd love to hear his voice. Instead, she emailed him, letting him know she finally had a cell phone, and asking him for his number and a good time to talk.

In a call to Victoria to share the news about her sister, she asked if she could request a ride to Carefree the next day. Victoria offered her condolences and agreed to drive her, suggesting that Caroline or Starr might be able to take her back.

Starr would be good, thought Laurel. Then I can talk to her about Betsy.

With those arrangements in place, she called her mom to say she'd like to come for the weekend, in light of what happened to Betsy, and to do whatever she might help with.

Joanne hesitated. "You don't have to."

Laurel insisted. So, her mom capitulated and agreed. Laurel had motored right through her resistance.

On Saturday morning Victoria picked her up. Laurel needed to catch up and talk to her about Betsy and her family in general. By the time they arrived in Carefree, Victoria knew most of the story. She offered to come in and meet her mother, but Laurel thought it wasn't a good idea. When she opened the front door, her mother was still in her pajamas.

"Hi, Mom, how are you?"

God, she looked like crap.

"How the hell do you think I am?"

Why did Laurel even keep trying to be nice? "I assume you're feeling bad about Betsy?"

"That's right, so why bother asking?"

Trying to keep her frustration under control, Laurel said, "Mom, I came here to give you help and support because of what happened with Betsy, and because I know you're thinking about putting the house on the market—"

"So, what, do you want, a medal?"

Shit, this wasn't starting off well at all. She struggled to figure out what to say that wouldn't throw gasoline on the fire.

"No, I'm not looking for a medal. Since I talked to you last week right after the police called, have you learned anything more specific about what happened?"

Sitting down gingerly at the kitchen table, her mother heaved a huge sigh. "Not much. They wanted to know what I knew about the men in her life. The answer is: not a damned thing. I told them you might know something. The cop left his name and phone number if you want to call him back. When did you last talk to Betsy?"

"It's probably been at least a couple years—"

"What was her situation then?"

"Not really sure. She didn't say much about it. I'm not even sure if she lived in Philly at that time. Frankly, the last time I had any real contact with her was about twenty years ago in Boston when Rick kicked me out. She let me stay with her while I tried to find a job and an apartment."

Joanne had a quizzical expression. "Rick, which one was Rick?"

Should she say the father of Ryan? "Rick was the guy who got me pregnant and made me have the baby."

She studied her mother to gauge her reaction and watched her consider it.

"Wait a minute. You got pregnant and had a kid? Wait— was that the kid who called here when you first were in prison?"

Laurel didn't respond.

"I asked you a question. Was that the kid who called here?" To herself, Joanne said, "What the hell was his name?"

Finally, refusing to look at her mother, Laurel said quietly, "Yes, his name is Ryan."

"What happened to him? I never knew you had a kid."

The Parkinson's must be really affecting her mental functioning. Laurel stalled for time. "Rick kicked me out and refused to let me see him. I haven't seen Ryan since he was about a year old. Rick raised him by himself."

"So, why was he calling here?"

"Trying to find me, curious about his mother."

Joanne frowned. "Trying to find his mother who abandoned him twenty years ago?"

The conversation went downhill from there. Laurel fought to keep her emotions under control, a battle she lost. For a minute or two, she tried to keep her mouth shut, but a thick red rage bubbled up in her that she didn't even try to stop.

Joanne continued to egg her on. "I can't believe you walked out on that poor defenseless baby."

"Mom, you have no idea what you're talking about—"

"What do you mean? I raised four kids—"

"And, look how they all turned out! Two had lives so fucked up they've been murdered. A drug addict, an alcoholic, a prostitute, two in prison. Great job, Mom!"

"I may not have been the best mom, but I never abandoned you kids."

That's when Laurel lost it. "What are you talking about? You absolutely did! What about that night you were at the bar and the boys, not even teenagers yet, were in charge? Remember when the neighbors ratted you out and Child Protective came? How about sending us to Aunt Alice's house without even telling her we were coming? She wanted no part of us! Have you conveniently forgotten how we ended up in three different foster homes, while you carried on with whatever lowlife guy was in your life at the time? How is that not abandonment?"

Unable to stop herself, Laurel had poured gasoline onto this raging inferno.

"First of all, that wasn't my fault. The boys *were* supposed to be in charge. I told them not to cook. Stupid neighbors had no business sticking their nose in where it didn't belong—"

"Mom, the fire department came! That's how Child Protective got there, not because of neighbors being nosy."

"Well, if my sister had just agreed to look after you kids for a few weeks it would have worked out fine. She owed me that."

"Who cares what she owed you! Sending four kids to a relative's house in another state, on a bus, by themselves, without even having the courtesy to let your sister know the kids were coming?" Laurel leapt up and paced, her arms waving, spittle flying from her mouth. "That's fucked up, really fucked up! You don't even know what happened to us after that. No wonder Betsy's life was a mess. Being the youngest, and having to go by herself, she had it the worst."

"That's why I took her back first!"

As if that made it okay.

"What about me? I was gone for almost two years! You refused to believe that I got sexually abused by one of the older boys in the foster family—"

"I *still* don't believe that! You're making that up to try to make me feel guilty. You always were a liar. If that happened, why didn't you tell right away?"

Laurel wanted to hit her. Almost screeching now, she yelled, "Because I didn't think anyone would believe me! Because I thought I'd get in trouble! Because I was scared! Because I was just a kid whose mother didn't care enough about her to not leave her home with two irresponsible brothers. A mother who couldn't get her shit together enough to be a half decent parent. Who cared more about going out and partying than taking care of her kids. And, *you* have the nerve to criticize *me* for abandoning Ryan? You have no idea what you're even talking about!"

"And, you have no idea what it was like to try to raise four kids by yourself!"

Her mom had unleashed a lifetime of venom. "Who asked you to have four kids? You weren't equipped to take care of even one!"

Finally, Joanne jumped up from the kitchen chair and charged toward her.

Laurel, afraid her mother might hit her, dodged out of the way.

At that point, Joanne yelled, "I want you out of my house! Now! Get out before I call the police!"

Chapter 32

At noon on Saturday, in the casita, pacing while on the phone to Starr, Laurel cried and yelled simultaneously. It felt like a million needles pierced her body.

Starr finally got her to calm down enough to explain what happened, which took a while since she hadn't yet talked to Starr about Betsy's death.

Laurel sniffled. "Any chance you could come get me."

"I would need to rearrange some things. Are you gonna be okay?"

"I'm not sure. I'm totally freaking out here."

"I can hear that. But, do you think you can calm yourself down until I can get there?"

"Maybe." At the moment, she was taking refuge in deep resentment.

"Are you thinking about drinking at all?"

"Yes!" she practically shrieked. "There is nothing I want more right now than a drink! Or ten."

"Is there any booze in your mom's house?"

"No idea. I'm not going back in there, regardless."

"Okay, that's good. There's none in the casita, right?

"Right."

"Okay good. Let me think. What about Victoria? Do you think she could get there sooner than I can?"

"Not sure what her plans were for the day."

"Give me her number and let me call her and see if she can come get you sooner than I can."

Starr called Victoria and left a message. She called Laurel right back, explaining she couldn't reach Victoria. They talked some more, and she managed to get Laurel calmed down to the point where she wasn't hysterical.

"Listen, you need to be honest with me. Are you still thinking about drinking?"

Laurel hesitated. "Kinda. But not really. Remind me why it's a bad idea. I mean, I obviously know, but I need someone else to spell it out right now. I feel like my whole brain and body are on fire. I want to spit, I want to hit, I still want to scream."

"But, you know that drinking's worse than pointless right now, right? It'll only make things worse. Remember your relapse. You need to deescalate your emotions right now, calm yourself. There's no way a drink will make this situation any better. And, the urge will pass. Is there somewhere you can go and sit and just close your eyes and breathe? Or, how about taking a short walk?"

"Maybe out back. That's a good idea. I'm walking out back now. Hold on . . . Okay, I'm sitting on the patio. I don't see my mother anywhere."

"Okay good. Now just sit there and close your eyes and breathe. If you have a safe place to go to in your mind, go there."

"What do you mean?"

"When I was in treatment, my therapist and I worked on what she called 'a safe place' for me. A place where I could go in my mind that had good associations when I felt really upset. For me it was the ocean. Do you have a place like that?"

"Not really, but it's pretty nice in my mom's backyard, actually. It's very green out here, shady."

"Okay, that should work. So just close your eyes and do deep breathing until you're feeling less agitated and upset."

"Okay, I'll try it."

She sat on a chaise lounge with her feet up, closed her eyes, and did some deep breathing. She listened to the birds chirp. She could smell flowers of some kind. She found herself continually returning to the argument with her mother, but tried to change her focus and let it go.

Amazingly, it worked. After she practiced it for a while, she started to feel more relaxed, less agitated. Although the thought of drinking still lingered in the back of her mind, like an app she couldn't turn off, she didn't feel desperate about it. She could hold on until Starr or Victoria arrived. Closing her eyes, she imagined herself at one of the AA meetings she liked and could actually hear people talking about why drinking wasn't going to change anything. When she finally looked at her watch she discovered it had been nearly an hour since she first called Starr. She needed to go around to the front to be ready when she arrived.

Fifteen minutes later, Laurel got into Starr's Toyota. She leaned over and hugged her friend behind the steering wheel.

Starr looked into her eyes. "Boy, sounds like you've had a really bad time of it."

"You got that right. And, here's the ironic part: I came over here to try to help her out, to support her because of my sister dying. And, to help her with the house."

"Wait. Start at the beginning. Sounds like there's quite a backstory here that I haven't heard."

"You're right, there is. First, thank you so much for rescuing me. I came this close to drinking," she said, holding her forefinger and thumb a quarter inch apart.

"But the point is, you didn't. You did what the program tells us to do. You reached out for help. While we're driving back to Hope House, tell me about your sister."

So, Laurel explained about her childhood, her mother and siblings, and foster care, including the sexual abuse. Although she'd told the part about the foster care and abuse to Krisha, it surprised her how much it helped to tell it again. Plus, Starr said all the right things at the right times.

By the time Starr got her back to Hope House, she'd pretty much told the whole story, including about Betsy's death and her mother's raging verbal attack about Laurel moving out and leaving Ryan to be raised by Rick. She felt a hundred per cent better, and no longer thought about drinking.

Starr asked about her plans for the rest of the weekend.

"I think I should go to a meeting tonight, for sure, and maybe tomorrow. I guess I'll read and take a walk, take advantage of the nice weather. Are you still up for that meeting tomorrow?"

"Absolutely."

After the meeting on Sunday, she and Starr sat outside in the backyard at Hope House and rehashed the run-in with her mom.

"So, can you see your part in it? How you made things worse by taking your mother's bait, rather than walking away or trying to deescalate the argument?"

Chagrined, Laurel nodded.

"What did she say that set you off?"

"Her judgments of me triggered my guilt about leaving Ryan."

"I think that's something you need to take up with your therapist."

Laurel couldn't make eye contact. Her own behavior had very nearly caused another relapse, after she'd worked so hard for her sobriety.

"It also seems pretty clear you haven't forgiven your mom about how she raised you," Starr said.

"Obviously!"

"Do you want to forgive her?"

Not this again. "You sound like my therapist."

"I'll take that as a compliment, although I'm not trying to be your therapist."

"I know. Starr, I really don't know if I *do* want to forgive her. It just infuriated me to hear her criticize me for leaving Ryan, which I didn't have a choice about. She was such a shitty mother. What a hypocrite."

"Honestly, Laurel, sometimes I can't help thinking the problem is you versus you."

Laurel raised her eyebrows and gave Starr a quizzical look.

"Sometimes you're your own worst enemy. What I'm trying to get you to see is, even if you're right that your mom is a hypocrite who had no right to criticize you for what you did, what did being infuriated at her earn you? Who ended up being a total mess after that encounter? You know, recovering alcoholics cannot afford to indulge in the toxic emotional state of righteous indignation."

A speckled cactus wren scolded them from the garden.

"What do you mean?"

"Did being right, having that huge argument, help you in any way at all?"

"Obviously not."

"What happened instead?"

"I ended up wanting to drink." She knew Starr was right. She had to learn to shut down this explosive anger.

"Exactly. You came pretty darn close, but you did the right thing by calling me. Lucky for you, we were able to get you calmed down and out of the situation. What if no one had been able to take your call? What if you couldn't reach anyone?"

"I know. I might have started drinking." Laurel sat with her head down.

"And, what happened the last time you drank because you were overwhelmed by your emotions?"

Laurel jerked her head up. "Are you trying to make me feel guilty? Because if so, it's working."

"Not at all! I'm trying to get you to see how your actions can make it more likely that you're heading *toward* a drink versus *walking away* from a drink. By taking the bait in that argument, you got really upset and escalated the situation. You can't afford to keep doing that, Laurel. There's too much at stake."

"I know. You're right. I'm sorry I'm being so defensive. I let her get to me."

"Yeah, you did. So, here's where forgiveness might help. If you could let go of that part of your past, accept that it is what it is, it might not trigger such an intense, emotional response in you. It can't be changed. Your mom did a lousy job, but maybe it was the best she could. Forgiving her doesn't mean you *approve* of what she did. It just means you let it go of that resentment, accept the past, and make a decision to move on."

Laurel contemplated that. "It sounds like what Krisha, my therapist, calls 'radical acceptance.' Have you heard of that?"

"No, but you mentioned it once before. What does it mean?"

"Well, I'm not sure I'll explain it right, but it's something like this. In life, pain is inevitable, but suffering is not. Suffering is what can happen when we refuse to accept negative things and, instead, fight against them."

"Okay. How does that apply here?"

"When I hold onto my anger against my mom, rather than just accepting I had a crappy childhood because she was a crappy parent, rather than just accepting it and moving on, I just prolong my suffering."

"That's right. Yet, I do see you moving toward what you call radical acceptance, or what I might call forgiveness, when you try to help your mother and work to normalize your relationship with her. The reality is, with your sister Betsy gone, you and your mom are all you have in the way of family. Who knows how much longer she'll be around . . ."

"Well, yeah, right. But there's Ryan . . ."

"Yes, there's Ryan. But, it's unclear what exactly will happen there. If you're lucky, the relationship may blossom. Think how much better you might feel if you were able to make peace with your childhood and your relationship with your mom."

"But, what if she won't meet me halfway?"

"That could happen. She sounds like a damaged person, and she just might decide to continue with her hostility toward you. There still might be some value in trying to work things out with her, though. Why don't you see what your therapist thinks?"

Sunday night, climbing into her pajamas, Laurel noticed a pink Post-it on her bureau. Momentarily puzzled, she walked over and saw a man's name and phone number penciled onto it. Sean Flaherty, the Philadelphia cop she was supposed to call back. Crap, because of the fight with Joanne, they never got to talk about Betsy. Laurel needed to follow up with the detective, find out more details about what happened to Betsy, try to communicate with her mother about what to do with her remains. Could she afford what it would cost?

"Detective Flaherty here."

"Hi, this is Laurel Peterson in Phoenix, Arizona. I'm the sister of Betsy Peterson. You called my mother Joanne Mc-Manus about her about a week and a half ago. Told her Betsy was dead, maybe a suicide. My mom said you left this number, and I should give you a call back."

Silence. Finally, "Peterson, you said?"

"Yes, Betsy Peterson."

"Yeah, right, okay. I know the case now. Found in her apartment by the landlord with ligature marks around her neck—"

"Wow, I didn't even know that much. My mother became so hysterical when she told me about it, she didn't even know how Betsy had died."

"First, let me say how sorry I am for your loss. Initially it looked like it was a suicide. Like she had hanged herself. But, the autopsy results came in yesterday. Hold on a minute." Laurel heard the sounds of papers shuffling in the background. "Okay, the coroner has ruled it a homicide."

"Homicide! What makes him say that?"

"She says here in the report that despite the ligature marks, the cause of death was strangulation not consistent with hanging. What can you tell me about your sister?"

Laurel struggled to gain her composure. Finding out about Betsy's death, probable suicide, was bad enough, but murdered? She already had one murdered sibling, her brother, many years ago. Betsy, too?

"Well, almost nothing about her recent life. In fact, I hadn't seen her in about twenty years. We had a pretty rough childhood."

"What about more recent times?"

"Can't tell you much about that. About twenty years ago, in Boston, Betsy let me live with her for a few weeks while I got back on my feet." He didn't need to know anything more than that.

"What was that like?"

"She lived with her boyfriend in a pretty nice apartment. She was very beautiful then. I found it uncomfortable, because this so-called boyfriend was pretty abusive."

"You said 'so-called' boyfriend. Why?"

"Around this same time, my mother told me that Betsy was turning tricks. Looking back on it, I'd say at that point she might have been a call girl. But, I also think this boyfriend was probably her pimp."

"What makes you say that?"

"Just a feeling I had after my mom said she was a prostitute."

"Was she doing drugs at that time?"

"Not that I could see, though she was drinking a lot."

"Well, I'm asking because the tox screen showed Betsy had high levels of methamphetamine and alcohol in her system at autopsy. We were wondering how far back the drug use went."

Neither of them said anything for a minute.

Finally, Laurel responded, "I have no idea. I wasn't aware she was doing drugs. What else did you find? Do you have any leads about who might've done this to her?"

"Here's the thing: We dusted the apartment for prints, and in addition to hers, we found lots of others, virtually all men's. Apparently, in addition to her, there was a guy living there, but the landlord doesn't know his name. We asked neighbors, but nobody admitted to knowing anything, although they did say a lot of different men came in and out of there over the past few months."

"Jeez."

"Yeah. So, she might well've been turning tricks to support her meth habit, or she and the guy might have been dealing drugs. I don't know if you want to hear this, but the autopsy also revealed physical evidence—lots of small tears—that she'd had vaginal and anal sex quite frequently, probably over a long period of time. That's consistent with prostitution."

Laurel could feel her stomach contents trying to come up in her esophagus. She swallowed a few times to keep it down, unable to talk. Poor Betsy . . .

"So, what's next?"

"Well, we're still checking those fingerprints, some of which are in the system, meaning that they belong to people—men—involved in the criminal justice system as offenders or ex-offenders. The most frequently found prints belong to a guy we think might've been her boyfriend or pimp . . . the guy living there. At this point, we consider him a suspect but haven't been able to track him down."

"So, bottom line, how likely is it you'll find her killer?"

"Ma'am, I wish I could be more optimistic . . . Even if we can find this guy, there's no other physical evidence linking him with the strangulation. So, catching him's not too likely."

Laurel let that marinate, trying to think if she had any more questions, still sick to her stomach. Add to that a massive headache. She mulled over how to approach her mother with this new information—or even *whether* to approach her mother.

"In light of all this, how can my mother and I find some closure on this? Can we even get Betsy's body back, or have her cremated, or what?"

"The body's been released by the coroner. I think your best bet would be to contact a funeral home here and have the body cremated. They can arrange with the morgue to do that and ship the cremains to you in Arizona."

"How long will the morgue hold on to her body? I mean, is there any rush to get her out of there?"

"No big rush, but when you decide what you're going to do, there's no point in dilly dallying. I'd say you probably have a couple weeks anyhow. Then the morgue staff might start bugging you to do something. Let me make sure I have a phone number for you."

Laurel gave him the number at Hope House as well as her new cell phone number.

After she hung up, she just sat on her bed awhile and finally cried, her head pounding. Amazingly, the thought of a drink never crossed her mind. Still unsure how to proceed with her mom, she decided to get input from Krisha to figure out what to do. *If I call Mom, what's the worst that could happen? She can start shrieking at me again and saying awful things about me. That's okay. I'll handle it.*

Better find a meeting.

Wednesday and Thursday passed in a blur. She saw Krisha on Friday, first explaining what happened over the weekend, the big fight, and how she dealt with her craving to drink. She acknowledged her part, courtesy of Starr, and talked about her phone call to detective Flaherty. Krisha listened quietly, complimenting her for how she handled the situation after the argument with her mother.

"Yeah, but I shouldn't have allowed myself to get sucked into that fight with her. I sank to her level."

"Yes, you did, but you're human. The point is you acknowledged it with Starr's help, and have learned from it."

"It's clear I need to figure out how to let go of my resentment and anger at my mom."

"Important realization. So, what would it take for you to be ready?"

"Well, on the one hand, I think about having her accept responsibility for being a crappy mother, but realistically, that's not going to happen.

"Actually, what I really need to talk about, is how to approach my mom regarding this situation with my sister being killed. Like, do I let her know what the detective said? I'm pretty sure if Mom knows all the details of Betsy's death, she'll totally freak out. So, at this point, I'm considering calling her, apologizing for the fight without getting into any details, and telling her I talked with Detective Flaherty."

She paused and took a breath. *This is so hard.*

"Then I thought I'd tell her about the plan to have her body cremated in Philly with the remains sent back here. I should ask her if she's willing to pay for that, or help me pay for it."

Krisha's head was down, listening. Finally, she looked up. "You know, that sounds like a good plan. I have no idea what it's going to cost, but WRAD might have some kind of emergency fund to help cover things like this. See what you can find.

"It might be worth rehearsing that phone conversation with someone before you have it, too."

"Okay, I'll plan to call Mom on Monday, maybe. That way I'll have group every other day for support, in case it's just horrible."

Chapter 33

Late Monday afternoon, after rehearsing what to say with her roommate Karina, Laurel called her mother. With her stomach in knots, she'd been dreading it but, so far, she'd kept it together emotionally. That could change the instant her mother picked up the phone.

It rang and rang and rang, and just as Laurel was about to hang up, frustrated by her inability to leave a message, Joanne answered.

"Hi Mom, it's Laurel. How are you?"

"Just as crappy as ever."

Okay, breathe, she counseled herself, *don't react.*

"First, I want to apologize for my part in the fight we had last weekend. I'm sorry the whole thing happened." That's about as much as she could muster in the way of amends. No response from mom. "Second, I did call that detective back, the one in Philadelphia, about Betsy. Are you interested in hearing what he had to say?"

So far so good. She wasn't talking, but she hadn't hung up on her. "Okay, so he said they performed an autopsy and concluded that Betsy had been killed rather than committing suicide."

She let that just hang there for a beat before continuing, to give her mother a chance to respond if she wanted to.

"You mean she was murdered?"

"It looks that way." No details.

"Do they know who did it?"

"Not really. They think it's probably the guy she was living with, but they can't find him."

"Oh, okay."

What? That was it? Laurel let out a big breath she'd been holding.

"The detective suggested we should have the body cremated and the remains sent to us out here." No response from Mom. "So, I went online and looked into it and called some places. I found one that will pick up the body from the morgue, do the cremation, get us five death certificates, and send us the remains through the U.S. Postal Service for a little over six hundred dollars." Again, silence.

"Should we pay for it together, go half-sies?"

Her mother didn't say anything at first. "Yeah, I'll split it with you."

"Can we do it from your house using your credit card? They need a credit card. I'll bring cash for my half."

"Okay. When do you want to come over?"

Whew, what a relief. Mom was being reasonable. "I'll have to find a ride up there. Let me call you back when I can find someone."

Thursday at noon, Victoria drove her to Carefree. They appreciated the gorgeous November day, warm, with a cobalt sky, a few puffy white clouds, and a soft breeze. They arrived and knocked. This time Laurel agreed to let Victoria come in, hoping it might keep Mom from going off if something unexpected happened and she got upset.

After introductions, Joanne got her credit card and they made the call. Everything went without a hitch. They'd pick up the body and send five death certificates as well as the cremains, which should arrive in four to five days at Joanne's address in a cardboard box.

Laurel ponied up three hundred dollars in cash, most of her savings.

Her mother frowned. "What's this for? I'll take care of it."

Surprised, Laurel bit her tongue to keep from saying something snarky. Instead, she took the high road. "Thanks Mom."

Now, let's get out of here before she can think of something to fight about.

As soon as the car doors shut, Victoria observed, "Well, that wasn't too bad. Your mom was kind of nice. She's in pretty bad shape though."

Laurel burst out with, "You have no idea! I was an absolute wreck about doing this today. Yes, today she was surprisingly nice. A couple visits ago when I came out to help her get the house ready to put on the market, she was pretty nice, too. The weekend before last, though, she was an absolute shrew. Part of what makes her so hard to deal with is her unpredictability."

"I wonder if that's partly the Parkinson's."

"It can affect mental functioning, and I think it might cause dementia, but I don't know enough about it to understand whether it might cause her unpredictability."

"Well, at least that part of this painful episode is over. I'm kind of surprised you don't seem more upset by the whole thing. You're handling it really well. I mean your sister was . . . murdered."

Laurel thought about that. "Well, a couple things are going on. First, Betsy and I haven't been close since we were kids, and I've barely seen her or even talked to her in about twenty years.

"Plus, having to make all these arrangements has just made me very . . . focused is the word, I guess. I did cry once, briefly, right after I got off the phone with the detective and learned that Betsy was a meth addict and a prostitute. That hit pretty hard, even if I wasn't all that surprised. And I feel guilty about the whole thing, regretting I didn't reach out to Betsy and try to stay in touch. Maybe I can grieve a little more now that this part is behind me. In a way, I think I'll be grieving the normal childhood Betsy and I never really had. Honestly, given what we went through, how could we have turned out in the normal range? Poor Betsy never even had a chance."

Just before Thanksgiving, she received a call from Jessica, the WRAD vocational specialist. "I might have a new job opportunity for you."

"Fantastic. The cleaning job's been okay, but it's been getting to me lately. Don't get me wrong, it's better than not working at all, and I've been able to save a little money, but I'm eager to find something where I use my brain."

"Let me tell you about this new possibility. Again, I'm going to warn you not to get your hopes up too high."

"Okay, hopes deflated." Again.

"So, here's the deal. It's a small graphics company called iGraphics. About ten employees, including the owner/CEO, a couple of other manager types, and a few worker bees."

Laurel sat bent forward, head in her hands. "Okay, so . . . small."

"It's an entry-level position, below your skill level and experience, but it would be a way to work your way back in."

She looked up at Jessica. "Still okay. What else?"

"Starting salary is fifty thousand dollars a year. Probably way below what you were making at your last real job, but it works out to more than twenty-five dollars an hour. Plus, two weeks paid vacation and the usual holidays."

"Well, you're right about the salary, but beggars can't be choosers, right? It's a lot more than I'm making now."

"And, the CEO knows your situation."

Laurel's eyes narrowed. "Meaning what?"

"Well, I explained that you were in our program for substance abuse and had been in prison for a year and a half. Turns out he's pretty familiar with substance abuse issues and is willing to take a chance and interview you. Doesn't mean you have the job—it's only an interview. I don't know how many other applicants there are, probably young people right out of college."

Laurel groaned.

"That could work in your favor. You're going to convince him how badly you want the job, how hard you're going to work for him. You've probably got a lot more experience than those other young applicants, if I'm correct about the competition. So, point that out in the interview. Tell him how much this job will mean for you. You can do this."

Laurel considered the situation. "Okay, you're right. I'm going to give it my best shot. It'd be a hellova lot better than cleaning office buildings. I've got to start somewhere."

"Here's his name and number, and the job description. You can be honest about your history. Tell him you worked in the prison print shop job, for example. Feel free, if you want to, to tell him about your program, that you have a safety net here, go to meetings, and so forth. In other words, sell yourself. Do you have the confidence to do that?"

Laurel had to think about that. "I think so. I may need a little more coaching from you. I don't want to blow the interview like that last one."

Laurel studied the iGraphics website. By the morning of the interview, she brimmed with confidence: comfortable enough to present herself and her history for what they were, and assured enough to sell herself as someone with experience, who'd work hard and be a good employee.

She arrived with time to spare, her nerves under control. *I'm just going to do the best job I can, be honest, be myself. If that doesn't do the trick, well, so be it. There'll be another job later.*

She interviewed with the CEO and the supervisor. Laurel talked matter-of-factly about her experience both in graphics and prison. When they asked her what she thought she could bring to the job, she sold herself effectively, talking about her assets without bragging, but with confidence.

She learned that much of the job consisted of routine graphics tasks and jobs that might be less sophisticated than what she'd performed at her last job. They told her the other employees she'd work with would be a lot younger and less experienced. How would she handle that?

"I can work effectively with people of all ages. What matters is how serious they are about doing the job, and if they can be part of a team. In a company this small, it's pretty important for people to get along well with each other, to communicate well. I can do that."

iGraphics planned to make a decision in the next few days. Walking away from the interview toward the bus stop, Laurel reviewed the past couple hours. The interview had gone well. She'd accomplished her goal: be confident, sell yourself, but be yourself. She liked the place, despite its small size. Yes, the jobs were pretty uncomplicated, but she felt like she could fit in. It might be fun working with a bunch of high-energy twenty somethings. Making more money would be nice, too. Now it was up to the Fates.

Two days later, they offered her the job. Thrilled, she called Jessica first thing to let her know and thank her. iGraphics wanted her to start as soon as possible.

Finally, some good news. She couldn't wait to tell Krisha, Victoria, and Starr—her support team.

She only saw Krisha every other week now. At her appointment, she burst out with, "Krisha, I got a new job! A real one. I'm so excited."

"I can see that. Congratulations. I'm proud of you."

"It means I don't have time during the day, though. So, I'm not sure how I'm going to schedule time to see you. I think you said I could go to group at night, right?"

"I'd suggest going down to twice a week for group, Tuesday and Thursday. Maybe you could see me once a month during your lunch hour, or at the end of the day, for a check-in for the next few months?"

"I think I could work that out. I'm going to be pretty busy, aren't I?"

"But, hopefully not too busy to continue with your AA meetings. Remember, just because things are going well doesn't mean that you can neglect your recovery. That's one of the things that can lead people to relapse, by the way . . . getting too busy to attend meetings. One of the things we teach clients here is how recovery *always* needs to come first. No matter how well things are going, you're an alcoholic forever. And, even if things are going really well, you'll hit bumps in the road, and bad things might happen—life on life's terms—that might make you want to drink. You need to have an infrastructure, as I like to call it, for when that happens. Meetings and a sponsor, and other supportive people, are part of that infrastructure."

Laurel thought about her past drinking, how far down she'd plunged, and how far she'd come since then. "You know, back in the bad old days, I didn't let anything get in the way of my drinking. I drank with reckless abandon."

"And now, you have to embrace recovery with that same enthusiasm. Which you've done so far. You just need to keep it up, even when things are good."

"Yeah, you're right. Thanks for reminding me. There've been enough times in the past few months where I've wanted to drink that I'd have to be nuts to think that won't happen again."

"That's right. It's not *if* it's going to happen, it's *when*, and *how bad* that craving will be, and how you're going to handle it. You need to be prepared."

"God, I wish it didn't have to be that way! I really hoped when I got my act together the desire to drink would vanish. *Poof.*"

"You need to be realistic. Maybe eventually, after a few years, that urge to drink will leave you once and for all. For some people, it does. For others, it's always lying in wait. So, you need to be prepared. Oh, I just thought of something else good that your new job means."

"What?"

"You'll be eligible to move out of the sober living house and into a supportive living apartment. Technically you are now, 'cause you're working, but you don't make enough money. Now, you can go on the list to move into a two-bedroom apartment with a roommate."

"Fantastic."

As Thanksgiving approached, Laurel had no idea what she'd do for the holiday in light of all that had been happening. She'd been thinking about her mother, but obviously Joanne couldn't prepare a meal. Without a car, Laurel couldn't even take her out for Thanksgiving dinner. She'd called a week ago to update her on the good news, but found her mother pretty dispirited and uninterested.

Probably should try to get up there more often and help, she thought guiltily. In the end, she shared a low-key Thanksgiving dinner at Hope House with a couple of other women who had nowhere to go. It kind of reminded her of prison, and she had to work hard to remember how far she'd come since those days not so long ago.

After Thanksgiving, Laurel met with her PO Trevor for her monthly appointment. She explained to her iGraphics job manager that she had a "doctor's appointment" and would need a couple hours off, which she'd be happy to make up. He said no problem. She could make up the time, or do a couple of hours of work at home on the computer. Laurel realized she'd actually be making enough money to buy herself a decent laptop.

She practically danced into Trevor's office, a huge grin on her face.

Trevor looked up. "You're certainly perky today, Ms. Peterson."

"I have some great news."

"Good for you. But, let's get some business out of the way first. Are you still in treatment and going to AA meetings?"

"Yes, and yes."

"Still employed?"

"I got a new job. A good one! A real one."

"Great. Tell me about it."

She told him the details. "So, I can start to make bigger payments toward my fines. I'd like to get those paid off as soon as possible so I don't have that hanging over my head anymore."

"Good for you. Great progress. Wish all of my probationers had such good news. See you next month then."

Chapter 34

Another Christmas approached, this one to be enjoyed, and not just survived, for the first time in a very long time. So different from last year at Sunstate. Still not religious, Laurel focused instead on how much she had to be grateful for. Sobriety, a new job she actually enjoyed, and friends, people who treated her well, and did nice things for her. Residents had decorated Hope House for the holidays, with a Christmas tree put up right after Thanksgiving, and all kinds of decorations—garlands and candles and a wreath on the front door.

The women did the Secret Santa thing, and it thrilled Laurel to actually *have* twenty dollars for her secret Santa gift. She also had enough money for gifts for Starr and Victoria. They'd all done so much for her these past few months. Victoria dropped her off at the mall for a couple of hours, so she could walk around and listen to Christmas music and shop to her heart's content. She thought about buying something for her mom.

She'd been thinking a lot about forgiveness and letting go of her resentment toward her mom. Starr and Krisha convinced her of the pointlessness of holding onto the anger about her childhood . . . it only hurt herself. She felt ready, having accepted that Joanne would not change. Why would she?

How could she? Miserable, without one good thing in her life. *Maybe I can be the one good thing in Mom's life, even if she doesn't appreciate it.*

So, she called her mother to see how she was, not having talked to her in a couple weeks. As usual, the phone rang and rang.

"Hi, Mom."

"Laurel, is that you?"

"Yes, Mom. How are you?"

"Well, you made me get up and answer the phone, so not all that good."

Try to be compassionate. "It sounds like it's getting harder and harder for you to get around. The Parkinson's is getting worse, isn't it?"

A long pause filled the phone connection. "It's kicking my ass. The medication stopped working. The doctor told me that would happen as I got to the later stages. But, I didn't think it would happen this soon. It's exhausting to just get through the day, doing virtually nothing."

"You sound kind of depressed." Laurel realized her mistake immediately.

"Of course, I'm depressed. Who wouldn't be in my condition? This sucks! I can barely walk. My hands shake so bad I can hardly turn on the TV, much less do anything else. You try eating a bowl of hot soup when you can't hold the spoon still."

"Oh, Mom, I'm so sorry. Is there anything I can do? By the way, did you ever get the box with Betsy's ashes from Philadelphia?"

No response. "Mom, are you still there?"

"Yeah. What did you ask me?"

"I asked if the box ever came from Philadelphia with Betsy's ashes."

"Betsy? What happened to Betsy?"

Jeez, this was bad. Really bad. Way worse than she expected. "Mom, remember how you got the call from the Philadelphia police detective? He told you Betsy had been killed? Remember how we called from your house and made arrangements to have the body cremated and the ashes sent to your house?"

"Oh, so that's what that box was that came a couple weeks ago. What did I do with that? Shit, I'm not sure what I did with it."

Now she sounded agitated, anxious.

Laurel hoped she hadn't thrown it away. "That's okay, Mom. We'll find it. I'm going to try to get a ride up there in the next few days, before Christmas, okay?"

"Okay, sure."

"And, Mom, if you need anything or want to talk, please call me, okay?"

Laurel had been in her new job for three weeks and loved it. As expected, she found the work itself unchallenging and routine—calendars, business cards, conference brochures, and the like—but it beat cleaning office buildings. She much preferred working during the day, and she liked her boss, not the owner/CEO, but the other guy from the interview. Although almost twenty years her junior, Adam Rockwell was a straight shooter. The other employees, also much younger, turned out to be fun to work with. All in all, a pretty good team atmosphere, everyone pulling his or her own weight.

The first couple of Fridays, she noticed that several co-workers went out together after work to a bar. Long ago, in another life, she enjoyed doing exactly that with her co-workers every Friday. That's fine, she thought, I hope I don't get invited, so I don't have to make any excuses. These days, she was satisfied with getting the bus back to Hope House for dinner, and possibly meeting up afterwards somewhere with Victoria.

She'd been wondering what had been going on with Ryan. They'd emailed regularly, but he usually took more than a week to respond, then didn't have much to say. She had sent newsy emails about how her life had been getting back on track, sharing news about her new job, telling about her new friends, et cetera. But, he had little to say in response. With each email since she'd gotten her cell phone, she'd asked for his phone number. He never offered it though. Finally, shortly before Christmas, she asked him directly why he hadn't given her his number.

He reported being busy with end of the semester school assignments and that Madison had broken up with him. It apparently surprised him how upset it made him, despite seeing it coming. He mentioned graduating in the spring and not wanting to be tied down during his job search. Lots of other kids were already job hunting, so that had him concerned and busy, too.

Although she'd smiled when she opened the email, and her heart went out to him as he described his first breakup, by the end she was tearing up. Sitting on her bed, she kept rereading that last paragraph, even though it was like a punch in the gut.

> *"I know you've asked me for my phone number a few times. I've thought about it, and I just don't think I'm ready for that step, actually talking to you. I've been*

worried that you might want to visit, or come to my graduation in May, but I'm not ready for that either.
Take care,
Ryan"

How did he intuit she had been thinking about a visit, either him coming here, or her going there? And graduation, yeah, she'd been fantasizing about how wonderful it would be to go to California and see her son graduate. But, he didn't even want to talk with her on the phone.

She wondered what happened. How could she have played it differently?

A staffer from WRAD informed her that, by February first, a spot would be open for her to move into a supportive living apartment in Phoenix. With that news, Laurel could hardly contain her excitement.

The place was furnished, but she'd be able to move in some of the things she left in the casita at her mom's. That reminded her that she never visited her mom before Christmas, and needed to work out a ride up there.

She made plans with Victoria to pick her up and take her to Carefree. While she visited Mom, Victoria would hang out and visit the cool little shops and galleries all over Carefree and Cave Creek. In the late afternoon or so, she'd come back and pick up Laurel, who'd treat her to dinner on the way back to thank her.

Victoria dropped her off in the driveway and Laurel walked toward the house. Although her mom knew about her visit, she knocked first. No answer, so she used her key, calling her mom as soon as she went inside. Still no response. Maybe she was still asleep, or taking a nap. She remembered that Parkinson's disease, or one of the meds for it—she couldn't remember which—caused insomnia, so her mom could be sleeping at any point during the day. She walked around the house trying to find her.

She discovered her in bed and, when she entered the room, Joanne woke up. Laurel apologized for waking her, but her mom insisted on getting up. She looked like a wreck—hair wild, stick thin, skin sallow-looking. An eggplant-sized purple bruise tinted her arm.

"What happened to your arm, Mom?"

"Uh, I must have fallen."

This was the worst Laurel had ever seen her. "How long ago was that?"

"Can't remember."

Not good. Plus, the house was a total mess, much worse than she'd ever seen it. What happened to Mrs. Hernandez, the helper? Laurel couldn't help with that today, because it looked like would take more than a couple hours.

They walked into the kitchen, Joanne bent over, shuffling, obviously hurting. Might be time for a walker. Laurel offered to get her mom something to eat. Then she noticed that, once again, there was barely any food in the house. Most of what she found in the refrigerator was spoiled. She knew she needed to dispose of it, but didn't want her mother to see her doing it.

"Mom, why don't you go into the family room and relax, maybe watch some TV while I get you some breakfast?"

"Okay."

As she left, Laurel started tossing out perishables long past their sell-by dates. After a few minutes, her mom stumbled back into the kitchen, startling Laurel.

"What are you doing throwing all that food out?"

"It's all spoiled, Mom. Look at these vegetables. They're all moldy." She picked up a cucumber that had deliquesced in its plastic bag. "This cucumber is so far gone I could practically pour it out of the bag. And, the milk and cottage cheese are all well by their use-by dates. They smell sour."

"Maybe, but you should have asked me first. You know how I hate to waste food I've paid good money for."

Laurel sighed. She did indeed remember that. "I guess you're right. I should have asked you first. I'm sorry. Fortunately, these eggs are okay, and I see a couple of English muffins here, so I'm going to make you some eggs, okay?"

"Yeah, sure."

While Laurel made breakfast, it became obvious how much her mother had deteriorated in the weeks since Laurel last saw her. She was still angry, but now the depression was glaring . . . not to mention her difficulty in functioning without help. When they finally sat down at the kitchen table, Laurel geared up to have a difficult conversation, which she wasn't expecting to have so soon, a conversation she dreaded.

"Mom, when did you last leave the house?"

Between bites, her mother said, "I'm not sure. Not for a while."

"When was the last time you saw the doctor?"

"No idea."

"Don't you think it might be time to schedule an appointment?"

Silence. Finally, she said, "Suppose so, but what he can do at this point?"

Laurel took a deep breath. "Mom, I'm really worried about you staying here by yourself. It's obvious you can't really take care of yourself anymore. I think you really need a walker. You need some help with the house."

Bracing herself, she thought, *Okay, here it comes.*

To her immense surprise, her mother nodded. "I know. Mrs. Hernandez quit, and I'm just falling apart." Tears leaked from her eyes.

Totally unprepared for weeping, and trying to remember the last time she saw her mother cry, Laurel was nonplussed. Should she go over and put her arm around her? What should she say?

"Mom, I'm so sorry. I can't imagine how difficult this is. Let's talk about possible solutions." She was buying time.

No response. Joanne still wept. Laurel got up to retrieve a box of tissues.

She returned and sat. "Well, as I see it, we've got two options, neither great, and both expensive. First, you could consider having someone come to the house every day. I'm not sure what that'll cost, but I'm willing to look into it for you. The second option is to consider assisted living arrangements. Unfortunately, I think you'll have to consider that option pretty soon, if not now. I know that'll be expensive, too, but you probably know more about it from when you put Bill in that facility. Do you know if there are assisted living places around here you can afford?"

Still no response.

"Okay, I'll look into both of those things for you, and see what I can come up with. Meanwhile, can I go online and order you some food from the grocery story? I'll do what I can do to clean up around here until Victoria comes back to pick me up later."

Since her mother didn't respond, she went to the computer and ordered groceries that would arrive soon. Then, she started cleaning the kitchen, dusting, vacuuming, and changing the disgusting sheets on her mother's bed. Was incontinence part of Parkinson's?

That took her the rest of the day. She stopped briefly for lunch, more scrambled eggs and the last English muffin. She opened up a can of soup and put it into a pan on the stove so all her mother would have to do for dinner was heat it up. But, would she actually do it?

While she cleaned, she found the box with Betsy's cremains and carried it out to the casita. *No point in talking to Mom about that. I think I'll just bring the box back to Hope House with me and scatter the ashes someplace nice. That's really about all I can handle.*

When Victoria pulled into the driveway at four forty-five, Laurel invited her into the casita to help put some belongings into the car. She wasn't sure how she'd store them until she moved into the apartment, but she also couldn't tell when she'd next be visiting. She thought guiltily it should be sooner than later, but it was so darn hard to get here. After carrying stuff out to Victoria's car, Laurel found her mother in the family room dozing in front of the TV set. She shook her gently and said goodbye, explaining that the food should be delivered sometime later today or tomorrow, and that she'd left some soup on the stove to heat up for dinner.

When she and Victoria got back into the car, she could barely contain herself.

"I gather it was a tough visit."

"Horrible! She's going downhill so fast. I don't know what to do. At this point, she really can't take care of herself, and I think she's starting to lose it mentally. Her memory is shot. I mean, she forgot that Betsy was killed, and when the box with her ashes arrived, she had no idea what it was. Thank goodness she didn't throw it out."

She grabbed some tissues from her purse.

"She either has to have someone come in, at least during the day, or move into assisted living. I know she doesn't have much money, so I don't know if she can afford either. I'm in no position to help her financially, since I'm just getting back on my feet and have to pay rent soon. I'm going to look into those options this week, but I think it's possible she won't be able to afford either."

"Oh, Laurel, that sounds terrible. I'm so sorry you have to do deal with this on top of all the other issues you've got right now."

"Actually, I'm feeling like my life is pretty stable right now, as long as I don't relapse again. I mean, I have my new job, which is going well, and I'm moving into an apartment in a couple weeks—"

"You are? You didn't tell me that. Congratulations!"

"Sorry, I just found out a couple days ago. First of February. That's why I wanted to bring back all this stuff. It's furnished, but there'll be room for more of my things there."

"Fantastic. So, we have something to celebrate at dinner tonight. Let's try not to have your mother's issues get in the way of celebrating this next phase of your recovery."

"Okay, deal. Can we go to that wonderful little café you took me too on my first day out of prison? My treat this time."

Chapter 35

"How's everything going?" Krisha asked. "It's been a while."

"A lot going on. Some good news is that I moved from Hope House into a supportive living apartment last week. So far, so good. It's been a long time since I've lived in an apartment with a roommate, but I think we'll get along okay."

"Congratulations. What else is going on?"

"Well, a couple things I really need to talk to you about. The first is Ryan, and the second is my mom."

"Let's do the shorter one first."

"Probably Ryan. I'd thought things were going well in my relationship with him, such as it is . . . limited to letters and now email, I mean. The last few emails I sent, I asked him for his phone number. I really wanted to hear his voice and actually talk to him. Each time, he ignored the request. Then he sent me this email." She handed a printed copy to Krisha. "Read the last paragraph."

Krisha read it. "So, how did you respond to that?"

"Naturally, I was pretty upset. Very disappointed, and surprised he somehow had figured out I was actually thinking about a visit, or at least attending his graduation. I am second-guessing myself about what I'd said in our correspondence. Do you think I've been pushing him too hard?"

"Hard to say, since I've not seen what you've written, but I haven't had that impression based on what you've said about him in our sessions. I'm wondering, since he visited his dad over Christmas, if it's possible his dad has continued to discourage him from being involved with you. By the way, did you ever get a response to the letter of amends you sent him a while back?"

"Nope. Didn't really expect to. I said what I had to say, owned up to my part, and as far as I'm concerned, I'm done with that chapter of my life. It was hard to do, and I'll cop to dragging my feet about doing it, but in the end, I did it, and it worked. Feel like I got some closure on that."

She ran an index finger along her forehead. "Now, what you said about whether Rick has continued to discourage Ryan from having a relationship with me . . . I'd say that's pretty likely, even though Ryan didn't say that in his email."

"So, what're you hoping to get from our session today?"

"Not sure. Some validation maybe? Advice on how to proceed? It's probably just one of those lousy situations in life we have no control over and just have to accept. Getting Ryan's email has made me realize I had some expectations about what might happen in the future with him—what I *wanted* to happen in the future. I probably didn't even know I had them until they didn't materialize."

She crossed and uncrossed her legs. "I guess I thought, as I got my life back together, my relationship with him would continue to develop . . . But, maybe he's gotten from me what he needed—an explanation of what happened. He was curious about who I was and why I left him. He found out, didn't he? Maybe he just isn't that crazy about what he found. I don't know. I'm having trouble making sense of the whole thing."

"Let me try to respond. First, I'm probably not going to give you advice on this one. I do understand your disappointment though. Anyone would be disappointed under the circumstances. And, I like your analysis of the situation—you've become aware of some expectations you had about the future that might not come to pass. This is a tough one. Don't forget, he's going through a difficult time now, and might just feel overwhelmed and negative about *everything* in his life for a while, including you. At the risk of elevating your expectations again, I'd say it's not over 'til it's over."

"Meaning what?"

"Meaning he didn't say he didn't want any more contact with you. He said he wasn't ready for the closeness of a phone call right now. He might not always feel that way. But, I think it'd be risky to assume it's just a matter of time until he comes around. I think the best place to be on this one is to have no expectations at all, if you can manage that."

"Okay, well that's advice in a way. Let me think about that. On to my mother."

"What's going on with her?"

"The short version? Her Parkinson's is progressing rapidly. She's gone downhill fast and really can't take care of herself. When I visited recently, she was mess, the house was a mess, the whole situation is a mess. She needs to have somebody come in to take care of her, or get into assisted living, and I'm not sure she can afford either. But, I feel like I need to do whatever I can to make that happen."

"I'm very impressed with how responsible you seem to be feeling for her in light of your history with her, and even her more recent behavior toward you. It almost sounds like you might be moving toward forgiving her."

"You know, I hadn't thought about it in terms of forgiveness, but maybe I am. I *do* feel responsible, and I'm really worried about what'll happen if she can't afford daily care. I can't really help her much, if at all, financially, and she can't live with me."

"I'm not sure what I can offer here. Obviously, you're feeling stressed by it. Anyone would. All I can say is, explore those options, try not to get too far ahead of yourself, and see what unfolds. If worse comes to worse, you could consider calling Adult Protective Services and getting their help figuring it out." Krisha leaned forward. "What I'm actually most concerned about in all this is your sobriety. How have you been staying sober through all this? This is a lot to deal with. Are you thinking about drinking?"

"I actually haven't been thinking about drinking over either of these situations, thank God. What I'm doing to stay sober is going to group two nights a week, and at least three AA meetings a week. I have my sponsor Starr and my mentor Victoria. Plus, working full time."

"So, you're staying very busy, but still involved with recovery activities."

"Absolutely. Very busy, but in a good way. Not much time to think about drinking. I'm spending time with good people and feel like I'm much more connected with recovering people than I ever was before."

"Okay, all that sounds good, and we're out of time. Laurel, you seem to be dealing with life on life's terms. Nobody promises us when we stop drinking or using that we'll have a life with no problems. But, you seem to be using the skills you've learned to deal with those issues in a healthy way. I'm optimistic you'll come to terms with both Ryan and your mother."

Krisha paused for a minute and continued, "I had another thought about Ryan and your reaction to the disappointment of the relationship not blossoming the way you hoped or expected. I wonder whether your disappointment stems from wanting to be the kind of mother to him that your mother never was to you, and you couldn't be when he was growing up because of your drinking. Is that possible?"

"Whew, that's huge. Going to need to think on that."

Laurel spent the next weeks adjusting to the new apartment and her roommate, working, going to group, attending meetings. The apartment worked out fine, and Laurel got along with Jenna. She got annoyed when Jenna's kids or grandkids visited, but Laurel was gone so much of the time it didn't matter. Life just chugged along.

Laurel's research on in-home care and assisted living in the Phoenix area revealed that assisted living, if she could find a decent one, might be the better deal, since it was twenty-four/seven and included meals. Because assisted living would be necessary sooner than later, Joanne might as well make the move and adjust to that. She wasn't sure of her mother's finances, but she might be able to afford it with a little financial help from Laurel.

She obsessed over the whole scenario: How to present it to her mother, what Joanne's reaction would be, helping her make the move if she agreed, and what to do about Bill's house. How much furniture did Joanne have, or was all of it Bill's? Could she locate Bill's children to tell them her mother was moving out and they'd have to sell the house? It felt like a tornado in her head as she spun out the various scenarios, and she procrastinated talking with her mom about it.

At dinnertime on a Tuesday at the end of February, Laurel finally worked up the courage to call her mother. She didn't answer and, of course, Laurel couldn't leave a message. Probably sleeping and didn't hear the phone. She called on Wednesday evening, but the phone rang forever with no answer. She started to feel concerned, and made a mental note to try the next day at work. Again, no answer. By Friday, when her mother failed to pick up again, Laurel concluded something was wrong. What should she do? Victoria couldn't drive her to Carefree until Sunday and suggested calling the police.

So, Laurel called the Maricopa County Sheriff's Department to see if they could look in on Joanne and make sure she was okay. The dispatcher sent a car out with a couple of officers to check. Someone would get back to her as soon as they knew something.

Breathing a sigh of relief, Laurel started thinking about dinner and an AA meeting in light of all that'd been going on. A good one at eight o'clock at a Lutheran Church took about fifteen minutes to walk to.

On her way there, she took her phone out to put it on vibrate. It rang in her hand, an unfamiliar number. A male voice asked if this was Laurel Peterson.

She frowned. "Yes, it is."

"Ma'am, this is the Maricopa County Sheriff's Department. My name is Andy Lawrence. My partner and I were just dispatched to check on a Joanne McManus in Carefree—"

"That's right," Laurel said. "She's my mother. I called a couple of hours ago about her, worried that something might have happened to her. I've been calling all week and she wasn't picking up."

"Well, Ms. Peterson, you were right to be worried. I'm very sorry to have to tell you we found your mother on the floor of her kitchen. It appears that she fell and hit her head—"

Laurel gasped. "Oh my God, is she all right?"

"I'm afraid not. The EMTs arrived about a half hour ago, and they're taking her to the hospital now but, from the looks of things, she's been deceased for some time. I'm sorry for your loss."

Speechless, Laurel stood stock still in the pitch dark on the sidewalk in downtown Phoenix. She shivered. A million questions swirled around in her brain like buzzing insects but, somehow, she couldn't seem to get her mouth to coordinate sufficiently with her brain to produce speech. Time just stopped.

"Ma'am, are you still there?"

She mouthed yes, but no sound emerged.

"Ma'am? Ms. Peterson?"

"Uh, yes, I'm still here. I'm just struggling to wrap my brain around this. I mean, I knew she wasn't doing well, and she'd fallen recently, but she's so stubborn I had trouble convincing her to get help. I'm not sure what I should do next."

"Do you have any other family around?"

"No, no one."

"Well, at some point I believe you'll have to come and ID the body. I'm not sure exactly where that will be, or when, but someone will call you. I suggest you try to contact somebody who can help you through this. And, again, I'm sorry for your loss."

With that, he hung up.

Laurel stood on the sidewalk, paralyzed. Her rubbery legs felt like they might collapse beneath her, her whole body jittery. She looked around in vain for somewhere to sit. She knew she should do something, but just couldn't seem to get her brain to work.

This was my fault. I knew things were getting worse. I knew she had just fallen. I could see she couldn't take care of herself any more. That was weeks ago, and I didn't do anything until it was too late. What's wrong with me?

As she stood there on the sidewalk, half a block from the church, dazed and confused, a man came along and, through a fog, she heard him ask, "Are you okay?"

She looked up at him. He looked vaguely familiar. She knew she'd seen him before.

He asked her again, "Are you okay? I'm pretty sure I've seen you at the meeting at the church. I'm on my way there. Is that where you're going?"

Laurel couldn't figure out what to do, but she slowly nodded her head.

"Okay, why don't I walk with you then. You don't look like you're doing too well. Have you been drinking?"

The question grabbed her by the throat. She stopped short and shook her head no. No, of course she hadn't been drinking. Did she say that or just think it? She was still struggling to make a connection between her brain and her mouth.

"Is there anything I can do to help?"

Oh my God, he was being so nice. Why couldn't she talk? She shook her head. She willed her legs to move, and together they ambled slowly toward the church. They walked in the door, and the meeting had already started. He took a seat toward the back, and she found an empty seat up near the speaker. She wished she could sit in the back.

The meeting unfolded in a blur. Dim awareness of people speaking, of conversations occurring around her. But, she couldn't seem to tune in. A heavy gray mist fogged her brain. She realized the man to her right was speaking.

He shared briefly and then said, "Thanks for letting me share. And, I'll pass to the lady on my left."

Everyone's gaze turned on her, waiting expectantly.

And as if by rote from attending so many meetings over the course of her lifetime, she heard the words come out of her mouth: "My name is Laurel, and I'm an alcoholic." Immediately she started to sob, the room went silent around her. Someone handed her a tissue. People waited. It took a couple minutes to compose herself.

"On my way here, I got a call from the Sheriff's Department saying my mother was found dead in Carefree. I'm afraid it was my fault." She couldn't manage anything more. She heard murmuring around the room, people saying things like, "wow" and "oh boy, that's awful."

Two women she'd never met helped her to stand up. With their arms around her, they escorted her out of the room. Once out in the hall, the floodgates opened, and Laurel started sobbing. Long choking sobs prevented her from talking, and snot dripped from her nose.

One woman introduced herself as Suzanne. The other, Nicole, just held her and let her cry, while Suzanne offered her tissues.

After a few minutes, Suzanne said, "Do you have a sponsor or close friend in the program I can call for you?"

Laurel retrieved her phone from her purse and called both Victoria and Starr. She talked briefly to Starr and left a message for Victoria. Starr agreed to come to Laurel's apartment. Nicole offered her a ride home. In the car, Nicole asked if she wanted to talk.

Laurel shook her head. "Not yet," she said, "but thank you so much for taking care of me. I think I'll be all right when Starr and Victoria come over."

She walked into the apartment, grateful that Jenna was spending the weekend with one of her daughters.

Chapter 36

"I don't know how I'm going to deal with another death," Laurel said to Starr. "I've barely had the chance to grieve for Betsy." Victoria hadn't arrived yet. "This is so hard. A million feelings are swirling around in my head. Now, I'll never have the chance to work things out with her. It feels like it's my fault. I feel so guilty, like I should have done more."

Starr looked into her tear-stained eyes. "Why would you think that?"

Just then, Victoria knocked on the door. "Oh Laurel, I'm so sorry. What exactly happened?"

Grateful not to have to tell the story twice, Laurel shared with Starr and Victoria the recent developments of her mother's illness and rapid deterioration.

"It's not like I wasn't doing anything. I researched both in-home health care and assisted living options in Phoenix. I wanted to have all the information in front of me when I approached her, so she'd be able to make a good decision. But, here's the thing. I knew she didn't want to do anything. She just wanted to stay there in that house."

Victoria handed her a tissue.

Laurel's words rushed out. "Her memory was failing. She couldn't take care of herself. There either wasn't food, or she wasn't eating what was there. The house was filthy. She didn't want to spend the money for food, or care, or anything. She didn't want anyone to know how bad she'd gotten. She was angry, she was embarrassed, she was depressed." Laurel sputtered, "And, she'd gotten really difficult to deal with. I knew getting her help was going to be a big argument, so I was procrastinating."

For a minute, neither Starr nor Victoria said anything.

Starr eventually turned away from Laurel. "Victoria, just before you arrived, Laurel asked me if I thought this was her fault. So, now that I know the whole story of what happened, here's my answer." She gazed straight into Laurel's face. "No, not at all. I personally don't think you have anything to feel guilty about. What about you Victoria?"

Without a moment's hesitation, Victoria added, "Your fault? Why in God's name would this be your fault? Your mom apparently fell. It was a tragic accident. You tried the best you could to help her a few weeks ago, maybe longer than that. Hell, you've been trying to help her since you got out of Sunstate. But she rejected most of your attempts. Probably for the reasons you mentioned—anger, embarrassment, maybe depression."

She leaned forward and put a hand on Laurel's arm. "I for one have been impressed with how much you've done to try to help her—especially in light of your history. I know she's been a pain to deal with through this whole illness. You did a good job of making living amends and working on forgiveness. So, I don't think you have anything feel guilty about. Sad, of course, on so many levels, especially in light of Betsy's recent death." She paused to take a breath and think. "This is a lot to deal with Laurel, but I'd say you're doing a great job. What do you think Starr?"

"I agree with Victoria. Good job of making some very difficult amends and good progress toward forgiving your mom, accepting a difficult past that can't be undone. I think you've really stopped fighting. And, I know how hard that's been. Having to take care of the arrangements after Betsy died really did throw a monkey wrench into that whole process. What I mean is, it made grieving so difficult."

Starr and Victoria stayed another hour, talking with Laurel about what had happened. After they left, Laurel stepped back and could see, as awful as it was that her mother had fallen and died, it really wasn't her fault. Although she felt guilty about thinking it, on some level this wasn't the worst outcome. Not that she wanted it to happen, of course.

There were actually some things even worse than dying from that fall, like having to move to an assisted living or nursing home you couldn't really afford, giving up your independence, losing control of your body and your mind.

She hoped her mother didn't suffer too much after the fall, that her death was quick. Because she knew her mother suffered plenty before the fall, and she would have continued to suffer after Laurel finally found someplace to move her. Away from everything that had become comfortable and familiar, living with equally compromised strangers and caregivers poking and prodding her as her body and mind deteriorated even further.

Two days later, the Sheriff's Department called to see when Laurel could come identify the body. As Laurel ran through in her mind how she'd get to wherever she needed to go, the deputy said, "Ma'am, if I recall correctly, you don't have a car.

Do you need someone to drive you from Phoenix to Carefree and stay with you while you make the ID?"

What a blessing. It would have been nice to have a friend with her while she did this thing she dreaded, seeing the mother she had such conflicting feelings about one last time. But, she had so imposed upon her friends over the past few months. It would be a relief to have someone, even a deputy, come pick her up and take her to identify her mother and say goodbye for the last time.

"Yes, that's correct. No car. So, I'd really appreciate a ride."

The identification turned out not as difficult as Laurel had imagined. She didn't actually have to be in the room with her mother's body. She looked at it through a window. Everybody involved knew it was going to be her mom. But still . . . She'd never seen a dead body before, and the first one was her own mother, the person who raised her.

The ride home with the deputy was endless. She couldn't define how she felt, but wanted it to be over, to be numb, to not feel anything. The thought of a drink . . . *No, I'm not going there.*

Krisha agreed to see Laurel sooner than their usual monthly appointment. In the intervening week, Laurel had made some progress. She'd let go of feeling responsible for her mom's death. She accepted that she couldn't really have prevented it, or done anything more than she'd already done and was trying to do.

She recounted all of that to Krisha—what happened to her mother but, more importantly, how Starr and Victoria helped her see she had done her best to help her mom, and was not in any way responsible for her accidental death.

Krisha complimented her on the good work she had done to get to that point. "So, how can I best help you today?"

"I need some help . . . grieving, I guess. You know, I don't think I ever really grieved Betsy's death either. I had to be the grownup in that situation, the one in charge, and it just seemed like I couldn't afford to get in touch with my real feelings about what had happened. Now, with my mother's death . . . I feel broken, wounded. I don't know what to do with all these different feelings."

Krisha didn't respond immediately. Finally, she said simply, "In my experience, conflicted relationships are much harder to grieve."

Laurel fiddled with a tissue in her lap and fidgeted in her seat, not looking at Krisha. Finally, she looked up. "What do you mean?"

"Grieving conflicted, estranged, or difficult relationships can be very confusing and complicated. Mourning isn't straightforward like grieving unconflicted relationships, where sadness and missing the person typically dominate our emotional responses to the loss. With relationships like the ones you had with your mother or Betsy, it wouldn't be unusual to experience emotions simultaneously that seem really incongruent: sadness and anger and relief. Does that make sense?"

"It does. I can already see that. It makes me feel weird . . . kind of . . . out of control."

"Sure, that's understandable. The other thing about conflicted or estranged relationships is that there is often unfinished emotional business. Things that'll never get said, that'll never get resolved. That was certainly the case with your mother, but maybe also with Betsy. The fact that you hadn't seen her in many years doesn't necessarily mean you don't need to mourn her loss, or perhaps the loss of the kind of relationship you never had, but wished you could have."

"I think I know what you mean. With Betsy, I've always felt guilty that I couldn't really protect her from my mother. With my brothers, it was different. They were older, for one thing. Betsy always seemed so vulnerable, even more than me. Hearing how she died, and that she was an addict and prostitute . . . I *do* feel guilty. I know I was a mess, too, back when she let me stay with her, but I *knew* she was in a bad spot and I didn't do a thing to try to fix it."

Very quietly Krisha asked, "Is it possible you had your hands full trying to fix yourself, trying to survive after Rick asked you to leave?"

By now, tears streamed down Laurel's face. She couldn't talk, and Krisha let her sit there, offering her the box of tissues.

"You're right, I was a mess. Drinking, trying to find a job and a place to live, furious that Rick had thrown me out, and ashamed I couldn't be a mother to Ryan. I was just like my own lousy mother. I was in no condition to try to help anyone else."

She blew her nose and wiped her eyes. "You know, I thought I'd made good progress accepting what happened in my childhood, what a crappy mother we had. But now, I feel all that anger all over again. Why did she keep on having kids? Why did not a single one of our fathers ever take responsibility for us? Why did she keep choosing men like that?"

Krisha nodded slowly. "That's the unfinished business I mentioned. Those questions can never be answered. By the way, you *have* made good progress on dealing with your childhood issues, but unexpected traumatic losses have a way of kicking our butts. They tend to stir up those issues from the past, even stuff we thought we'd packaged away nicely. You're not unique in this regard, not that there's much comfort in knowing that."

She leaned forward gently. "So, here's my advice, even though I usually don't give advice. Give yourself time to grieve these losses. It's going to take a while, easily more than a year. Maybe longer. Grief doesn't really have a timetable. Find trusted people you can safely talk with about these complicated, often ambivalent, emotional reactions. People who won't judge you. It's okay to feel these profoundly confusing and conflicting feelings. If, after a while, people seem tired of hearing you talk about it, and you still need to talk about it, join a grief support group."

Laurel wiped away more tears. "Okay, thanks."

"Another thing that helps some people is a journal where you can write about your feelings to your heart's content. No one is going to read it but you, Laurel. No one is going to judge you."

After Laurel left the session, she walked to a park in Phoenix and sat down on a bench, thinking about everything Krisha had said. She decided to have a final mental conversation with her mother and tell her all the things she couldn't say in life. This time, though, her mom wasn't going to get angry at her.

Mom, I'm so sorry about all of this. Sorry I couldn't have helped you more. Sorry you had to put Bill in that place. Sorry you got Parkinson's disease. You were right, having Parkinson's sucks. I'd've been angry and depressed, too. In fact, your whole life pretty much sucked. The fact that your actions are partly what made it suck is beside the point, I guess. It's too bad it worked out the way it did. Too bad for the boys and for Betsy. Too bad for you, too, although these last few years you had with Bill were one of the few bright spots in your life.

Too bad for me, too. You know, Mom, I just wasn't equipped to deal with life, none of us were. And, just like everybody else in our family, I kept making bad choices and wondering why bad things kept happening to me. The drinking was just a symptom. Right now, it looks like I'm the last man standing. I think I finally might get it. I guess it took that last relapse, arrest, and going to prison to get me on this path.

I don't know whether I could or should have done more to help you or not, Mom. I guess it doesn't matter now, does it? I hope you forgive me, because I'm trying really hard to forgive you.

Epilogue

Another Thanksgiving approached. Laurel had so much to be thankful for. She had a good job, a decent apartment. She and Jenna got along, and Laurel felt grateful for the chance to save money because of the reduced rent and shared utilities.

She still saw her probation officer, who supported her driver's license being reinstated. Soon, she'd be eligible to get her license back and could start driving her beloved old Beemer. She was fine with having to see Trevor once a month for a while longer. The appointments usually didn't take long, and it was a good reminder of where drinking would take her if she relapsed. It amazed her she still did think about drinking occasionally, and not necessarily when something stressed her out. It truly baffled her that she could actually think about taking a drink after all that had happened.

Not much in Bill's house had belonged to her mother. Joanne had moved into Bill's furnished house from a tiny studio she rented when she worked for the Four Seasons. Laurel had contacted Bill's son and daughter through his attorney and told them they would have to deal with selling the house.

Bill had transferred from the assisted living to a nursing home, with no telling how much longer he'd live. According to the lawyer, Bill had left a considerable part of his estate to Joanne. With her passing, though, it was unclear what would happen to that. Nor was it clear how much, if anything, would remain after paying for Bill's care in his final days—or weeks or years.

Although Joanne knew something about Bill's financial situation, Laurel herself certainly didn't. However, she learned from the attorney that his children fully intended to challenge the will if any assets remained after Bill eventually died. Otherwise, according to the lawyer, Joanne's portion would eventually be passed on to Laurel, even though her mother died without a will. Laurel never expected to see a penny of it, and thought she wasn't entitled to it anyhow.

She hadn't heard from Ryan for months. Then, he got back in touch with a new email address. He graduated from Caltech with honors and found an engineering job with a nice salary in Providence, Rhode Island, allowing him to be near his father in Boston.

In the months when she didn't hear from him, she had pretty much made peace with the fact that she might not hear from him again, and she felt okay with that. She had accepted their relationship wouldn't grow closer over time. It still disappointed her, of course, but she reasoned that Ryan had discovered what he needed to learn about her—why she'd left him and what happened to her. If he had any sense at all, he was saying to himself, "Lucky I was raised by my dad. My mom had serious issues."

Still, she wished it could have been different.

Sitting in her bedroom after work one Wednesday night, Laurel's phone rang, a Scottsdale or Tempe 480 prefix she didn't recognize.

"Hello."

"Hi, is this Laurel Peterson?"

She narrowed her eyes. "Yes, who's this?"

"Scott. Scott Harris."

Scott? Was he kidding? After all this time?

Once she recovered from the shock of hearing his voice, she said, with as much snark as she could muster, "You mean Scott the jerk who dropped off the face of the Earth without the courtesy of telling me why? The Scott who wouldn't take my phone calls, and texted me to stop calling and leave him alone? That Scott?"

After a moment, Scott said, "Yep, that Scott. The Scott who behaved like an asshole to a nice lady who didn't deserve it. I'm actually calling to apologize."

Laurel couldn't respond. Really? "How the hell did you get my number?"

"I've actually had it for over a year. It's taken me a while to get up the courage to call. What I did was drive up to your mother's place in Carefree. She had no idea who I was, but she gave me your phone number when I explained why I was there. Boy, she was in pretty bad shape, by the way. How is she?"

Whew, where to begin? Do I even want to talk to this guy, after what… three years, the most difficult years of my life? Relapse, jail, prison, Betsy dying, mom dying. What would Victoria say to do? What would Starr say? How can I even begin? Do I want to reopen that chapter of my life? Do I want to risk destabilizing my life?

As these questions zinged through her brain, she could hear Scott talking in the background.

"After my dad died, I just fell apart. Totally and completely came unglued. I know you called and called, and were concerned about me. I'm not sure I can explain exactly what happened, but I became almost paralyzed and just couldn't seem to function. God, I was practically catatonic. I started drinking again, and then things really came apart. My niece eventually . . . Hey, you know what, I haven't even asked you how you are. How the heck are you? I've missed you. The relationship we started. Would you be interested in getting coffee?"

About the Author

Bonnie E. Carlson was born and grew up in Central Connecticut. Before her junior year in high school, she had life-changing experience when she was selected to travel to Malaysia and live there with a family. Among other things, it gave her the experience of being in the minority, though white, and learning another language. This adventure led her to major in Asian Studies at the University of Michigan in Ann Arbor, providing an opportunity to learn about the Midwest.

After completing a master's degree in social work and a Ph.D. in Social Work and Developmental Psychology, also at the University of Michigan, she became a professor at the University at Albany, State University New York, where she remained for 28 years. There she taught graduate social work students and conducted research on domestic violence, child abuse, sibling sexual abuse, the impact of incarceration on families, and related topics. Toward the end of her tenure there, her focus shifted to studying factors affecting relapse in women trying to recover from drug and alcohol abuse.

After falling in love with the desert in Scottsdale and Phoenix, AZ, she took a faculty position at Arizona State University, where she stayed until she retired.

After retiring, she pivoted to writing fiction. Her short fiction has been published in literary magazines such as *The Normal School, Broadkill Review, Foliate Oak, Down in the Dirt, Across the Margin,* and *Blue Lake Review.* Now she lives with her husband, dog and too many cats in Scottsdale, AZ and writes fiction and hikes to her heart's content in the beautiful Sonoran desert.